Keeper
of the
Tower

Brett Scott Ermilio

ISBN(Paperback): 978-0-9863512-5-9

Edited by Bonnie Ermilio

Cover Design by Amy Beth Kunze, Art From The Heart

*Dedicated to the Barnegat Light
Museum and Historical Society
who keep the light burning*

ACKNOWLEDGEMENTS

I am thankful for the following people and their support:

First and foremost, my love, my wife, Ashley. She enables everything that I am.

To my children, Phoenix, Bailey, Tyler and Ella—you are my little dreamers.

To my mother who is my constant editor (literally on this project!) and greatest supporter.

To Sue Aeling, the best mother-in-law in the world! Thank you for your help!

To Kaitlyn Johnson, thank you for your help and support on this wonderful book.

To Reilly P. Sharp, your information and help was invaluable.

To Gerry and Jim Perko, thank you for the stories and tales surrounding Old Barney.

And finally, a very special thanks to local artist Amy Beth Kunze; an extraordinary talent who created an original painting for this cover. I thank you so much for your talents!

Introduction

Lighthouse keepers and their families lived among the most beautiful scenery in the world. Keepers were on call 24 hours a day and were responsible to work every night without fail. In times of poor weather, keepers would need to man their stations throughout the storm and keep the light on. It didn't matter whether they saw a ship or not; the keeper had to keep the light on to provide a beacon for those at sea. Their lives were often boring and routine. Their families made clothing, worked on gardens and fished in the ocean's waters. However, there were times when lighthouse keepers would be faced with other kinds of challenges. They would be faced with life and death decisions.

And…sometimes they had to risk their own lives to rescue people in terrible weather from shipwrecks.

One

GRINDING metal scrapes across cement. Thomas's eyes open, his tired, aching body turning slightly on his small dirty prison cot. His cell door has been dragged open.

"Let's go. Time to rise, Dent." The voice of Officer Bullocks calls to Thomas. Thomas is groggy and slowly rolls up to a standing position. "It's moving day!" the young baby-faced officer excitedly states.

Thomas straightens up, his unshaven face covered with a thick scraggily beard. Behind his beard is a young man's blue eyes and soft skin. He drags himself over to Bullocks. There is a sizable difference between Thomas and Bullocks. It's not that Thomas is really tall; it's more that Bullocks is short and stout. Thomas is athletic and has above average height and a broad-shouldered build.

"You really need a bell." Thomas jokes.

"Ha-ha. Let's go, Dent." Bullocks urges with a chuckle. Bullocks is the happy-go-lucky type working in the dark catacombs amidst the dreck of society. He enjoys his job and smiles, not a sarcastic or evil grin, but a joyful smile thoroughly relishing the opportunity to serve as a corrections officer.

Thomas turns and sticks his hands between two of the metal bars, knowing the routine all too well. Bullocks ties Thomas's wrists with rope. Officer Whitmore, a stern looking older officer stands nearby, peering over Bullocks's shoulder. He watches with a bent eye, closely inspecting all the actions around him.

"I'm going to miss you, Dent. Just one last hurrah." Whitmore relates in a dark devious tone, enunciating every syllable with the utmost perfection.

"No offense, Whitmore, but I don't feel the same." Thomas musters the energy to allow a smile to momentarily drag across his face.

Whitmore pulls out a long bullwhip off the side of his hip where it had been nuzzled in its belt holder. He has it out in his hand, rolling between his fingertips, ready for a crack if need be.

"Just make a wrong move for old time sake," Whitmore's sinister tone challenges Thomas. His words drip of evil and his smirk is worthy of a firm smack.

Bullocks finishes tying off the rope and uses his black club to gently push Thomas forward. "Let's go." Bullocks wipes his smile and firms his expression for his intimidating boss.

Whitmore trails from behind, enjoying his position of power, as Bullocks ushers Thomas along.

A few of the prisoners rise and watch as Thomas makes the fateful steps through the long walk; the dark mile with no light at the end of the tunnel.

"The big house! Congrats on your graduation, Dent. Trenton!" Whitmore sarcastically plays up Thomas's new home. "Ten more years. That's quite a stretch up there. A rough crowd in *that* house."

"You worried about me, Whitmore?" Thomas sarcastically asks.

"Oh, no. You're going to get your fill of me long before you get there. We're handling the transport. I specifically asked the warden for the honor."

"Great. Looking forward to it," Thomas sarcastically states. His eyes roll knowing he is in for a long ride.

Thomas is led out through a side metal side door. The entourage moves outside, exiting the prison, stepping out into the middle of nowhere. Tall pines surround the warn down structure and home to many delinquents. Thomas looks up and smells, closing his eyes, taking in the damp heavy air. He smiles and nods, a thought striking his mind. *It's going to be a rough one.*

It is dark outside and the sky grumbles as if stating its bad intentions for the evening. Thomas stops and one more time gazes up at the deep grey clouds blanketing the world above him. There are no stars in the sky, only thick darkness, Mother Nature's pall extending all across the world's ceiling.

"There's a storm coming," Thomas senses the danger above.

"Get moving, *Sally*. We don't need your weather prophecies," Whitmore sarcastically snaps back.

Bullocks gives Thomas a shove in his back. Thomas glances over his shoulder, angrily snapping a look at Bullocks. It is an uncharacteristic action by the officer and catches Thomas off-guard.

"Easy on the tough-guy routine, Bullocks," Thomas requests.

"Just keep moving, all right." Bullocks all but concedes he is performing tough for Whitmore. He wants no problems with his superior.

Whitmore walks ahead and cracks his bullwhip for fun. The snap causes everyone to flinch as if a grenade just went off.

"Gonna be a great ride, boys!" he shouts with excitement, his villainous voice filling the crisp night air.

They reach the police transfer wagon. The cab in the back has bars and is attached to four horses. The rickety door is opened and Thomas is shoved inside. Two other men are sitting inside the transfer cage. The back cab has chains and shackles ready to lock themselves upon its tenants. Bullocks steps in and chains Thomas's feet and then proceeds to lock in his arms. He takes out a knife and cuts the rope he had tied around Thomas's wrists for the walk over.

"Those feel all right?" Bullocks asks. He now shows some compassion with Whitmore not leering over his shoulder.

"I'm all good, Bullocks. Thanks."

Bullocks nods and turns to step out of the car. Pratt jumps forward out of his seat, the dirty prisoner with numerous missing teeth nearly scares Bullocks half to death. Bullocks jumps as the shackles reach their limit and Pratt's face stops just a few inches from the young officer's.

"Gotcha," Pratt chuckles, amused he scared Bullocks; his raspy voice comes from years of enjoying cigars and cigarettes.

"Somethin's wrong with you, Pratt," Bullocks shakes his head. He continues out of the back cab and closes the door behind him. He looks back at the prisoners one last time and walks away.

Thomas is staring at Pratt with an unimpressed glare.

"What? Don't like a little fun?" Pratt sports his twisted lips and cocky smile.

Thomas shakes his head and sits back, seeking to enjoy the ride and the scenery on the way to their new home. Pratt turns to the other man in shackles, Ben. The nearly six-foot four inch massive black man is quiet and keeps to himself. His lips are tucked like well-secured sheets on a bed. His stare is idle, looking off to a distant sanctuary for his troubled mind. He displays no interest in Pratt's games.

"How about you, Negro? You like a good prank?" Pratt chooses to play with Ben, seeking attention wherever he can get it.

Ben turns away, not wanting to entertain Pratt.

"Gonna be a long ride, boys. Might as well enjoy the air. It's gonna be the last we taste for a long while," Pratt narrates the terms to his fellow inmates. He then sits back and closes his eyes.

Bullocks sits beside Officer Martin. Martin grabs the reigns and looks behind him for orders. Whitmore places a black-rimmed cowboy hat upon his head and makes eye contact with Martin. He subtly nods, propping his feet up.

"Let's ride," Whitmore subtly commands, comfortably settling back in his seat.

Martin nods and snaps the reins. The horses' hooves pound the dirt road, the chains around them clanking as they trot down the road. The wheels to the carriage roll across the ground, the wagon creaking as it's pulled along. The wheels move up and down over the uneven ground.

The wagon travels from a clearing in a forest through the middle of a dark empty nearby town. Distant grumbles of thunder mock the prisoner transfer from a distance. Soon, the town turns to forest again as the police coach makes its way down the long dirt road carved through the thick brush. Thunder rumbles once and lightning strikes to the north are setting an ominous tone for the ride as they head directly toward the storm.

"You think we should settle up somewhere, sir?" Bullocks expresses concern to Whitmore.

Whitmore is relaxing by himself in the second seat, his face concealed by his hat. A single eye peeks out from underneath his hat with an annoyed glare accompanying the look.

"If I wanted to suggest that, Bullocks, I would have recommended such an action. We ride on. We have a schedule to keep." Whitmore disappears back under his hat.

"Yes, sir." Bullocks glances over at Martin. They share a concerned look as thunder continues to crackle and grow louder. The lightning strikes, once distant, are no longer so far away.

"YOU still sore with me, Tommy boy?" Pratt opts to break the silence in the back of the prisoner cab by verbally poking at Thomas.

"I am my own man. I make my own decisions." Thomas turns away, not wanting to engage in discussion with Pratt.

Pratt laughs and shakes his head. "Cocky kid," he sarcastically states. Pratt turns his attention to Ben.

"What are you in for, big fella? Heard you violated a woman." Pratt smiles, anxiously awaiting some dirt from Ben.

Ben slowly turns toward Pratt, his eyes squinting, his face dull and expressionless. He is a younger man, in his early 20s, full of anger, and is disinterested in Pratt's need to chat. Ben, like Thomas, carries a great deal of distain for Pratt.

"I ain't ever violate no woman," Ben states, the whites of his eyes growing along with the pulsating veins in his neck. His fists clinch and he brings his arms forward, the chains clanking around him. If Ben wasn't restrained, he would tear Pratt to shreds.

"Easy, big fella. You almost as angry as my boy over here," Pratt gives a nod to Thomas. Thomas bitterly flashes his eyes over at Pratt and then turns away.

"We were in relations," Ben justifiably states. "We were going to be married."

"But you a Negro and she was white—right?" Pratt advances into the details he already possessed.

"She was *Laura*—that's what she was. And I am Ben. And we were to be married."

"You got some set of balls, Benny. Some set of balls. Good for you." Pratt turns his attention back over to Thomas. "And my partner over here…"

"I ain't your partner, Pratt. We're done," Thomas snaps bitterly at Pratt.

"See that, Ben? That's what immaturity gets you. I've lived nearly double this young fella over here. I can tell you that you might as well enjoy life now because it ain't gonna come no easier. Don't be bitter, Tommy. Forgive and forget I always say," Pratt starts to chuckle, amusing himself.

Both Ben and Tommy tune the annoying *fly* out and look away. Rain starts to fall, light at first, then heavier. Large drops of water and the stiffening of the wind quickly up the ante. Loud thunder crashes above them with lightning bolts firing down dangerously close to the wagon's location. Pounding rain is teaming down from the sky and the wind whips with bad intentions. The prisoner transport is moving into the eye of a nasty storm.

"Sir, the horses are getting spooked out here!" Martin hollers as the horses are snapping their heads with angst and loudly snorting through their noses. Bursts of warm air, visible in the cold, emit out of the snouts of the mighty beasts. The officers all have their rain gear on, with heavy coats and hats providing them some protection from the storm.

"Sir?" Bullocks turns to Whitmore.

Whitmore is looking ahead and around. "About five miles up there is a small town. We can shelter up there until the storm passes!"

Martin and Bullocks each give a sigh of relief.

The rain water is starting to collect in the road and makes it very difficult for the horses to pull the police cab. Lightning shoots down from the sky and strikes a tree nearby, causing the horses to rise up and panic, strange screams coming from their lungs.

"Whoa!" Martin struggles to control the reins, the horses now lifting up off their front hooves in a panic.

Bullocks's eyes flare open with concern as he grips the sides of his seat as if his life was in imminent danger, the front of the wagon getting raised by the strength of the frightened horses.

"Relax, Bullocks!" Whitmore shouts as the horses continue to panic. Whitmore rises despite the chaos and then thunder pounds their position again. The horses wildly rise into the air and when they come back down, the right front wheel snaps. Whitmore is tossed off the coach and pancakes on the wet mud. The transport carriage comes to a complete stop and Whitmore slowly lifts up from his mud-marinade.

From inside the back of the cab there is laughing, a dark amused cackle. It is Pratt, but the men are concealed inside their dark cage. A muddy wet mess, Whitmore glares up from the ground and stares with beady infuriated eyes at the cab. Bullocks jumps down to help his fallen superior as Martin settles the horses.

"Are you all right, sir?" Bullocks rushes to Whitmore's side to help him up.

"Get away, Bullocks!" Whitmore shouts, embarrassed. He rises up on his own, mud sliding down his clothing, dripping like thick blackened pancake mix. Whitmore's scowl pushes through the mud as he looks for someone to confront.

The ground is pooling with water as the rain soaks the already oversaturated terrain. The heavy rains are quickly filling the road as the thunder continues to relentlessly crackle and bolts of lightning streak across the dark skies.

"Are you hurt sir?" Bullocks again attempts to appeal to his boss with concern.

"Bring them out here," Whitmore angrily growls to Bullocks. "Chain them to the side of the coach," he orders, his bright white teeth grinding with fury. His teeth shine compared to the mud streaked all across his face.

"Okay. Yes, sir." Bullocks moves quickly, sensing Whitmore's discontent. He unlocks the prisoner cab and opens the door.

As more thunder rumbles above, Whitmore unfurrows his bullwhip and snaps it angrily on the muddy terrain. The loud sound brings Bullocks's head around with concern. He gulps, knowing Whitmore has bad intentions.

"Chain them and remove their shirts!" the muddied officer demands, his warm breath visible in the cold night air.

Martin pulls the brake on the transport coach and hops off. He moves over to the horses to try and calm them down, patting their faces, easing their nerves. "Easy, girls. Easy."

Whitmore angrily looks over the broken wheel and turns back and watches as Bullocks finishes chaining the shirtless men to the side of the cab. The men are shivering, the cold rain and steady wind causing them an unbearable chill. Their backs are all scarred with marks from Whitmore's bullwhip. Ben has the most healed lash marks, with Pratt and Thomas only having a few.

Whitmore snaps his bullwhip on the ground by the men, water and mud splashing up from the wicked strike. They slightly flinch, all trying to remain as strong and brave as possible.

"I want the man who laughed at my unfortunate accident. I want the man who thinks it is funny to fall into mud. I want to hear that man laugh now. I want him to laugh right into my face—right at my eyes." Whitmore's cheeks raise, his eyes bulge out of his sockets and he waits as the sounds of hard driving rain and the rattling branches of the forest dominate the atmosphere. The prisoners all stand silently—shivering from the cold. His eyes slowly scan each and every one of them, hoping to read a tell.

The men barely flinch, none of them willing to rat another prisoner out. Thomas and Ben have every reason to point their fingers at Pratt. But they will not. They stand with their cold chests out, their chins raised just slightly up into the air; a quiet trio awaiting the evil taskmasters next move.

"Come on, gentlemen! Just a name! I want to know who has the best sense of humor! Is it you, Big Ben? I know you would get a kick out of mud striking my face!" Whitmore snaps his bullwhip and it strikes the edge of the cab right near Ben's face, wood trim exploding off the cab from the sharp strike. He flinches but manages to keep his head and eyes straight forward. He is expressionless, harboring his hatred for Whitmore deep inside of him.

"What about you, Pratt? You are a sick son of a bitch!" Again a snap of the bullwhip, this time right by Pratt, the whip cutting into the rain soaked air. Pratt flinches and smiles to himself, amused by the whole production.

"Thomas Dent. How would you fancy a free shot at me?!" Whitmore snaps the whip right by Thomas's leg. Thomas shies away, wanting no part of the end of Whitmore's sinister bullwhip.

Martin comes over, his hands clinched around the outside of his jacket, the cold getting to him. He leans down and checks the broken wheel over, inspecting it with Bullocks by his side.

"It's got a crack!" Bullocks points out.

"We gotta get the spare from under the coach!" Martin advises.

Bullocks gets up and looks at Whitmore. "Sir, we're going to need to change the wheel. It's cracked straight through!" Bullocks shouts amidst the loud storm.

"I'm busy, Bullocks. Do what you must," Whitmore cares little about the wheel at the moment. He is focused on being disrespected and salivating over revenge.

"How about five lashes a man? I can beat the truth out of all of you!" Whitmore shouts.

"Fine! It was me," Thomas blurts out, stepping forward with his chest pushed out.

Pratt looks over at Thomas with a confused look. Ben follows suit. Whitmore moves slowly towards Thomas and stands right behind him, whispering in his ear.

"You, Dent? You think it's funny to fall into mud? You think it's funny I almost broke my neck?" Whitmore's tone is to dig into Thomas, trying to penetrate his psyche. His words are meant as an appetizer proceeding the main course; the lashing of his whip against soft skin.

"I have a weird sense of humor, sir. What can I say?" Thomas replies with a deadpan stare out past the police cab toward the *sticks*. Thomas watches the trees bend and look as though they are about to snap in half. The rain pounds the side of his face with the wind doing equal damage. Thomas squints through the chaos; a welcomed view versus the side of his jail cell. It is worth the lashes and worth ending Whitmore's demented show.

Whitmore smiles, amused, enjoying Thomas's little bit of sass. It will make the beating worth so much more to him. His mouth fills with saliva as he relishes his evil role.

"Ten lashes then," Whitmore enjoyably states, savoring each of the words that fall from his lips as if they were a finely chewed piece of meat.

Whitmore backs up and lines Thomas up for a whipping. Ben stares angrily at Pratt. Pratt averts his eyes with an uncaring roll away from Ben's stare and smirks. His cocky smile is victorious in a way; enjoying the fact that Thomas is about to take a beating on his behalf.

"I'm really going to enjoy this," the evil officer continues to relish the moment. Whitmore grins, showing his pearly whites and snaps his whip in the air above his head as lightning strikes behind him. The crackling of a loud thunder clap follows; the entire world spinning into a dark chaos.

Martin is under the coach attempting to untether the spare wheel. He is knee deep in water and struggling to get the spare loose. Bullocks is standing to the side of the cab, waiting to help him with the weight of the wheel once it's loosened free. The snap of the bullwhip and a slight shriek from Thomas brings Bullocks's head around. Whitmore crows in enjoyment. But it's not Whitmore's laugh through the rain he hears. It's a different kind of thunder that concerns the young officer. He steps away from the wheel and moves forward, looking up the road. The sound is coming towards them like a herd of cows and he cocks his head to the side, trying to see into the dark night what is making that forceful groundswell. Soon, Bullocks sees with his widening eyes. A raging river is bearing down the road; a flash flood charging toward them, causing weak trees to snap, swallowing everything in its wake.

"Flood!" Bullocks shouts at the top of his lungs.

With his bullwhip in the air about to strike Thomas for a second time, Whitmore turns to his right and stares in shock as the raging water heads right at him.

"No!" he screams.

Thomas looks up just in time to see the water strike the horses in front of him. Thomas braces himself, clinching his hands tightly against the cab as the water strikes the helpless prisoners as they cling for their lives. Cuffed to the cab helps them maintain their balance upon the first strike of water. Martin can't get up as he is pinned below the coach by the water and disappears immediately, swallowed up by the flash flood. The cab is picked up off the ground and the entire traveling party is swallowed into the raging river.

Bullocks grabs the side of the cab and is holding on with all his might as the cab is a floating death trap bobbing violently down the road, getting pushed and pulled by waves of water. The raging water encompasses the entire vicinity with no quitting in sight.

The snap of a whip and Whitmore is dragging behind the cab, his bullwhip wrapped around some of the wood, enabling him to bob up and down and attempt survival.

The prisoners are clinging to the side of the cab, securely attached by the chains which keep them temporarily above water, riding the flood.

The raging water takes the cab and tosses it at the forest by the tree line. The wood statues present a deathly problem for them if they strike one of the large immovable objects. The men shout as the coach uncontrollably heads towards the large pines, getting steered by fate. Bullocks yells as his body is headed right for a large tree trunk and he is slammed firmly against it. The first blow knocks the wind out of him and crushes a few ribs. He slowly turns his head and the back of the coach is hurled into his body, smashing him up against the tree. The force causes blood to spout out of his mouth like a sprinkler head. His insides are crushed and Bullocks's lifeless body slumps in the water. He slowly is getting carried away and ping-ponging off a few trees before disappearing below the water line.

With the coach snapped into pieces, three prisoners flow through the trees, hanging on to whatever wood they can. Thomas is just ahead of everyone else and uses his chains to catch upon a solid tree stump. He holds on firmly and turns and sees both Ben and Pratt on either side of the tree quickly coming towards him. He knows he cannot save both men with the force of the water. He turns and sticks his hand out for Ben.

"No!" Pratt yells as he is whisked by Thomas, helplessly reaching for him. Pratt misses and his head dips below the furiously moving water, his body quickly disappearing into the dark tree line.

Ben grabs Thomas's hand and hangs on tightly. Thomas does his best to hold his position at the tree despite the force of the water and Ben's large size. He starts to pull Ben in and almost has him to the tree.

"I got you!" Thomas shouts.

Ben is holding on tightly in the raging river when the bullwhip is snapped around his other wrist.

"Ah!" Ben shouts as the whip digs in and Whitmore, struggling to stay above the force of the water, attempting to save himself. He slowly begins to pull himself over to Ben, trying to cut down the distance between them and reach Thomas and the safety of the tree.

Thomas is struggling with all his might to hold onto both men; their weight straining him to his limits.

"Let me go!" Ben insists.

"I won't let you go!" Thomas shouts back.

Whitmore is pulling himself over slowly but surely, clawing his way up his whip over to Ben's arm. He is nearly to the large man, smiling with each clasped pull forward.

"Let me go! He will kill us both!" Ben shouts.

"I'm not going to let you die!"

"No, but I'm going to make sure you live!" Ben swings his arm and gets loose of Thomas's hand.

"No!" Whitmore and Thomas yell in unison as Ben and the sadistic officer go floating away in the raging water tied to one another. They disappear into the dark forest along with the remaining wreckage from the coach.

Thomas does his best to hold on in the pouring rain and brisk wind. The water is cold and Thomas does all he can to brave the elements and wrap his body around the tree. A horse wildly *neighs* as it floats by, struggling to keep its head above the raging river. Thomas watches in shock as the beast floats away into the darkness. He looks around, dark forest and flowing water are all he sees; no more lightning to provide flashes of illumination in the pitch black forest. Distant grumbles of thunder echo in the madness, the storm moving on to claim more victims elsewhere. Thomas clings tightly for thirty minutes until the water slows and starts to subside, the wind calms, and the rain ceases.

Two

THOMAS, scratched, cut and bruised, releases his grip from the tree. He is cold and shivering with his chains limiting his movement. He takes tired strides through the manageable six inches of water. The water is receding quickly but still leaves deep puddles and a lot of mud to trek through. Thomas shuffles his feet along, dragging his chained legs slowly through the muck.

About a half mile up, he spots something; someone. Exhausted and cold, Thomas plods his way over. He arrives and sees Bullocks's dead body sitting in a muddy puddle. His face is bloodied and his skull partially caved in. The sight is grotesque. Thomas leans down and slowly pulls Bullocks's jacket off of his limp torso. He hears jingling and searches the pockets with his shaking frigid fingers. There he finds the keys to his shackles. Thomas undoes his shackles and drops them by Bullocks's body. He places the jacket around his shoulders, aching from the pain inflicted upon his back and plunges his fingers quickly into the pockets for warmth. His eyes flash open and then squint down as he finds something in one of them. Inside the pocket is a leather object; a wallet. Thomas pulls out the wallet and looks inside. There is money and his cheeks subtly raise, the makings of a smile emerging on his long tired face.

Thomas looks over the area and stares down at Bullocks. He is conflicted with multiple thoughts. Survival is the first. Another thought is plaguing Thomas's mind. He doesn't want to leave Bullocks out in the open; his body mangled and ripe for an animal to tear apart. Off to the side is a metal rod off the links that attached the cab to the horses. It is sitting in a puddle stuck in a soft layer of mud. Thomas walks over and grabs it. He pokes at the ground to find the softest point. Satisfied he has probed well, Thomas stabs at the soft surface. Again and again he stabs, digging slowly but surely into the marshy terrain. He digs and digs creating a shallow grave. He goes at it for nearly an hour. Then he rolls Bullocks's lifeless body inside. He starts to cover him back up again, slowly but surely, giving the young officer a proper burial, flinging handfuls of mud to cover him up. Thomas finishes, exhausted, and tosses the metal rod down. He looks up at the crisp beautiful night's sky. The stars shine brightly and are on full display. Thomas shakes his head and smiles, the irony of the extremes giving him pause. After a moment, he walks through the forest, heading in what he believes is east. He looks up at the now clear sky and locates the stars through the tree tops and reads the constellations. He is well-versed and spots Virgo, the blue-white star of Spica, guiding his way just as he thought; east.

THOMAS marches all night into the morning hours. Muddy and beat up, he comes across a two-story home standing in a clearing. It is unfamiliar to him and he has no idea where exactly he is; *possibly the Pinelands*? He is lost somewhere in the forest.

He lumbers toward the home and moves to the porch, stepping up on the deck. A rocking chair is on its side, tossed and broken by the storm from the prior night.

They may not be home. Thomas curiously peers around, bending his head to the right, then to the left, trying to spot any distinguishable clues. He steps forward and knocks on the front door. There are some downed leaves and trees in the area, but nothing that looks like the clutter Thomas encountered on the road the night before. He patiently waits, knowing it is early in the morning. Hungry and thirsty, he can't wait any longer and moves to a nearby window. He attempts to look in through the glass, but the shades only allow him to see outlines of furniture.

Thomas inspects further and rubs his chin. He moves to the back of the house and he can see the kitchen through the window panes on the back door. He reaches for the door handle and pushes in, the door opening freely, it slowly creaking inward. Thomas's eyebrows rise up in surprise. He hesitantly steps inside the quiet home, inching ahead, his eyes bursting open to locate any danger. He is breathless as he surveys his surroundings. Satisfied there are no waiting evils in the corners of the room, he eases up and stands tall. Thomas waits, deafening silence dominating his senses. He grows impatient and curiosity sinks in deeper.

"Hello?" he calls out. "Hello?" he asks again. Thomas waits, frozen. He looks over his shoulder to ensure he is still close to the back door. He has an easy escape route to the forest if something comes charging down the stairs with a shotgun. There is no answer and he slowly and quietly closes the door. He moves around the downstairs, cautiously inspecting it. There are some family photos of three individuals, an older man and woman and a young man. There is a rug and couch in the living room. The home is quaint and nice with recent flower-patterned furnishings. Dust has settled in many areas giving an indication that someone hasn't been here for a while. Of course, they could just be poor cleaners.

Thomas makes his way over to the stairs and sticks his head out.

"Hello?" he once again calls. He waits and gets no answer. Once he commits to the stairs he is a sitting duck.

Thomas takes a small step up and then stops. He looks behind him in the living room and spots a vase. He carefully moves to the vase, the floor ever-so-slightly creeping beneath his feet. He secures the vase in his hands as the only viable weapon around and turns back to the staircase. Thomas takes creaking step after creaking step, the moaning wood painfully giving away his position with each landing of his moist shoes. He holds the vase high into the air as if he were about to unleash it at someone's head at a moment's notice.

He reaches the top of the stairs and sees a thin rug running across the floor. There are three doors and Thomas nervously takes step after step toward the first door. He opens up the door and sees a perfectly made bed. There is no one in the room with freshly painted white furnishings. The faint scent of paint causes Thomas's nostrils to tingle, an indication someone may in fact still live here. Thomas steps through the doorway and sets the vase down on the bed. He makes his way over to a Victorian style white dresser and finds men's clothing in the drawers; pants in one drawer, shirts in another, underwear in yet another. Thomas quickly undresses and gets out of his muddy old clothing. As he arches his back, he cringes. A dried fresh wound running between Thomas's shoulder blades from Whitmore's single lashing gives him some fits. He carefully maneuvers and cringes momentarily as he puts on a clean shirt; then underwear and pants. He looks in the narrowest drawer on bottom and finds clean socks. Thomas takes the socks out and presses them against his nose. He closes his eyes and thankfully squeezes the thick cotton against his cheek. He looks down on the ground, staring at his grey, thin, torn socks. There is no comparison. He quickly pulls his worn socks off and happily places the fresh socks on his feet. He moves over to the closet and sees a single hanging suit. Below the well-kept suit are two pairs of shoes; a single perfectly shined pair of black dress shoes and a pair of worked in walking shoes. Thomas takes off his muddied shoes and tosses them into the closet, placing the walking shoes on his feet.

They fit, he happily boasts to himself. He grabs the rest of his dirty clothes and tosses them into the closet as well and slowly closes the door. He stares at the door for just a second, the closed closet representing a closed chapter in his life. He looks around, remembering he is a foreigner and someone could still be in the house. He refocuses and picks up the vase. He exits the first room, now dressed more comfortably and feeling like a fresh man.

Thomas closes the door and moves to the second door. He cautiously opens it and sees a small room with a half-finished painting on an easel. There are numerous paintings up on the walls, many of them are of flowers in vases and fruit in bowls. Thomas closes the door and looks down the hall toward the final room. He is drawn to the third room and slowly opens the door. His heart drops as he sees a bulge in the bed. *There is someone in this room*! There is an odd scent as he makes his way inside, noticing a few buzzing flies by the bed. Thomas takes slow steps as he tries to see who is underneath the covers.

"Hello?" he asks softly, with a nervous hesitation in his tone. Thomas holds his breath, his head dipping just slightly back as he reaches the covers. He leans in with his lower body leading the way, his face bending back away from whatever may come. His hand extends and grabs the edge of the cover. He pulls the sheets back and sees what looks like the decomposed body of an old woman. She is under the sheets as if she died there and hasn't been touched. She looks like she is becoming mummified.

Thomas goes over and lifts the sheets slightly more, the passed away woman dressed in her white pajamas; grey and dead. Thomas is grossed out, dropping the covers and backing away quickly. He heads out of the room, slamming the door behind him. *Oh, my god!*

Maybe it's her place and she passed here a long time ago. He attempts to rationalize the situation. He heads back down the stairs and moves into the kitchen. He searches the cupboard and sees a few jars of jam and a glass container filled with crackers. He smells the jam and it contains a delicious scent. Thomas brings the jam over to the table and begins to eat, stuffing his face with the sweet treat and crackers. He uses his fingers and grabs clumps of jam. He piles food into his mouth as quickly as possible and then savors the mouthful of flavor. He chews with his cheeks pushed out like a chipmunk, filled to the maximum. It has been a long time since Thomas has tasted something so flavorful; so sweet.

"So good" he says with crackers spitting out. Thomas smiles, enjoying the comforts of a home. He eats some more and then moves over to the refrigerator. He opens up the cold box and sees three pints of milk inside and some vegetables. He stares curiously at the milk and brings it to his nose. He tests its freshness. He smiles, the milk's just right. He takes a sip, savoring the goodness of the cold milk. Thomas drinks amidst his confusion as he tries to figure out what's going on. His deafening silence is intruded upon by the sound of something from outside.

A car motor hums and is growing louder as it arrives by the front of the home. Thomas quickly moves over to the window with the milk in his hand. He sees the car parked by the front of the house and his eyes pop out of his head. He turns every which way in a panic. He rushes into the kitchen and puts the milk back inside. He grabs the jelly and crackers and quickly puts them back into the

cupboard. He goes toward the rear door when he hears a
voice call out-

"I'm checking the garden, pa!" the voice of a
younger man states. The voice is moving right toward the
back door with accompanying footsteps.

"Thanks, son!" an older voice calls right by the
front door.

Thomas races to the stairs and rushes up the steps.
The front door is unlocked and is pushed open just as
Thomas safely reaches the top of the stairs and freezes.

Thomas stands quietly in the hallway pressed up
against the wall, attempting to hide in the shadows away
from the light. The front door closes. One step after another
brings the creaking wood floor to life. The aching wood
also gives away the location of the older man who moves
deeper into the living room downstairs. The back door
creaks open and then closes. A second set of heavy
footsteps enters the home.

"You make a mess in here?" the father questions.

"No. Whatcha mean, pa?" the son asks in a
confused tone.

"Look at this table. You got crackers and jam
everywhere!" he shouts.

Thomas peeks his head out and looks to make his
way down the stairs as he listens to them argue.

All of a sudden there's silence. Thomas waits by the
top step, wanting to make a run for the front door. It is all
but one flight of stairs away from him. Then there is a click
and the sound of a shotgun snapping shut. Thomas's eyes
open and his mouth drops, knowing he is very much in
danger.

"I'm checking upstairs on your mama. Keep your
eyes open!" the father intensely orders.

Thomas slowly and carefully moves backward away
from the stairs as he hears the father's footsteps charging
toward the living room.

Thomas stops at the first bedroom door, freezing. The steps downstairs have seized as well. Thomas isn't sure if the creaking floors have given his position away. Thomas doesn't move, listening intently. He wants to move only when the man downstairs moves.

A very quiet step; then another and another. The man downstairs is slowly moving to the staircase. He is softly stepping like a hunting big cat, the floorboards barely creaking beneath his feet. Thomas has to make a move and gently opens up the first bedroom door. He does all he can to carefully slide his feet inside the room, the gentlest of creaks sounding. He does all he can to close the door, like a pillow laying down upon a mattress. Once inside the room, Thomas holds his breath. Then an explosion of pounding feet, charging footsteps of the father, comes roaring up the stairs.

"I think he's up here!" the older man shouts.

Thomas prepares himself as the footsteps come right to the first door. He doesn't move, not wanting to make any unnecessary noises, but holds his fists up, preparing to pounce.

The footsteps stop, a pause, and then swiftly move by the first door. They head right down the end of the hall by the third bedroom. A second set of footsteps come charging up the stairs toward the bedroom where Thomas is. The doorknob turns and Thomas backs away as the door opens. He hides behind the door as it opens, doing his best to stay out of sight. A foot moves forward into the room and the end of a long shotgun appears.

"Boy! Somebody touched your mother! Somebody was here!" the older man shouts in anger.

There is a pause, a moment of doubt filling the air. There is a creak of the floorboards bending back toward the hallway; the shotgun nose reversing away from Thomas and the first bedroom. The younger man leaves his bedroom door open and rushes down the hall toward his father's voice.

"Oh, baby. Tell me who was here. Tell us who violated our home!" the older man beckons in the far bedroom.

Thomas is beyond unnerved and makes a decisive decision; he makes a run for it. He goes sprinting out of the bedroom and nearly slides down the stairs and he rushes as fast as he can to the front door.

"He's on the run, pa!" the son shouts from upstairs as Thomas opens the front door. A shotgun blast narrowly misses Thomas and blows a hole in the door frame, the wood torn to shreds.

"Oh, crap!" Thomas stumbles out the front door down onto the porch. He uses his feet and kicks the front door shut. He turns with eyes bulging, a panicked expression on his face. He sees the car and leaps up, rushing over to the automobile trying to stay as low to the ground as possible. He dives inside and searches all around for the keys. The front door of the house is kicked back open, the swinging door an alarm bell for Thomas. The son has his shotgun aimed and is looking around in all directions. Thomas quickly ducks, not sure if he was spotted. His breath is short and quickened, his mouth hanging open trying not to make a noise as he inhales and exhales small amounts of air. He hides his head under the steering wheel and spots the keys on the floor. He reaches slowly for the keys, two in total on the chain. He carefully snatches them in his fingers, not wanting to make any noise. Outside the car is silence, the young man with the shotgun is still looking, still hunting—not committing in any direction.

"You see him?!" shouts the father, emerging out onto the porch.

Breathing ever-so-quietly, Thomas carefully brings the keys to the ignition. He holds his breath, knowing a sound—any sound, would signal his doom. He places the key in the ignition and closes his eyes. He takes one deep breath and quickly turns the car on, the machine purring like a kitten.

"He's in the car!" the son yells.

A shotgun blast blows through the front window as Thomas frantically lifts his head up and shifts the car into reverse, backing up as quickly as possible. Another shotgun blast strikes the right front light, causing it to shatter and Thomas to duck. He continues to blindly reverse backwards and then pokes his head up again. He looks and sees the father and son team trying to hopelessly run after him. Thomas glances over his shoulder and sees he is bearing down on a tree and tries to hit the brakes. He is too late and slams into the tree, the back of the car caving in.

Thomas pulls his face off the steering wheel, a fresh cut above his right eye causing blood to streak down the side of his face. He is momentarily stunned and grabs his neck, trying to regain his bearings.

"Hurry!" the father yells to the son.

Another shotgun blast strikes the tree Thomas planted the car against. Thomas wakes right up and he refocuses. He sees the strange father-son team rushing toward him. He shifts the idling car into drive and quickly pulls around and drives away down the road, leaving the strange duo long behind in a whirl of dust.

Three

THE car stalls out and dies as Thomas emerges
from the forest. He sits at the edge of a small bustling
town. He pulls the dying car over to the side of the road,
smoke pluming out of the engine. He focuses his eyes on a
distant sign reading *Restaurant.* The sign is jetting out over
the sidewalk where businesses are lined up, one after
another, making up the quaint bustling town. Cars, a few
horses, and a decent smattering of townies and travelers are
moving through the roads on foot. The townies are
enjoying the beautiful sea-driven air wafting over the
quaint city.

Must be by the ocean, Thomas nods, smelling the
familiar scent of the sea. He looks around further and sees
travelers who are happily shopping, dressed in fine outfits
from New York City. They don't look like small town folk.
The women look overheated in their cloche hats and
flapper dresses, waving decorative fans by their faces. The
men are in their white suit pants and light colored jackets,
also looking a bit heated. It feels as if it is almost 70
degrees and the sun is perfectly hot on this fine spring day.

"You need a hand, fella?" a man approaches
Thomas. He is looking over the dying vehicle, watching as
steam rises out.

"No, sir. That's quite all right. I'm just gonna let her settle a bit and enjoy the town." Thomas keeps things light and innocent.

"You new here? I mean no offense. I can guide you in the direction you want to head if need be." The man is kind, far kinder than the people Thomas is used to dealing with.

"I'm okay. But thank you. Much appreciated." Thomas squints into the sunlight, attempting to ascertain where exactly he has landed. His head pans around, trying to get a read on his surroundings.

"Not a problem! Just holler if you need a hand or two," the man offers. He nods and continues walking down the street.

Thomas looks around with a perplexed look on his face. This isn't the big city he is used to. It's a calm, peaceful, happy world.

He walks past the American Stores Company and continues onward, strolling by a church. He sees a hanging street sign reading *Main Shore Road* and comes to an intersection. A sign reading *Bay Street* heads north and south in front of him. The Great Atlantic & Pacific Tea Company draws Thomas over to their store front. He smiles, a calm feeling settling upon him, recognizing the business. He crosses the street and heads into the company store. Thomas knows the name from New York City. The familiar market chain must have expanded down here to this coastal town in New Jersey. It is a sight for sore eyes for Thomas. It is the only store he recognizes.

He shuffles inside and looks around for a drink and some food. He moves through the aisles and starts to grab food as he sees it, his eyes growing bigger than his stomach. It has been a few years since Thomas remembers being inside an A&P. He is happy to pick out everything his heart desires.

"Sir," a man behind Thomas states.

Thomas freezes for a moment, uncertain of what the man may want. Why is another stranger approaching him? He slowly turns, food piled in his arms. The man is a store clerk and he happily offers a hand-held wood shopping basket. "Try this. I can get you a second one if you need." The clerk is dressed in a long sleeve collared shirt and dress pants. He is wearing a sparkling clean apron and has a pencil tucked in by his right ear.

"Thank you, sir," Thomas kindly replies. He sets the items down, keeping an eye on the clerk. Thomas is weary of the man despite his kindness. He keeps a good eye on him as they place the food into the basket. Once finished, the store clerk looks up at Thomas with a big smile.

"Let me know if there's anything else you need, sir!" he happily expresses.

Thomas subtly nods and the man walks away. Thomas places just a few more items in the basket and looks toward the front door. He sees the daylight of the door and a basket filled with wonderful food. He has an urgency to run. He wants to walk right out the door with the food. It is Thomas's first instinct. The clerk is laughing and jabbering away with a woman. They seem to know each other and are exchanging stories. He could leave and no one would be any wiser.

Thomas, intensely staring at the door, takes a step toward the light; then another. He moves to a stack of canned food closest to the entrance and pretends to look around. He turns and is half-facing the light from the street shining into the store. He takes a step when-

"Can I ring that up for you, sir?" the clerk, again with a kind tone, offers.

Thomas freezes and then turns to him.

"Yes. I'm curious how much this all is."

"Well. Come on over and I'll take care of that for ya!" The clerk turns to the woman. "Talk to ya later, Cheryl!"

"Bye, Bob!" she happily returns and moves past Thomas and walks out the front door.

"Let's see what you got, fella."

Thomas places the basket of food up on the counter. The clerk pulls out a small pad and the pencil off of his ear. He begins to add up the total of Thomas's bounty.

"You moving in for the summer months?" the chatty clerk asks.

"Um, not sure. I'm visiting."

"You have family here?" he asks.

"Just visiting." Thomas tries to keep things as plain as possible.

The clerk flashes his eyes up at Thomas for just a moment and then returns to focusing on the food items being purchased. Becoming a little paranoid, Thomas tries to correct his answer and be less evasive. "I like the town. I'm thinking of maybe moving my family down here— from Philadelphia."

"Big city! Yeah. We move just a bit slower down here but are awfully happy about it. Great town," the clerk states.

"How do you pronounce it again?"

"Barnegat. Originally Berende-gat and then Barndegat. But now just Barnegat; the vacation destination for anyone who loves sun and sand," the clerk pitches the city like a commercial.

"New Jersey, right?" Thomas tries to make certain he knows exactly where he is.

"Of course! Only one Barnegat. And across the bay is Barnegat City. She's a beaut! I highly recommend a trip out there."

Thomas nods and looks around as the clerk finishes ringing up the total.

"That will be two dollars and ten cents. If you are going to stay a while, you can start an account here." The clerk offers Thomas a way out of not paying.

"Um…wow, that sounds great." Thomas looks down and remembers the wallet in his pocket and quickly pulls it out. He hands the clerk over three one dollar bills from inside the fold. "I'll come back and start that account if I stay," Thomas says.

"Suit yourself. We'll be here," the clerk happily states and gives him his change.

Thomas nods.

Thomas exits the A&P with a brown bag full of his food. He walks down the road, reaching inside the bag and pulling out a piece of bread. As he chomps on the bread he continues to enjoy the sea breeze of this kind coastal town. He sees a sign reading *Post Office* down the street. He thinks to himself, stopping in his tracks. He stares at the sign and debates the merits of walking over to the store. He takes a deep breath and marches, with his bag, across the street and heads to the Post office. There's an adjacent larger sign reading *Groceries* next to it. He makes the decision to go inside.

He enters the store and a bell rings. An older woman stands behind the counter. She is holding a book in her hands, reading. Behind her is a flip board with the date reading: April 20th, 1919. The store is filled with a variety of supplies: brooms, clocks, bags of flour, jars and cans of various foods stacked in shelving behind the counter as high as the ceiling. There are a few chairs in the corner of the room and a small stack of lanterns and candles. The store seems to have a little of everything. Thomas looks around the shop and sees all the various supplies.

"Can I help you, sir?" the woman pleasantly asks.

"Is this the post office entrance?"

"It's just next door. I handle that as well. I'm Mrs. Buttersworth."

"Okay. Do you have paper and a pencil to write with?" Thomas asks, not having any of the necessities he needs to construct a letter.

"I have plenty." The kind old woman bends down, disappearing behind the counter for just a moment. She reappears with a piece of paper and a pencil.

"How much do I owe you?" Thomas offers to pay, wanting to do the right thing.

"Oh, dear, I have plenty. Just let me know where you want to mail the letter to." Mrs. Buttersworth smiles and continues with her perfectly calm pleasant tone.

"Thank you." Thomas looks down at the piece of paper and pencil as if he were taking a test, his face pulling in with some anguish. There is indecision behind his expression. He looks back up at Mrs. Buttersworth and she has gone back to her book. He feels intimidated and unsure of himself. He takes the paper and folds it up and places it in his pocket. "May I take this and bring it back?" Thomas asks.

"Of course dear. Not a problem."

"I'm just not sure what to write yet."

"I'll be right here when you figure that out. There's no rush."

Thomas nods. "Thanks, again."

"You have a wonderful day."

Thomas bobs his head again, feeling the need to persistently nod, and exits the post office. He looks out at the light of day, enjoying the sunlight on his face. He stands there, almost as if posing, letting the beautiful day soak in on his deprived skin.

"I've missed you," Thomas whispers to himself, the sunlight providing a beacon of hope upon his soul.

A steam engine sounds from the east. It's distant, but brings Thomas's head around. He is curious and takes a step in that direction. He stops in his tracks when he sees a policeman on horseback riding toward him. He looks down, nervous, not wanting to make eye contact with the officer. Thomas lifts his brown paper bag up high to cover his face. He peers around the bag up toward the officer on horseback. The policeman's eyes glance over at Thomas and he barely gives him a second thought. He continues to ride down the street with a smile on his face.

Thomas relaxes and walks down the road, heading east toward the smell of sand and the shore.

The walk gives way to dusk as Thomas reaches the docks. He looks around and sees a few people fishing off a small dock. A boat is tied down with an older man standing upon it. Thomas decides to move in the man's direction. The old man has a sea captain's hat on and a long grey beard. His face has been weathered by the sun and time. He possesses sturdy hands as he plays with a fishing net.

"Sir?" Thomas asks, uncertain if the man welcomes communication with strangers.

The man doesn't say a word and continues on with his fishing equipment.

Thomas takes a step closer. "Sir?" he asks a little louder. Thomas's shadow starts to reach the tip of the man's boat and he instinctively looks up with curiosity. He sees Thomas staring at him.

"Hello, there," the man states.

"I was just wondering if you give rides?" Thomas asks.

"Rides? What, you mean like a charter boat?" the man asks.

"Where is Barnegat City?" Thomas asks.

The old man smiles and looks up at Thomas with a gleam in his eye. "Right past my head."

Thomas stares at the old man, confused at first. He straightens up and turns, pointing out toward the island across the bay where the lighthouse stands tall. It's as clear as day on this beautiful late afternoon.

"You may have not been able to see her yesterday, but right out there on yonder is the lighthouse. That's Barnegat City."

"Can you take me there? I can pay you."

"Oh, I was just gonna tie down for the night," the old man rubs his chin.

"I can give you a dollar."

"Oh, it's not the money. The misses will be sore at me."

"I bet a new dress bought with that dollar will solve that soreness," Thomas negotiates with the man and sports a big smile.

"It sure would." The old man thinks for a moment and then nods. "All right. You got your things? I want to make it back to shore before dark."

"Yes. Thank you, sir. You are too kind."

The old man nods.

Thomas gets into the boat with his brown bag of food and the old man unties his rope. He shoves off and pulls the string to ignite his engine. It takes a couple of tries and then it fires on. The old man's motor boat is off and they head east to the island and make a heading for Barnegat City.

Four

"I'M PROUD of you. You did great yesterday—shined *real* bright. You did good, ol' girl." The keeper praises his lighthouse, gently cleaning the giant 12 foot Fresnel lens as he prepares for dusk and another evening of work. Dressed in a bright yellow cleaning coat, the keeper works carefully on the lens. "My time is gonna be over soon. You know that. I can't be with you forever. And after Felicia, well, you know I don't have long left, either." The keeper continues to clean all around the lens. "I know-I know. But I like to clean you twice a day. Once in the morning is not enough. You will shine for me. You will shine for all." The keeper finishes cleaning the glass around the large lens.

"Time for your feeding, my dear," he states. He takes a brass oil measuring can of kerosene and fills the lamp. "Is this what you wanted?" he asks the lighthouse as if it were his closest friend. He finishes and sets the brass dispenser down. He turns and looks out of the windows of the tower at the ocean around him. The vast blue water is turning darker in the distance. The golden sun is starting to dip in the west and the scattered blues and purples in the east welcome in the evening and the darkness to come.

"I think it's going to be a grand night, Barney," he states. The keeper smiles and stares at the view, soaking in the world around him.

The keeper takes a seat upon a wood padded folding chair. He watches as the world slowly grows darker; the blues becoming purples, the deep purples turning to blackness. He takes out a small paper bag and begins to eat a slice of bread. He grabs a tin cup and pours out steaming hot coffee. He takes a sip and smiles, enjoying the peaceful moment.

"Breakfast is served, darling. Would you like some?" he asks, smiling at his own joke.

He waits and receives no answer except the whistling wind and the sounds of waves crashing up against the rocks below.

"More for me then," he states. He drinks and eats.

After a few minutes, the keeper finishes up his food and removes his yellow cleaning coat. He reveals his uniform; a sharp clean blue jacket with numerous brass buttons. The lapel is finely creased over. He moves to the furthest corner where a hat is hooked upon a coat rack. He places his yellow cleaning coat on the rack and swaps it out for his navy blue lighthouse keeper insignia hat. He carefully places the hat upon his head, treating it like fine china. He pulls his jacket down and props his head proudly up; chin raised, chest out. Two lanterns are sitting on the ground. Their light is starting to shine more and more as darkness arrives. He grabs one of the lanterns and removes the glass lid.

"All out of matches today," he says. "I'll get to the store soon—I promise." He gazes fondly upon the inside of the prism lens as if it were his own beating heart.

He reaches out and lights the wicks. The five wicks ignite together to form a single bright light. The lens projects the light out toward the darkening seas and the keeper smiles.

"I never get tired of that," he states. He takes out his telescope and looks through it, seeing the last of the limited light the world has to offer. As God's light dies down the keeper's tower light pours into the ocean. He surveys the entire eastern sea with his spyglass. "All quiet on the eastern front, Barney. Let's keep'em safe tonight," he says aloud.

THE road is darkening and the temperature dropping. Thomas is carrying his brown bag walking north. He sees a few large structures and the beacon in the night; the lighthouse. The Barnegat Lighthouse stands tall, piercing up nearly two hundred feet into the dark sky. Its light is shining deeply into the darkness across the ocean and it is drawing Thomas closer to it with every step he takes. He approaches 8th Street and sees The Barnegat City Inn. The quaint building looks inviting to Thomas. He takes out Bullocks's wallet and checks inside. Only a dollar remains. Darkness has fully immersed the island and Thomas can't take his eyes off the lighthouse. He sees the outline of a large structure up ahead just before the tall beacon. He opts to walk away from the inn and head further north, moving toward the tower.

A cluster of houses and shanties lay nestled tightly by the shore with only a few faint lights signaling life inside. The burning of small wicks inside cloudy hanging lanterns draws Thomas's eyes as he lethargically passes by. The wind howls through their crevices, their wood skeletons moaning and growing as the men inside snore in perfect harmony with the breeze.

The cool wind is bringing chills to Thomas, similar to that of the cold brought to his core by last evening's storm. There is a serene sense about this world that brings

Thomas to a place of peacefulness. There is just enough wind to make a crooning sound in the eaves and a steady whisper in the sparsely placed cedars. The trees and structures are scattered on either side of the road, darkness cloaking much of their exteriors. The star of the island continues to be the flashing beacon of the lighthouse.

Thomas plops his tired feet one after another in the direction of a large building just off the ocean. He begins to kick up dirt, his heavy cement-filled legs unable to lift sufficiently up off the ground. He is only fifty yards from the lighthouse, but Thomas's legs feel like hundred pound weights. His body is finally surrendering to exhaustion. In the lighthouse's immediate gaze, a large dark building calls to Thomas. It lacks the life of an occupied four-story hotel. The darkness surrounds not only its outsides, but its insides as well.

The building is grand, huge in stature—four stories standing proudly into the night. The light from the plentiful stars gives Thomas a good view of the building's outline. As opposed to the large structure being a bustling mecca here in the spring, it is dark and dead silent. The ocean's waves and the whistling breeze are the only sounds heard beside this local skyscraper.

A broken sign reading *Oceanic* sways ever-so-slightly in the wind by the front entrance. The sign has been torn to shreds with only the one word remaining; *Oceanic*. Thomas, with his brown bag in his hands, slowly steps through some broken wood and moves to the chained front doors. A wood sign stating the premise's clear purposes is hammered right above the front entrance; *CLOSED*. Thomas looks around and moves to one of the nearby bay windows. He tries to see inside the hotel but it is dark and deserted. Dust has built up by the window sills and gives further indication of abandonment. He looks around as if someone could see him; a good samaritan may think he is a lurking robber up to no good. But there are no takers on this spring evening. There isn't a soul outside; just Thomas. Satisfied he is by himself, Thomas reaches back and kicks the window, busting a hole in it. He uses the bottom of his foot and kicks more of the window off. Once the window panel is safely cleared of glass, Thomas slowly edges inside. He moves into the dark lobby which sports weathered and beat-up red carpeting. He takes a few steps forward and sees a closed door. Thomas opens the door and sees an empty desk with a chair behind it. The darkness doesn't provide much more context than that. The light from the clear night's sky draws minimal illumination into the lobby but is blocked from penetrating the darkened office.

Thomas turns back and makes his way to the hallway where he finds an opening to a large room. With a few tables scattered about and chairs stacked awkwardly in one corner, the grand room looks like the former inhabitants of a dining room. Large chains hang a few feet down from the ceiling, dangling with nothing at their ends. Perhaps chandeliers or beautiful lamps hung down at the ends of those chains. Now they just dangle hopelessly in the darkness. Thomas exits the room and continues the self-guided tour, searching for a place to rest his tired legs.

He moves up a set of stairs to the second floor. He strolls across the red carpeted hallway, a running theme throughout the hotel, and sees a few small empty rooms. He steps into another large room; a ballroom. The old dusty parquet floor runs all the way through the spacious room. A covered piano sits as a hidden gem in one far corner, slightly raised on a two foot high platform. More chairs and a few tables are clustered together in the other corner of the room. Thomas curiously walks over to the piano and he smiles as he approaches the musical instrument. He sets his bag down and removes the cover. Thomas stares at the perfectly clean body and keys. His brows furrow in and his cheeks rise slightly with a confused half-cocked grin. He doesn't feel an ounce of dust or see any dirt on it. Thomas pulls the piano chair out from underneath the piano and takes a seat. He presses into a few keys, the piano perfectly tuned. Thomas looks around, perplexed by this perfectly kept musical instrument. Thomas listens and looks around, suspicious of the piano's presence. All he hears is the whistling light breeze and the crashing waves by the shoreline.

Satisfied, Thomas places the cover back on the piano and carefully pushes the chair back under the musical instrument's body. *Another time.*

Thomas walks back into the hallway, his feet dragging. The intrigue of the hotel carried him this far, but he needs a place to lie down. The wind and ocean continue to provide a beautiful backdrop to the abandoned hotel. Instead of further inspecting the third and fourth floors, Thomas's exhausted body and mind give in. He finds a nearby empty room, the remains of what once was a hotel bedroom. The room has been stripped naked, just four walls and a curiously clean floor. Thomas looks back at the hallway and moves toward the red carpeting. He leans down and presses his hand against it. It isn't as thick as it once was when they laid it upon the grand hotel's floorboards. But it will do.

"No rougher than the cell cot," Thomas jokes to himself. He places his brown bag down beside him and lies on the carpet. He closes his eyes to the softly crashing waves and whizzing wind of the night.

THOMAS opens his eyes. He looks around confused, not knowing where he is. It is dark and his eyes pierce through the darkness in an unfamiliar bedroom. The furniture is dark oak and there is a large vanity mirror atop a dresser. Sitting up in bed, Thomas is staring at his own reflection. The moon outside provides plenty of illumination despite the darkness of the room. Thomas looks to his left and sees a beautiful woman; a brunette. She is sound asleep. He gets up out of bed and walks, drawn toward a bad feeling; an evil sixth sense. Thomas looks around to grab something—a weapon. He goes to his dresser near the bedroom door. He carefully opens up the drawer and his pupils increase in size as they fixate upon something. He reaches inside and pulls out a revolver. He pops open the barrel and makes sure it's loaded. He snaps it closed like an experienced gunslinger. Satisfied, he prepares the gun to be fired, cocking the hammer back.

A brisk wind finds its way into the bedroom and Thomas now realizes he has no shirt on. He is topless, cold, wearing only his flannel pajama bottoms. Thomas holds the gun out in front of him as he walks through the red carpeted hallway. He looks to the left and sees an empty room. There is nothing but four empty walls and a small wooden box in the middle. He stops, drawn to the wooden box. There are black childlike painted letters on the top of the box. It reads *Thomas.* He walks to the center of the room, leans down and hears something from down the hall; a shriek of some kind from a small boy. Thomas looks back down to the ground and the box is gone.

He rises back up to his feet, the gun steadily drawn before him. He slowly sticks his head out into the hallway, making no sudden moves. His bare feet take careful steps upon the red carpeted floor. But with each step upon the carpet, a creak is brought to life. The creaking floorboards only seem to increase in loudness the more Thomas tries to dull their aching.

"Help," the muffled sound of a helpless boy calls out.

Thomas hears the cries and takes more determined steps, increasing his speed. He looks into the next bedroom and sees two people asleep. He pokes his head inside and moves toward the two lumps concealed underneath the covers. He slowly peels the covers back and sees the dead old woman, decayed and long gone, lying in bed next to a man who is turned away from Thomas. Thomas backs away, not wanting to disturb the man and needing to get away from the old corpse. He backpedals into the hallway, carefully shutting the door.

He continues on down the hall and enters another bedroom. Water is flowing out of the room, pouring into the hallway, soaking Thomas's feet. The cold water makes him shiver as he looks up and sees a man dressed in a raincoat holding a large hook with a swordfish dangling down, dead. The man, with a full beard, looks over toward Thomas with an angry glare. After a moment, the fisherman turns away from Thomas in disgust.

Thomas backs out of the room, closing the door, more water pouring out from under it. The door springs more leaks, higher up, near the knob. The wood begins to bend into the hallway as a large amount of pressure is building behind the door. The crackling of wood being pushed to its limits gives way to snapping and pieces of the door shredding apart. Thomas backs away, heading deeper down the hallway as the water fires out of sprung leaks. The door has become a badly damaged dam; the leaks multiplying one after another.

Thomas runs, sprinting away down the endless hallway. The red carpet keeps going no matter how fast or far Thomas runs. Water explodes out of the doorway behind him and rages toward Thomas.

Thomas runs and runs but is no match for the river of water chasing after him. He is swallowed up into the cold swell. It engulfs the entire hallway, a giant flash flood infiltrating the structure. He tries to stay afloat and desperately reaches for anything. He swipes, once, twice and finally is able to grab a random piece of wood to help keep his face just above the raging river.

A bullwhip is snapped and wraps tightly around his right wrist. Thomas's head bows back in pain.

"Ah!" he screams.

"You're mine now, Dent!" Whitmore's evil voice crows. He is standing just inside a doorway, safe from the flood. His door is raised above the flow of water and provides him an excellent view as he looks down upon the helpless Thomas. Whitmore pulls his bullwhip in like a rope, dragging Thomas through the water toward him.

Thomas tries to break free of the bullwhip but cannot loosen its grip on his wrist. The whip cuts into his skin.

"I've told you a thousand times before, Dent, once I have my man, I always have him," Whitmore maniacally laughs for effect as he continues to pull in Thomas.

Thomas lifts up out of the water and sharply drops down, pulling hard on the whip with his other free hand. He uses his body weight to surprise Whitmore and drags him down into the water with him. Whitmore is submerged with Thomas. It is an ocean of dying artifacts flowing by them; wrecked pieces of wood, Bullocks's dead body, fish and other life seen only at the bottom of an ocean. Thomas and Whitmore begin to fight under the water. Whitmore does all he can to prevent Thomas from getting a breath, holding him down in the flowing rapids. He ties the bullwhip around a randomly placed old rusted anchor sitting in a pile of sand and swims away, laughing.

Thomas is stuck, the bullwhip not releasing off his bloody wrist and now the other end tied to an anchor. He swims to the water's crest but is just short of it. He struggles for oxygen, his breath nearly gone. His face feels as if it is reddening, pressure building all around. He feels his eyes bulging out of his skull. He takes a mighty push forward and emerges just a little from the water, getting brief, but needed, oxygen, gasping for as much air as possible. He fights with his upper body to keep his head barely peeked out of the water as his right wrist drags him down below. It is a battle of survival for Thomas.

He is doing his best to pull the anchor up out of the sandy bottom. He tugs and tugs—pulls and pulls. He makes some progress and gets his hand free of the bullwhip; it snapping off of his wounded wrist. He bursts his head up out of the water. He gasps for air and again hears a distant sound. He listens to the familiar wail of the young boy's cries. Thomas treads water and looks down the hall. The young boy's shriek is heard once again.

"I'm coming! Daddy is coming!" Thomas yells.

A loud rumbling is raging from behind Thomas, gaining in strength. He turns, continuing to tread water, curious over the sudden loud noise. Thomas's eyes bulge open, his heart drops. A huge wave is cresting and drops right on his face.

"No!!!" he screams, throwing his hands up into the air.

Five

THOMAS sits up in the hallway, gasping for air. He is trying to catch his quickened breath and slowly but surely does so, calming himself down. He looks around, seeing he is still in the abandoned hotel. Dawn has arrived as light from the east is pouring through the bare windows. The crisp crashing waves are a serene reminder to Thomas's location. The sun hasn't begun its arc in the sky; just light from its oncoming presence.

About 6 in the morning, Thomas thinks to himself. He knows the sun and he knows the time.

He looks in his brown bag and finds some bread and jam. He makes himself a small sandwich; a quick treat to start the morning.

The dawn is breathtaking. Thomas hasn't seen one in a long, long while. The sun crests over the ocean's horizon and beams of sparkling light glisten upon the world, slowly altering it to wake up. Thomas makes his way out to the beach and faces the magnificent sunrise. Thomas drinks in the cool ocean breeze slamming against his cheeks. He closes his eyes and raises his chin up into the air. The wind blows his hair back away from his face, an intoxicating inhale of life.

Thomas looks to the north and gazes at the large lighthouse. He sees the keeper's house nearby, a two-story home just a stone's throw away from the tower.

Thomas looks back at the empty hotel, a tall grand-standing building pressed firmly up against the sloped shoreline. It's the first time his eyes have gazed upon the structure in the light of day. Its paint is peeling, the walls getting worn down. The backside of the structure shows markings near its base of a dangerously close waterline. There is little beach left between the Oceanic Hotel and the waves of the Atlantic.

Thomas is finished with his satisfying moment and walks toward the lighthouse. He looks out at the ocean and can see a few fishing vessels moving through the choppy waters of the rippling Atlantic.

As he gets closer to the keeper's house, Thomas sees a number of ships sailing out of the bay. The ships are heading by the tower on their way out to sea for a day of fishing. Thomas curiously looks around, no one there to bother him. He is a free man. He takes a deep breath and slowly exhales; his cheeks rising up a little, a smile emerging on his face. *Freedom.*

Thomas is standing right behind the keeper's house. He doesn't want to go inside. He doesn't want to trespass here. Then he hears a voice.

Thomas rushes over to some nearby shrubbery and hides. He slowly moves toward the origin of the man's voice. It is by the lighthouse. He curiously looks through the brush and sees the keeper, wearing his yellow work jacket and painting by the bottom of the tower. The bright white paint is brushed on by the keeper who appears to be talking to himself.

"Yes, old girl. You look gorgeous. Must get you ready for the summer. They will be coming to see you; certainly not me," the keeper jokes.

Thomas curiously watches the old keeper talking to himself as he carefully paints the side of the lighthouse. He paints for almost an hour, talking to the large structure. Every stroke is perfect; a smooth coat of paint evenly smoothed on just right. The keeper takes his time to ensure the paint is flawlessly applied. Thomas looks on, curious what the keeper will do next.

After he is finished painting, the keeper removes his yellow jacket and his lighthouse keeper uniform. He has a t-shirt and pants on and tends to the nearby garden.

"You have to look nice for Barney. She needs a good season," the keeper states as his flowers are just starting to grow, buds forming, getting ready for warmer weather. He waters his vegetable garden, carefully inspecting tomatoes on their vine to see if they are ripe for the picking. "Almost," he states.

Thomas continues to watch the older man until he finishes with his morning chores and heads back to the keeper's home. He enters the large house by himself with no one in sight. Thomas looks back at the lighthouse and slowly moves over to the large structure. He again glances back, making sure the keeper is out of sight. Thomas edges closer to the lighthouse door. He looks around and tries to jiggle it open. It's locked.

The sound of a train engine blasts, startling Thomas. He whips his head around like he was just caught trying to break into a bank. He relaxes and looks past the trees and sees the smoke rising just a hundred yards away from a train nearby. He looks back at the locked lighthouse door and concedes to staying on the outside of the tower. He steps back and looks all the way up to the top.

"I'd like to see you," Thomas states aloud for no one to hear but the wind and the tower.

After a second, he turns and begins to head back over to the Oceanic, passing the keeper's home on the way. Thomas looks the home over closely as he passes by, curious about this man. He sees and hears nothing and continues on his way.

Thomas steps through the back door of the Oceanic, just as he left it. The breeze whizzes through the empty halls. He starts to walk down the red carpeted hallway when he is tackled out of the clear blue. He is knocked into the abandoned dining room, sliding along the floor. Thomas looks up to see which linebacker just laid him out and sees a thin young black man.

Thomas jumps up to his feet, readying for a fight. The man doesn't say anything and also prepares his fists up by his chin, readying to brawl.

Thomas and the young man slowly circle around one another. They each alternate jab steps forward, but no punches are thrown. Neither are experienced brawlers and both look hesitant as they eyeball one another.

"This is my house," the man says in an impassioned tone.

"Unless your name is *Oceanic* it don't belong to ya," Thomas returns.

The men lunge toward one another and lock up, starting to wrestle. Neither man can get the upper hand as they struggle and lose their balance, falling into a pile of the old chairs. Both men shake off the fall and slowly get back to their feet. The dark skinned man sees a snapped piece of wood off one of the chairs and grabs it, holding it up as weapon. Thomas looks around for a weapon of his own. He grabs one of the chairs and holds it up as if he were taming a vicious lion.

The men once again circle one another.

"I'm gonna have to ask you to leave," the man says.

"I ain't got nowhere to go, friend," Thomas replies.

They continue to circle around one another and then the man swings his piece of wood at Thomas. His wood slaps against the chair a few times. They are warning shots, not meant to hit Thomas, just to scare him. Thomas easily uses his chair as a shield, calmly deflecting the man's swings.

"Don't make me hurt you," the man states, defending his cherished territory.

"The feeling is mutual," Thomas replies.

The man lunges forward again. Thomas is able to neutralize the man's wooden weapon and smacks it out of his hand. The man rushes after his lone weapon. Thomas hurls his chair aside and tackles the stranger. He knocks the man to the ground and falls on top of him. The two men roll around on the ground, once again jockeying for position with poor wrestling tactics. Thomas is able to gain the upper hand and pins the man's arms down.

"I just slept here. That's all!" Thomas yells, the two men continuing to struggle with one another.

The other man uses his legs, pulling his knees in and pushing Thomas up into the air and off of him. Thomas flies back a few feet and tumbles away. The man rises to his feet.

"You ain't no payin' customer and this hotel here is closed, mista." The man rises up, his big white eyes flaring open. "This hotel is mine. And you ain't welcome."

Thomas stands up. "Well, I ain't got no place to go, friend. And you don't own this hotel. All I want is shelter. That's all I ask for. I need this place."

The two men slowly start to circle again, but it is clear they are both growing tired of their fight.

"You ain't ask me anything. You just went ahead and did as you please."

"Listen," Thomas begins, attempting to appeal to the man's sense of negotiation. "...how about I make you a jam sandwich? I'll make you that sandwich and I'll make myself one. Then I can properly ask you if it's all right if I stay here for a bit; just a bit."

They circle for just a moment more when the dark skinned man stops. He straightens up and extends his hand.

"Okay. The name is Zander, Zander Wilcox."

Thomas thankfully straightens up and extends his hand, firmly shaking Zanders.

"Bullocks. Thomas Bullocks."

Zander nods and the two men shake hands.

THEY sit on the back deck overlooking the ocean waves crashing against the shore. They each are chomping on a jam sandwich, enjoying a good meal with a fantastic view.

"This is good," Zander compliments.

"I'm a chef at heart," Thomas jokes.

The two men quietly eat for a moment, each staring off at the ocean. Thomas glances over at Zander with curiosity. Zander senses Thomas's eyes, and without even looking over, responds.

"You're wondering what I'm doing here?"

"I am," Thomas curiously replies.

"I am the caretaker of this beautiful establishment," Zander proudly boats. "Been here ten years now. I started when I was fourteen. This place has been my home and I've known no other as a man. I clean her, fix her and keep her ready. She will rise again. The Oceanic Hotel was once great and she will rise again. And I will be here ready to serve her every need. This is my home." Zander speaks, his words full of pride. He stares out at the ocean, silently reminiscing about better times. His face draws down, his eyes pan down to the side, life's realities marring his optimistic hopes and dreams.

"What happened? Is this place haunted or something?" Thomas sarcastically asks.

"A few years back, the fever came though. Killed a guest. The hotel was closed and we cleaned and cleaned. We made sure everything was like new. But, it wasn't meant to be."

"Typhoid?" Thomas asks.

"Yup," he confirms.

"It's so quiet up here. Was the hotel busy?"

"In the summer season, a little. Mr. Archer went ahead and built The Sunset across the way a few years after the Oceanic went up in '81. Called it the Sans Souci. But the two big hotels right near one another just weren't drawin' enough crowds. The fishing is good, but the south part of the island has them really nice sandy beaches. They get a few more folks down there. And, with the fever hittin' Archer closed both hotels. He sold the Souci and it became The Sunset. It's open now. Not too busy yet. But it will get busier soon."

"Why didn't you go work over there?"

"Because the Oceanic is my home," Zander smiles, again bustling with pride.

Thomas nods, respecting and understanding Zander's position.

"What about you? What's your story, Thomas Bullocks?" Zander asks.

"I used to be an officer at a jail. And um…I just got tired of it, ya know. So I wanted a change." Thomas keeps his lies short and simple.

"I can see that. Jail can make a man go a little mad."

"Yeah. It sure can." Thomas's eyes repeatedly flash over at Zander and inspects his response. With no change in expression, he is satisfied Zander isn't on to him and relaxes back into their casual conversation.

The two men finish their sandwiches. Soon after, Zander shows Thomas his fishing poles and they head up near the lighthouse by the inlet where fishing is the best from the shoreline. They cast out and sit side by side; fishing in the beautiful spring sun.

As they fish, a quiet pair of eyes are taking a look at the two men from inside the nearby house. The keeper is curiously watching, wondering himself who Thomas is; this new face that has come to occupy a space near the tower.

A FIRE burns by the beach in the dark of night. Thomas and Zander are chomping on fish. They happily eat and Thomas's eyes can't help but be drawn to the lighthouse and its stunning flashing light. Zander catches Thomas periodically glancing over at the tower.

"You ever been up one?" Zander asks.

"One what?" Thomas asks, not realizing Zander saw him look up at the Barnegat Lighthouse.

"You've been staring at that thing all day. I figured you been there before; or maybe one like it."

"No. Never been. But there's something about it. I've always been a seafaring man and I don't know." Thomas stares out toward the lighthouse and then out at the ocean, cutting off his sentence.

"Well…that man over there, the keeper, he's a mean sonofabitch. I heard he killed a man for trying to sneak into that tower. Killed him with a blade; gut him like a fish." Zander finishes talking and shakes his head.

"He gut a man?"

"Like a fish," Zander repeats. "He just isn't a man to trifle with. He was a soldier. Went off to war just before the turn of the century. He came back crazy. That's why he talks to himself. He walks around and talks to himself all day long. Most lighthouses have more help. They all keep disappearing; quittin' I'm guessing. He is alone again. I think that's how he likes it. Ever since his wife past, that's how he wants it."

"His wife died?"

"Recently. She passed not too long ago. Whole town came out for the funeral. They love that keeper."

"That's sad. He didn't have children?"

"A girl. She is older. And he had a little boy. He lost him young—long time ago. That alone is enough to drive a man mad."

Thomas nods in agreement, looking back over at the top of the lighthouse. He looks at the light shining from within its cylindrical walls and wonders about the man in charge of it.

"He's crazy?" Thomas haphazardly asks.

"As far as I know, friend; he's crazy angry. Not a man I'd mess with. He's got nothing to lose."

Thomas turns to Zander as the light from the fire shines upon his face, reflecting in his eyes. "We all got nothin' to lose." His serious tone comes from deep in his gut.

"True is that, brother. True is that," Zander agrees.

The two men go on chomping on their catch of the day and enjoy the cool breeze and refreshingly chilly night air.

THOMAS awakes to smooth piano keystrokes. The Blues is being echoed through the abandoned hall of the Oceanic. He rises up off the cot he slept on, a single wool blanket draped over him. There is another cot in the room with a blanket folded neatly upon it. Thomas's new bedroom is courtesy of Zander. The two have become bunkmates, castaways occupying the abandoned dreams of a once vibrant hotel. Somehow, the Blues makes it easier to rise up and start the day. Thomas has a smirk on his face as he gets up out of bed, knowing it's Zander's perfect musical fingers pressing the piano keys. Thomas makes his way to the ballroom.

Zander's eyes are closed as he pounds away at the keys in the grand ballroom, the music infusing emotion into his soul. Zander's face looks almost pained as he plays the song, an emotional release of epic proportions. He plays and plays until he softens the keys and finishes his emotional journey, the song coming to an end.

Thomas, leaning by the entrance of the ballroom, starts to applaud.

A smile breaks across Zander's face and then his eyes open.

"Thank you," he modestly states.

"That was great. I could tell someone kept good care of that piano."

"Yeah. It didn't make it on the truck out. And I didn't report it here. I wasn't gonna let her go. She is my pride." Zander gently runs his fingers across the top of the piano as if he were caressing a woman's back.

"Jack of all trades and an entertainer!" Thomas jokes in a complimentary tone.

"Something like that. My papa taught me when I was young, before he died. I never forgot it. He was good. He could *really* play. And if it wasn't for his accident, he would have been somethin'. I was young when he passed, but he was awfully good. My mama told me he was the cat's pajamas. A real cake-eater too. The women couldn't stay away. He was a cool cat, man. He didn't just play. He could get hot on that dance floor. He was something else. Could tap and swing with the best." Zander speaks fondly of his father; proud memories pouring out.

"What happened to him?"

Zander pauses, thinking to himself, biting his lower lip. "They hung him, Thomas. They hung him cause a white woman that belonged to a white man flashed him eyes. So one night, they waited until he finished his set and they strung him up on a tree. Just like that he was gone. Them drunk boys, they didn't even bat an eyelash. And the police said they couldn't find them boys after. Just like that…my papa was gone forever." Zander looks down, his eyes glossy, tears welling behind them. But the young man is far too proud to cry. He instead places his hands on the piano, gently touching the tops of the keys without releasing any sounds. "This is my center. Always brings me back home. Brings me right back to my daddy."

"What was that song?" Thomas asks with curiosity.

"Ah. A good jam. *The Memphis Blues*. A little 'southern rag.' It always gets my blood movin'."

"I liked it."

"What about you?" Zander asks as he casually begins to play random notes on the piano that somehow seem to flow together.

"What do you mean?" Thomas plays hard to get.

"Who is Thomas Bullocks?"

Thomas smiles, shaking his head at the last name. He swallows, considering the moment and having pause.

"Just Thomas."

"Bullocks isn't you?" Zander curiously asks, as if already knowing the answer.

"No. It was the name of a good man, though. But that man died. So…I left behind my bad name and told you a good one instead. I don't know why I did." Thomas feels foolish now that Zander has shared so much.

"Because you runnin'."

"What's that?" Thomas nervously replies.

"You runnin' from your past. You feel you gotsta get away from somethin'. So you run. You run as far as you can. That's how you ended up here. Can't go any further east unless you a fish."

Thomas smiles and nods. "This is true."

"You don't have to tell me. Just know, until you stop runnin', you won't feel whole. You gotsta find peace, my friend."

"Play me another Handy. Maybe some *St. Louis Blues* this time." Thomas lets out a smile.

"Oh, so you know it! You know the Blues! My man, Handy! Ha!" Zander smiles, bending his head back, impressed. He focuses back on his favorite instrument and fixes his fingers to play. "All right then…let's dance."

Zander starts to strike the keys as Thomas happily listens to him playing the *St. Louis Blues.* The new friends share the perfectly played Blues together, the music bringing them both back to something special.

Six

THOMAS and Zander are fishing on the rocks as they have every day for the past two weeks. The skies are ominously cloudy with three quarters of the sky covered. The thick grey puffy clouds insinuate bad intentions. Thomas is continuously glancing over his shoulder at the lighthouse.

"Just go talk to him." Zander smiles at Thomas, knowing his curiosity won't end until he musters some bravery and speaks with the keeper.

"You said he doesn't much like people."

"No. I think he is quite pleasant to visitors. He gives tours to people in the summer all the time. I've seen him give it in the spring and fall seasons too. I've never had a bad word with him—or any word for that matter. Our lives have been parallel to one another; no cross sections."

Thomas looks up, studying the weather in silence. He turns and looks behind him, watching closely as the pall of black clouds encompass part of the sky. He pays attention to the low cloud formations and then the larger, higher cloud tops.

"Maybe another time," he finally replies.

"Suit yourself," Zander shakes his head, amused by Thomas.

"What?" Thomas defensively asks of his new best friend.

"Well, he is a stone's throw away. If you want to speak to the man, if you want to see the lighthouse, all you gotta do is walk on over. You use your feet; you just go left, then right, then left and right again," Zander giggles, amusing himself.

"Yeah-yeah. But it's gonna rain soon. It's gonna rain hard. And that keeper is gonna have to go into the lighthouse and work a long day." Thomas scans the sky for more reassurance on his prediction.

Zander looks up and sees a partly cloudy sky. "Clouds look a little thick, but they don't look so bad. Half the sky is clear. The other half is just saggin' a little."

"See those clouds over there," Thomas points off to the southeast.

Zander looks over and sees the flat-topped anvil shaped thick clouds forming. "Yeah. I see those. They look pretty nasty."

"See how the top of the cloud, the one shaped like an anvil, is pointing toward us?"

"Yeah. I see."

"Well, that's because the air is blowing that cloud this way. And more are gonna follow. Those are storm clouds—strong ones at that. My guess is we will get some thunder, lightning and maybe even some hail."

"That's pretty specific," Zander looks over at Thomas, wondering how he knows so much.

"I know the clouds and I know the stars. I know the sky. I know it well," Thomas shares.

"You were a fisherman?"

"My father was. I spent a lot of years down in the Gulf; Mississippi, Louisiana and Alabama. Listened to a lot of Blues down there."

"Yeah, you did. I'm jealous. A lot of good tunes played in those parts."

"Yeah." Thomas takes a long deep pause, something bothering him. "Yeah, there were," he finishes up.

Zander recognizes his new friend had a troubling thought from the past haunt his mind. Instead of probing further, he moves on.

"So, you think rain?" Zander switches gears back to Thomas's strength.

"Yeah. And by the looks of it, I'd say some heavy drops are coming our way."

"All right. I guess we'll see."

The two men share a smile and continue to fish.

TWO hours later, hauled up safely under the torn up awning of the Oceanic deck, Thomas and Zander watch as thunder and lightning explode in the sky and rain soaks the world. Each lightning strike displays the raging ocean waters as the surf crashes against the shore.

"You're right. Damn, you a good read," Zander compliments.

"I read the sky like you read the piano, my friend. We all have our things."

"We sure do." Zander smiles and agrees wholeheartedly with Thomas.

Thomas glances over at the lighthouse, the bursts of light cutting through the dark sky like a carefully calculated knife. Thomas looks over and stares, watching the lighthouse closely.

He cannot see, but from inside the lighthouse, the keeper is looking down at Zander and Thomas. He is watching them as well. There is a mutual curiosity developing among the men.

Boom! Thunder crackles and a lightning strike fires down from the sky, striking the coastline not more than a mile away from where the men are sitting.

A thousand small objects start raining down from the sky. It sounds like stones are being tossed everywhere. The cacophony of banging occurs all around and Thomas turns to Zander with a smile on his face.

"You son of a..." Zander smiles and shakes his head, thoroughly impressed with Thomas's skills. "How did you know it would hail?"

"You can't know that for certain. But the air was cold and getting colder. I just had a feeling."

"You felt right." Zander nods and watches the grand storm continue to pound away.

The horn blows from atop the lighthouse. And then it blows again.

Thomas rises to his feet, wondering who or what the keeper is alerting. Zander follows suit behind him, also staring out at the ocean with curiosity.

"I wonder who is crazy enough to be out there in this weather?" Zander queries.

"A man desperate to feed his family," Thomas replies, all-the-while staring out at the sea.

Zander thinks about Thomas's words, potentially a glimpse into his past. He casts his eyes back out to sea, wanting to find the ship struggling in these conditions.

"Do you have a boat?" Thomas asks.

"A boat? I don't do the water, man. I swim like a stone," Zander shares.

Thomas senses something is wrong and again the horn sound confirms it. The sea is foggy, the clouds are low and with the rain and hail pounding the ground, it is near impossible to see anything out in the ocean. The wall of deep dark grey conceals any ships which may be out in the chaotic waters.

A wave crashes—then another. The water rises and charges forward, nearly to the deck of the Oceanic. The storm surge is pushing the water dangerously close, something that doesn't get by Thomas as he stares, wide-eyed, at the ocean swell.

"Is that normal?" Thomas asks, concerned the water is coming dangerously close.

"No. They moved this here hotel back before. The beach gives way. Not like the south side of the island. Holds better down there."

The horn sounds again; Thomas takes a step toward the water. The outline of an object becomes clear. A fishing vessel is getting tossed around in the sea. Up and down, it dips and climbs over the rolling waters of the Atlantic.

A lightning strike fires down from the sky and strikes the ship. Almost immediately, the ship catches fire and numerous distant voices yell. Their screams carry just far enough through the stiffening wind and storm to reach Thomas's ears. He takes a determined step toward the shoreline.

The ship is highlighted by the keeper's light. The lighthouse now has the limping fishing vessel in the spotlight.

"Oh, no." Thomas watches the ship with great concern.

"Did that ship just catch fire? You see that lightning?" Zander is in shock over the theatrics playing out before him.

Just fifty yards out, the ship is now dead in the water as the men aboard frantically try to put the fire out. But despite the rain and poor weather, they struggle to get the flames down. The fire spreads and they are in big trouble.

Thomas looks and sees the keeper, with a life vest around his neck, dash toward a small boat. He braves the conditions without regard for himself and gets his flat-bottomed boat quickly into the water.

"Look!" Zander points to what Thomas already sees. "Look at how small that boat is that he's getting into. He'll get tossed in the sea!"

"No. That's a jon boat. It's made for choppy waters." The keeper gets in the boat, his yellow coat on and life vest around his neck, and begins to paddle into the chaotic waters without an ounce of fear. He forges ahead into the teeth of the storm; into the rabid sea.

Thomas watches the keeper row and row against the current with all his might. He is determined to reach the men on that boat. When Thomas's eyes pan back over to the ship at sea, he sees a smoky heap starting to sink in the Atlantic. Men, like small ants, are bobbing up and down in the ocean, abandoning the sinking ship.

"I gotta help them," Thomas mumbles to himself.

"What?" Zander can't believe his ears.

Thomas takes his shirt and pants off, stripping down to just boxers.

"That water's freezing! You won't make it twenty yards!" Zander yells, his mouth drawn open, his eyes widening with confusion and concern.

"I've been in colder," Thomas confidently states and takes off into the water, racing out with stroke after stroke. He shows little regard for his safety as he swims up and over the rolling waves.

"Thomas! Thomas!" Zander yells twice, concerned over his friend. He stands by the shore not knowing what to do, watching as Thomas swims out to meet the struggling fishermen, disappearing into the chaotic abyss.

The keeper is out in the water and gathers one man—then another into his small boat. He looks around and can't see any other men. Then he sees Thomas, his white skin momentarily visible in the wavy dark waters. The keeper is shocked seeing Thomas out in the water and he vanishes. Just as quickly as he disappeared behind a rolling wave he reappears. Thomas has his arms wrapped around a fisherman who looks unconscious, and is swimming back to shore. He struggles to pull the man along with him, but fights the water and keeps them both from dipping below, slowly paddling in, the strong current greatly aiding his efforts. The keeper intensely stares until he realizes his own safety and that of the two men in his boat are at risk. With the weather terrible, he begins to paddle back to the shore, getting the two fishermen safely to land.

Zander steps out a few feet in the cold water, going waist deep. He is nervous and doesn't want to go any further.

"Come on, Tommy!" Zander shouts. He looks around, hoping and praying for Thomas to appear. Then, coming forward in a crashing wave is Thomas and the man. Thomas is using all his might to save the one unconscious man in his arms. He is exhausted, the ocean tossing him back and forth. The ocean repeats, another wave carrying him further. Zander sees Thomas and breathes a sigh of relief, his arms extending out.

Thomas reaches Zander and hands the fisherman off to him. Zander drags the old fisherman to the deck.

Thomas is on his hands and knees catching his breath in shallow water, as the tide momentarily pulls back to sea. Then a wave crashes into his body, almost knocking him over. He tries to muster the strength to walk and moves to the deck of the hotel, sheltered by the awning.

"He's all right!" Zander shouts with exhilaration. "He's gonna be all right!"

The fisherman groans and holds his head. He has some blood trickling down from a nasty bump, but he appears to be okay.

Thomas drags his exhausted body over by the injured man's side. "That's great," Thomas states, exhausted. He slumps to the ground, rolling onto his back, his chest heaving. He attempts to catch his breath, his eyes closed.

"I can't believe you saved him! I've never seen anything like that!" Zander shouts with excitement. Then Zander's face grows silent. His smile flees like ants to the light and he looks nervous, staring above and beyond Thomas.

Thomas opens his eyes, curious over Zander's sudden silence. He can see a shadow before him, a light shining over his shoulder. He turns and locates the keeper holding a lantern. His face is covered by his yellow jacket and its hood. Standing beside him are the two other fishermen. Their beards are long, but their faces youthful. They are standing on either side of the keeper. Thomas struggles, but uses his jelly-feeling arms to push up, his sore tired legs propping his spent body upright. He proudly stands despite still attempting to catch his breath.

The old fisherman in Zander's arms groans, holding his head.

"Pa!" one of the younger fisherman yells. He lunges down and gives his father a big hug.

"Oh, thank you!" the other fisherman states to Thomas. He moves right up to Thomas with thankful, tear-filled eyes. Thomas, with his hand extended, is expecting a handshake, and his exhausted body is caught off guard when the man wraps his two hands and arms around him. Thomas gets a big appreciative bear hug.

The two sons then turns and gratefully hug their father; the family pulling in close together.

Thomas glances over at the keeper. His face is quiet, still concealed in part by his yellow rain suit. He doesn't say a word.

"What about Riley and Cooper?" one of the son's asks.

Zander looks over at Thomas.

"You're missing two more?" Thomas's face sinks, upset to hear the news.

"One can't swim. The other I don't know." The other son chimes in and gives some details.

"Well…" Thomas looks behind him and the keeper is already gone. He is headed quickly to the shore with his lantern. He gets back into his jon boat and rows. He rows as if he hadn't just rowed fifty yards through chaos to save two men's lives. He rows like he has the strength and energy of a hundred men.

The keeper rows out into the Atlantic by himself to search for the two other men. He rows into the dark chaos. Despite the keeper's efforts, those men would not resurface again, swallowed whole by the storm. Just as quickly as it arrived, the storm quells and leaves. By early nightfall it is quiet. The storm is gone, the ocean recedes back. By dawn, the damage is clear. The beaches are left with the remnants of an angry encounter. Pieces of boats stirred up from the ocean's bottom are spread deep across the shoreline like fallen seeds from a tree. The chaos and destruction left behind are a stark reminder of what has been lost in the past and a warning for what may be lost in the future.

AFTER a decent night's sleep, Thomas awakes before Zander. He has a towel wrapped around his body as he makes his way to the deck of the Oceanic. He looks out at the shoreline, taking in what Mother Nature has left behind. He sees the destruction and then notices something curious. The fishermen from the night before are lined up along the shoreline, spread about fifteen yards apart. They are looking out at the ocean waters for a glimpse, any clue, as to where their two other shipmates may be. Stacked in a small pile beside them are a few of the belongings they have recovered from their wreckage.

"Riley!"

"Cooper!"

The men call for their friends with frequent shouts met by only the whisking of the waves crashing against the rocks and shoreline. The chaos of the night prior has given way to the most beautiful of days. Mother Nature's only response to the men is the whipping of a few wind gusts and the serene sounds of the ocean kissing the shoreline.

Deep out into the sea at dawn, just as he was at dusk during the storm, the keeper rows, tirelessly searching for the missing men. Thomas watches the courageous keeper go. He watches the keeper with beaming pride. His facial expression is awed, his mouth hanging open, his eyes slightly squinting to focus out across the ocean and into the rising sun. Light shines poetically upon Thomas's face as he watches the actions of a man he respects greatly, but knows nothing about.

Zander steps up from behind Thomas.

"Look at the crazy man go," Zander states equally with respect.

"He's still out there because *they're* still out there," Thomas refers to the fishermen, his eyes remaining fixated out to sea.

"It's hopeless," Zander predicts.

"Their hope may be futile, but it's all they can cling to at the moment. Everything else has been lost to them," Thomas boldly points out. He glances over at the three men, their arms around one another, holding each of their exhausted bodies up.

"Let's get some breakfast," Zander pats Thomas on the shoulder.

Thomas agreeably nods but can't take his eyes off the keeper searching the ocean's waters. After a few more lasting moments, he reluctantly breaks away and heads inside.

Seven

ANOTHER two weeks pass and summer is quickly approaching. Barnegat City is starting to get busier with fishermen and tourists beginning to arrive at The Sunset Hotel and down toward the southern end of the island. A terrific find by Thomas searching through the hotel's attic netted the men some hidden china. It was completely out of place there, perhaps a former employee was intending on stealing it. Zander had no idea the china was in that small attic. He assumed the attic was reserved for spiders and nightmares. But the two men score some china to sell and swap for money and supplies. They head out for the best form of transportation on the island; the train station.

Standing by the train station, Thomas feels nervous. He bounces his leg up and down as he and Zander await the arrival of the morning train. Heading into town isn't just a day trip for Thomas. It's showing his face in the greater public; exposing himself. A voice in the back of his head constantly reminds him that he is an escaped convict at large.

Zander dances as he waits. He taps his feet on the ground and dances around to the beat of his own drum. He always enjoys going into town. And with money on the horizon, this is an especially fun trip for him.

The train horn sounds, smoke billowing out of the top of the engine car.

"You nervous?" Zander asks.

Thomas looks up, caught in a thought.

"What's that?"

"You nervous to head into town? You're bouncing your leg like a bottled up tap shoe," Zander jokes.

"Trains, I guess," Thomas jokes.

"Yeah. They used to get to me. Now they're fun. I like the ride."

Thomas nods. Zander picks up a sack, the contents inside clanking a bit from the movement. He carefully tosses the sack over his shoulder. The train arrives and the two men board and head into Barnegat to do a little wheeling and dealing.

After the short train ride and some walking, Zander enters a shop. Thomas chooses to stay outside and sits on a bench. He watches the people around town shopping, moving about their day. He is by himself and leans back, once again basking in the enjoyment of freedom. With his eyes closed, the sun bakes his skin just right; a warm touch to balance out the cool breeze. His nerves are calmed as the world seemingly moved on from his past, so why shouldn't he?

As Thomas relaxes, a shadow casts over his face. Thomas has bad experiences with shadows being cast upon him. His heart sinks and he becomes unnerved. Paranoia quickly parks itself right inside the forefront of his mind. He doesn't want to wake up from his dream of freedom. He wants to keep his eyes closed to enjoy the world one last moment before it is ripped away from him once again. He takes a deep breath and opens his eyes to the inevitable.

Instead of a police officer standing above Thomas, it is the face of a ten-year-old boy. The boy is staring down at him with a big smile on his face. Thomas has no idea who the boy is and slowly pulls his head back.

"Hey, buddy," Thomas curiously states.

"Hey," the young boy quietly returns, his words almost unrecognizable as they are mumbled so low.

"Whatcha doin'?" Thomas asks of the boy with a welcoming smile on his face.

"Visiting," the boy perks up slightly.

"You like it here?"

"Yeah. It's nice," the young boy steps back, looking toward the ground.

"You're quiet," Thomas states an inference he believes to be true.

"Sometimes," Jackson looks up at Thomas with a smile.

"What do people call you?"

"Huh?" the young boy barely looks Thomas in the eye as he replies.

"Your name. I'm Thomas. What do they call you?"

"Jackson."

"Well, Jackson, I found something. It's old, but pretty neat." Thomas reaches into his pocket and pulls out Bullocks's wallet. He hands Jackson a bronze badge that had belonged to Bullocks. "It's a badge. It's real too," Thomas gifts the badge over to the young boy.

"Thanks." Jackson gazes over the badge, entranced. He sticks it into his pocket.

"Your mom or dad nearby?" Thomas curiously asks, concerned the boy is out by himself near the road.

"No." Jackson's eyes flare to the ground, the question causing him to shell up.

"Jackson!" A beautiful brunette in a lovely spring dress comes jogging over. She is struggling to hold her matching hat atop her head. "I'm so sorry he bothered you," Sarah apologizes.

Thomas rises to his feet. "No trouble ma'am," he respectfully states.

"I'm sorry. My manners. This is Jackson and I'm Sarah—Sarah Jones." Sarah extends her hand to Thomas.

"Thomas."

They shake hands.

"Well, we have to run. Just got into town and this little guy has to get to his grandparents' house," Sarah continues to struggle with her hat as the wind is making it difficult for it to remain on her head. She grows annoyed and whips it off, crumbling it into her hands. "Sorry, I can't stand hats."

"It's quite all right." Thomas is amused by Sarah and drawn in by her authentic display of emotion. Her personality shines just as brightly as her beauty. "You have a nice boy there."

Sarah starts to walk away with Jackson when she stops.

"Jackson, wait here."

Jackson stands in the same spot and Sarah, with an inquisitive expression on her face, leans toward Thomas, getting close so only he can hear her.

"What do you mean, *nice*?" Sarah asks, her eyes squinting with curiosity, her face leaning in even closer to Thomas.

"I didn't mean anything by it," Thomas gets a little defensive, unsure of what Sarah is fishing for.

"You said *nice*."

"Yes."

"As in speaking nice?" Sarah cross-examines Thomas, cocking her head to the side, her eyes remaining poised and anxious for a reply.

"Yeah." Thomas smirks and squints, wondering what is going on. "We spoke to each other. Just a simple conversation. I apologize if I imposed." Thomas puts his hands up, not certain he has done something wrong by communicating with the boy. He doesn't want any trouble.

"Well…it's just that, I mean…he doesn't talk. And never to strangers"

"He spoke to me, ma'am. Sarah—sorry."

"You're not pulling my leg, are ya fella? Thomas is it?"

"I wouldn't dare, miss," Thomas respectfully replies.

Sarah looks back at Jackson who is staring up toward the sky and then back at Thomas. She has a look of disbelief on her face, squinting her eyes, smiling at Thomas.

"Okay. If you say so." Sarah steps away from Thomas, still not certain she believes him. But there is an unspoken spark between them, an obvious connection. They don't dare speak of it, only their eyes do the talking.

Thomas watches Sarah walk away with a curious look of his own. He wonders what she meant with her strange line of questioning, while at the same time admiring her beauty and brash style of speaking.

Jackson glances back and gives a quick wave goodbye to Thomas. Thomas raises his hand and gives Jackson one in return.

Sarah looks down at Jackson and he looks forward. She glances over her shoulder to see if Thomas is watching. She doesn't make eye contact, but can't help but give one last look at the kind stranger she met on the street.

"What's up?" Zander comes over to Thomas. He sees him in a trance, watching Sarah and Jackson walk away down the street. The two of them step into a waiting horse and carriage parked on the side of the road. She innocently kisses an older man on the cheek as she enters the carriage with Jackson. The man is at least thirty years her elder. He snaps the reins and the horse-drawn carriage is whisked away.

"Nothing," Thomas states with a stare that is anything but *nothing*.

Jackson pokes his head out of the carriage, looking back at Thomas as the horse carriage turns the corner. Sarah's head pops out behind his, just for a split second, getting one last visual exchange with Thomas. Then the carriage disappears out of sight.

"You fall in love?" Zander asks, looking at Thomas with a crooked smile.

Thomas breaks his trance and turns to Zander. "How'd we do?"

Zander is holding an empty sack. He pulls out a handful of money.

"Not bad!" Thomas excitedly states.

"Yeah. I'm glad you found that spare china. I didn't even know there was storage left in the attic. Now we can get new poles!"

"And I need a razor," Thomas rubs his rough face.

"Make that two," Zander smiles, rubbing the sides of his face.

The two men look around town with a smile on their face.

"I think you're good luck," Zander speaks sincerely with an optimistic smile.

"No one's ever accused me of that," Thomas jokes.

"You found the china! You saved a man's life. You're doing pretty good by my accounts," Zander points out Thomas's recent accomplishments.

"The one thing I know, my friend, is there is always stuff in the attic. Never fails." Thomas speaks from great experience.

"You got all *these* things," Zander's eyes slant and his head tilts as he playfully tries to get a read on Thomas.

"What things?"

"These sayings. These things. You got a whole lot of life experience but you ain't shared more than a drop or two. We friends, aren't we?" Zander asks.

Thomas nods, understanding Zander's frustration. "Yeah. We are, Zand."

"All right. Then tell me. Tell me who you really are, Tommy." Zander appeals to Thomas. But as soon as Thomas considers opening up to his friend, he sees something that causes him concern. His eyes open wide and he takes a breathless step backward.

"What?" Zander turns around and looks a few feet away. He sees an officer hammering up a poster on a wood post. He finishes hammering and turns to Zander. Zander looks down and away from the officer, wanting no part of a stare down with the police.

"Good day," the officer says pleasantly to Zander as he passes by.

"Same to you, officer," Zander respectfully nods to the officer as he walks by. Zander moves up to the paper. It is a *Wanted* poster. It offers $500 per head for a rough sketched picture of Thomas and Pratt. "Well, I'll be damned." Zander looks behind him and Thomas is no longer there. He turns and looks all around. "Tommy?" Zander asks, confused.

Zander searches around by the nearby storefronts and can't see Thomas. He walks behind the stores and sees him sitting on a rock. Zander walks over to Thomas and takes a seat next to him, the two sharing silence. After a few moments, Zander breaks the silence.

"I ain't no rat," Zander speaks first. His declaration is comforting to Thomas. Seeing the poster has made the escaped convict feel very uncomfortable. It is a reminder that his past is just a moment away.

"It's a long story," Thomas begins.

"Zander Wilcox." Zander extends his hand, reintroducing himself to Thomas.

Thomas rises to his feet and shakes hands with Zander. "Thomas Dent."

"It's a pleasure to meet you, Thomas Dent."

The two men look eye to eye. Thomas apologetically nods, his eyes fading to the ground, his lips squeezing together.

"I'm sorry, Zander. It's just…"

"We got plenty of time for that. Right now, we're gonna get a little moon shine, a couple of poles, razors and some damn good food. Then we going back home."

Thomas agreeably nods, a slight smile emerging on his face, trying to bust through the embarrassment and regret he feels.

A TRAIN ride back to Barnegat City and a series of explanations follow. Thomas spends the better part of the afternoon and early evening telling Zander about his sorted past. By the end, they are sitting by a fire in the early evening eating sandwiches and drinking moonshine. The two laugh and exchange stories. Thomas tells Zander everything, the first person he has ever trusted with his entire past; all of it. The two lost souls, the newly minted best-of-friends, enjoy their moonshine and have a great night by the Jersey Shore.

THE next morning arrives and Thomas is out early. Fresh off his clean shave, the first for him in a long while, he takes in the morning air. He jogs down the road, anxious energy he needs to exert. He sees the lighthouse and turns, jogging right by the tower. He stops, exhausted, catching his breath. It is the perfect place to fill his lungs with air as he gazes upon the tall structure.

"I've seen you run by here nearly every morning for a week now," the raspy powerful voice of the keeper states. He is wearing his perfectly pressed keeper's uniform, looking Thomas over.

"I like to run. Keeps me sharp," Thomas explains.

"You like to swim too," the keeper remembers Thomas's heroic moments at sea.

"I can swim a little," Thomas humbly replies. He stands tall, his chin up, chest out, as if standing before his commanding officer.

"And I saw you fixing the hotel; helping the black fella over there. You own it?"

"No, sir." Thomas knows where the keeper is heading before he even asks the question.

"Then why are you staying there? The two of you are stowaways."

Thomas smiles and nods. "You remind me of my father," he states with some bitterness dripping off his words.

"You sir, do not remind me of my son," the keeper is stern with his tone. He turns and walks away from Thomas.

Thomas shakes his head as the keeper walks away. Thomas looks around, surprised to be disrespected by the keeper in that way. His mouth hangs open, his brows furrow, stunned, uncertain of what to say; but he feels compelled to say something. His mind scrambles to regroup.

"I can help you, ya know!" Thomas's words marinate in the wind for a few moments. The keeper slows to a stop, letting the young man's words sink in. He keeps his back to Thomas as he ponders the offer. He then slowly turns the top half of his body, only giving Thomas the satisfaction of seeing his face and his front shoulder.

"No, son. You cannot." He turns and walks away, leaving Thomas alone. The keeper heads back to his house and goes inside, never once hesitating or looking back at Thomas.

Thomas shakes his head and smiles, brushing off the keeper's rudeness. He jogs back over to the Oceanic Hotel.

THOMAS and Zander are using their new fishing poles as they cast out into the water. A man wanders over toward them. Thomas grows nervous and looks away. Zander sees the concern on Thomas's face.

"Play it cool, man. I got this," Zander states.

The inspector makes his way over to Thomas and stands near him with a clipboard in hand. The inspector doesn't say a word. Thomas, uncomfortably, continues to focus on fishing, not wanting to react.

"Hey, sir! How are you?" Zander excitedly welcomes the foreign man to their fishing spot.

"I'm going to need your signature on this line, son." The inspector holds out his clipboard. He patiently waits for Thomas, his arm remaining extended.

Thomas curiously turns around and sees the clipboard. His eyes pull in as he focuses on the information on the page.

"Me?" Thomas asks.

"If you want the job, you're gonna need to sign. Hank has never been good with paperwork." The inspector glances over his shoulder toward the lighthouse with a smirk and then turns back to Thomas.

Thomas takes the piece of paper and signs it by the _X_. He hands the clipboard back to the inspector. The seal on the man's official navy blue coat reads: _United States Light House Service_.

"My name is Gus Philips. I'll be by from time to time. You'll see me around. We appreciate your service." Gus pats Thomas on the shoulder and turns to walk away when he hesitates, staring down at the clipboard. Thomas is wondering if the man recognizes his name; his signature. Gus peers back up at Thomas and cracks a smile. "Oh, just print your name below your signature. We need it on file. Things are changing now that we are Bureau instead of the Lighthouse Board. Things are easing up a bit. Always gotta keep good books though. Hank will tear your head off if the books aren't kept perfect. You got a great keeper to learn by. He holds high expectations, if you know what I mean? He can get into you a bit. Scares people off."

Thomas takes the clipboard back and hesitates for a moment. He makes brief eye contact with Zander who wonders what Thomas will write. Thomas spells out his first name and uses Bullocks as his last.

"Sort of like his bark is bigger than his bite?" Thomas asks.

"No-no. They'll both get ya. You don't wanna see his bite. His bark is bad enough," Gus jests.

"Okay," Thomas nods, nervously agreeing.

"You got any identification around?"

Thomas nods. "Certainly." Thomas places his fishing pole down and heads back inside the hotel to retrieve the wallet he now carries as his own.

Gus patiently waits with a smile on his face.

"Nice day," Zander tries to make casual conversation.

"Beautiful. It's a wonderful time of year."

Zander nods in agreement, uncomfortable and unsure what exactly is going on.

Thomas comes jogging back out and shows him an official officer's card with the last name Bullocks on it. The first initial on the first name is F.

"What's the *F* for?" Gus asks with curiosity as he looks the card over.

"Francis. I go by Thomas, my middle name."

"All right. My apologies on the paperwork. It happens. Hank tore into me pretty good about it. But I promised I'd get this expedited for you both."

"Thanks," Thomas mutters under his confused breath, uncertain of what is going on.

"Hank said he already started you off on some of the protocol, but allow me to officially welcome you to the United States Lighthouse Service!" Gus extends his hand.

Thomas reaches out and shakes Gus's hand, still a little awestruck by what is happening.

"Soon they'll be getting rid of all of us. I heard they are trying to make everything electronic. Always trying to replace good men out there," Gus shakes his head. "I wish you luck while it lasts, son. Be proud of her," Gus flashes his eyes toward Old Barney, the beautiful one hundred and sixty-three foot lighthouse.

"I will."

Gus flashes his palm and walks away. He leaves Thomas and Zander confused in his wake. Zander walks up next to Thomas as they watch Gus head back over to the keeper's home.

"What just happened?" Zander asks.

"I think I got a job," Thomas states with confusion.

"I didn't even know you applied."

"Neither did I."

TWO hours later, with the inspector leaving on the afternoon train, Thomas makes his way over to the keeper's home. He goes to knock on the front door and hesitates. He knows the keeper may be asleep. He looks through a window but can't see past the thick drapes. He wants to talk to the grumpy keeper about what transpired with Gus and figure everything out. But he doesn't want to wake the man up and out of respect, starts to walk away.

The front door is cracked open and Thomas stops in his tracks. He looks behind him and sees the door slightly askew. He looks around and doesn't see a soul. He slowly moves back toward the door and gently pushes it open.

He steps into the first story of the large two-story home. He looks around and is struck by the clean, nice furniture and grandfather clock in the living room. A large floor rug covers the nearby dining room and a beautiful long hand-knit rug runs from the doorway all the way down toward the kitchen at the end of the hall. Thomas's eyes are initially captivated by the environment, attempting to get a read on the world he just entered.

"Close the door," the grumpy man's distant voice orders.

Thomas does as he is told and curiously takes steps deeper into the keeper's home.

"In the kitchen!" It's another barked order from the keeper.

Thomas moves slowly through the hallway and slowly moves into the kitchen. The keeper has suspenders on, a white T-shirt, reading glasses and his face is buried in the *Trenton Times* newspaper.

"The Volstead Act," the keeper shakes his head, staring down at the paper.

"What's that?" Thomas asks.

"The Volstead Act. You know it, don't you?"

"Rumors. I've heard people complain about it," Thomas attempts to make conversation about topical news.

"They are outlawing booze—or so they say. You aren't permitted to drink on or off the job. Weak men drink. You must be strong-minded at all times. Are we clear?" the keeper asks the question in the tone of an order.

"Yes, sir."

"You must understand, you now represent more than yourself. You now represent the United States Government. You represent Barnegat City. You represent the lighthouse; Old Barney. We will accept nothing less than professional behavior. Are we clear?"

"Yes, sir."

"I have no time to train failures. I have no time to teach another man what I know unless he is mentally and physically prepared for that job. Do you understand?"

"Yes, sir."

"You have questions for me?" the keeper asks as his head continues to be buried in the newspaper.

"Yes, sir. What exactly is happening?"

"Beyond the Volstead Act I presume?"

"Yes, sir. Beyond that," Thomas replies.

The keeper lowers the newspaper down. He looks Thomas over, staring at him, expressionless. The keeper shows no emotion, no indication of happiness or sadness. He just stares and waits. Thomas stands firm and doesn't say a word, waiting for the keeper to say something—to say anything. The stare down lasts nearly two full minutes, nothing being said; no words exchanged. The silence grows uncomfortable, Thomas is barely breathing as he agonizingly waits for a response.

"You think you can be me?" the keeper asks.

"No, sir. I think I can be me."

"But you want to be me?" the keeper queries with squinted eyes.

"I want to stand atop that tower and shine a light to the world. I want to help those who are lost find their way. I want my life to have more meaning. I want to try and be the keeper. I want that chance." Thomas gives a rousing short speech.

The keeper doesn't flinch. He just stares at Thomas with the same stoic face, the lines of time standing out more than ever. Thomas can't help thinking to himself as he looks at the keeper, *the man has lived.*

"Do you think this job is easy or difficult?"

"I think it's the hardest job around and I can't wait to try my hand at it, sir." Thomas is fiercely passionate with his words and refuses to be intimidated by the keeper.

"I don't care what brought you here. I don't care who you were. I care only who you will be. I care what you will do when you place the uniform on. That is what matters most to me. Either way, you will most likely fail. You probably won't last the week. The others didn't last long either."

The keeper raises his newspaper back up in front of his face. Thomas remains standing in the room, again unsure of exactly what to do next. He looks around, wondering if he should leave or say something. He waits nearly two more minutes, doing nothing.

"You can go," the cranky voice blurts out. "Be back here in an hour. If you are one second late, you are fired," the keeper blandly states.

Thomas is about to answer back when the keeper continues on.

"Young people these days want the world handed to them. Nothing will be handed to you. You will have to earn everything; you will earn every step you take. Are we clear?" The keeper dips the paper down and stares intensely at Thomas, showing a disapproving glare.

"Yes, sir."

The keeper whips his paper back up and reshuffles it between his fingers, once again tossing up the barrier between himself and Thomas.

Thomas starts to back away out of the kitchen.

"Thank you, sir," he says with some hesitancy.

The keeper continues to read his paper, not responding to Thomas. Thomas is almost certain the conversation has ended and slowly backs away. There is a slight hesitance to his step, not fully concluding the conversation with a *good-bye* or some other kind of finality. The keeper continues to read his paper, the news providing a distinctive wall between him and the rest of the world.

Eight

"WHAT'S going on?" Zander asks with a bit of jealousy behind his tone.

"What do you mean?"

"You got a new friend now?"

"I got a job," Thomas clarifies the situation. He senses Zander's touch of bitterness.

Zander nods and can't help but feel hurt. "What about here? What if we open this season?"

"Zander...this place isn't going to open. There isn't going to be an Oceanic Hotel anymore. They have The Sunset open across the way. Benjamin Archer is gone and he isn't coming back. The men who own the hotel next door have no interest in buying a sinking ship." Thomas is brutally honest with his overly optimistic friend.

"No, faith," Zander jabs back, his friend's words are like a knife driven between his shoulder blades.

"No. It's not that. You see the ocean. You see how close it's getting. I overheard men in town talking about this place. They said it's gonna get swallowed up by the sea someday. I think they're right."

Zander turns and walks away, wanting no part of the truth and even less contact with Thomas at the moment.

.

"Zander!" Thomas calls out.

Zander continues and disappears down the hall, heading up the stairs to another level of the hotel.

Thomas shakes his head.

THOMAS arrives back at the keeper's house a few minutes early. He knocks and curiously enters the home.

"Hello?" Thomas calls out.

There is no answer at first and Thomas feels stuck in the mud by the front door. He waits a full minute, anxiety creeping on his face. He silently debates stepping deeper into the home. He decides to take the initiative and forges ahead. He wanders into the home and looks around. He moves past the dining room.

"Upstairs!" the keeper calls out.

Thomas strolls through the living room and finds the perfectly painted white stairs by the front entrance of the home. He heads up the stairs, taking one step at a time, uncertain of what he may see next. He emerges on the second floor to the glorious light of the dipping sun in the west. The sunlight pours in through the window at the top of the stairs. Thomas moves down the second story hallway and sees scattered paintings on the walls. The lighthouse is on two of them with two different looks at the tower. The first painting is on a sunny day and the other on a stormy night. There are a couple of paintings of various ships at sea, the boats nearly getting crushed by pounding waves.

"In the second bedroom!" the keeper firmly calls out, drawing Thomas's attention away from the seafaring paintings.

Thomas moves past the first bedroom slowly. It is neatly kept with a bed made and houses perfectly white painted furniture along the walls. He continues on to the second bedroom. There, the keeper is just finishing up, putting the final touches on getting ready for work. He is flattening out his jacket against his body. Under the jacket his navy blue collared shirt pokes out, the edges crisp enough to cut glass. The keeper's outfit is complete minus his hat. He is staring into a mirror at his own reflection as Thomas stands by the doorway.

"Are you ready for work?" the keeper asks.

"Yes. I am just curious about one thing," Thomas carefully speaks, keeping his tone light and respectful.

"Speak freely. Go ahead and ask," the keeper barks.

"Your name. What do I call you?"

"You will call me *keeper* or sir. Any other questions?" the keeper turns to Thomas and looks like a commanding officer peering down at a private.

"No, sir," Thomas respectfully replies.

"Your clothes are laid out in your bedroom down the hall. This is your new home. You sleep here. No more heading into the broken down hotel. Do you understand?"

The breath leaves Thomas's lungs. He is saddened by the clear ultimatum. He glances down and hesitates to speak. The keeper senses his hesitation and turns to him.

"Are you deaf?"

"No, sir."

"So you hear me just fine, then?"

"Yes, sir."

"Are we clear?!" the keeper more firmly asks.

"Yes. I sleep here. I understand, sir."

The keeper steps toward Thomas and moves within a few inches of his face. They are now nose to nose. His stern glare is an indication that he has little patience for insubordination.

"You sleep here. You eat here. You work here. You are here. There is no there. If you have a few hours off, you can scurry where you'd like. But our job here, *young man*, our job here is twenty-four hours a day and seven days a week. If you want another job, go find one. There is no wiggle room. You won't parse words with me. I am a traveled man. I will not be played a fool. Are we clear?"

"Yes, sir."

"I have no time to waste. I told you this. This exchange is setting us behind. Do you think you can live by the rules I have set forth or not?"

"I can and will."

"All right. Then get dressed and I'll meet you by the front door in exactly five minutes—not a second later."

The keeper goes back to fixing his clothing. He looks into the mirror and swats off a piece of lint he sees on his shoulder. Everything must look perfect.

Thomas turns and moves to his new home. It is a big upgrade from his previous two homes. No more cots— no more small rooms. Thomas enters a spacious bedroom with nice furniture. On the bed is a fresh bagged set of underwear; a package of three. A suit is laid out with a tie and a blue keeper's hat beside it. Then there is his uniform; a navy blue jacket, just like the one the keeper wears; a new pair of finely shined black shoes and black wool socks to round out the outfit. *He won't break me*, Thomas tells himself with determination as he gets changed.

Thomas meets the keeper downstairs in full uniform. He looks snappy and ready for any challenge.

The keeper steps up to Thomas and looks him over as if he were a stern father looking down upon his son. He picks off a piece of lint and helps flatten out Thomas's suit. He stands back and looks satisfied.

"You look like a keeper," is all the stern man says. It is the first and only kind words he has spoken to Thomas.

"Thank you, sir."

"You will wear this uniform today, and today only. Just because you look the part does not mean you have the part."

The keeper turns and abruptly walks away. Thomas is left in the keeper's verbal dust, thinking over his tough talk. The keeper stops and peers over his shoulder.

"You gonna make the first few steps or are you quittin' already?"

Thomas gathers himself and quickly goes after the keeper, jogging to catch up.

The keeper leads Thomas over to the lighthouse. Thomas stares at the tower with grand dreams. He is ecstatic to shine the light brightly across the sea. He can't wait to sound the horn and alert ships passing by that he is there for them. He wants to stand high above the ocean's crashing waves and be the protector in the night. The keeper carries a black bag with him over to the lighthouse door. Thomas can barely contain his excitement and his smile. He knows better than to show the keeper he is too eager. He doesn't want to seem like an immature child. But he has never been to the top of a lighthouse.

As the door to the lighthouse is opened, the keeper turns back to Thomas. "217 steps," he simply states.

"What sir?"

"There are 217 steps from the bottom of Barney to the top."

"Yes, sir."

"These 217 steps mean something. These steps are the difference between life and death. Do you understand?"

"Yes, sir."

"Every journey begins with one step. Today, you will take those first steps."

"Yes, sir."

"You will take exactly 205 of them tonight and not one more. Do you understand?"

"No, sir," Thomas's brows furrow with a bit of confusion.

The keeper points to a closed door leading to the vestibule house at the base of the tower. "You will carry seven full buckets of oil from this room up the stairs. You will reach stair 205 and leave a bucket just above the top step. You will not climb up to the top step. You will not step foot in the watch room. You will not step foot in the watch gallery. You haven't earned the right to step foot in my tower. You haven't earned the right to be the keeper. This isn't a game. What you will do, is the job I tell you to. You will bring me seven buckets of oil and leave them for me. That is your first order of business. Do you think you can handle that?"

"Yes, sir."

"Good. Then get me my oil. Seven full buckets. Not five. Not six and a half. Seven full buckets."

"Yes, sir."

The keeper turns and makes his way up the winding cast iron stairs, heading toward the top of the tower, his feet pounding the iron like he was a solider marching proudly into battle. His footsteps echo through the grand tower; each boot strike a reminder of the aura surrounding the stern keeper.

Thomas looks over to the vestibule house and moves inside the attached room. There, he sees the perfectly cleaned white buckets. The buckets look as though oil has never touched them. He sees a large supply of oil and starts to fill his first bucket.

"217 steps," Thomas says under his breath, mocking the keeper. He is upset he will not be entering the greatest view on earth tonight. "217 steps," he mocks again.

Thomas begins up the stairs, carefully carrying his first bucket of oil. He goes slowly as the oil splashes just a little and Thomas sees he must keep the bucket very steady. As he walks he reaches a window at the landing and pauses. He stares out at the ocean as the sun is beginning to descend in the early evening sky. He is only fifty feet up but enjoys the only view he will apparently get on this night.

"No time for that!" the keeper shouts from the top of the tower, as if knowing Thomas paused at the window for the view.

"Aye-aye," Thomas grumbles under his breath and carries the bucket to the top.

He heads down and back up. Down and back up. He makes the seven trips, hauling each oil filled bucket up exactly 205 cast iron steps.

Thomas, out of breath, is standing on the stairs, setting the last of the buckets up for the keeper. The keeper emerges and looks down at him with a smirk on his face, amused by Thomas's exhaustion. Thomas smiles upon seeing the keeper mock him with his expression.

"That's a lot of steps," Thomas jokes, defending himself.

The keeper smiles and nods and then moves the lesson forward.

"The air flow is important inside the tower. It is the air flow that causes the flame to dim just slightly. And a dim light means less distance out to sea. The other interesting thing about the airflow inside the tower is that voices tend to carry up. You can almost whisper at the bottom of the tower and your tiny voice could echo all the way up to the top to my two ears. Isn't that interesting?"

Thomas's heart sinks a little. As he has mocked the stern lighthouse veteran, the keeper subtly intimates he can hear every word spoken.

"Those facts would have been more interesting before I started tonight," Thomas jests.

The keeper smirks and nods. "Aye-aye, assistant keeper," he playfully mocks Thomas.

Thomas shakes his head, embarrassed.

"There is a broom in the vestibule house. Sweep the floor at the bottom of the lighthouse. Then get a rag and the cleaning spray. There are two bottles on the shelf. Use the clear soapy liquid—not the other one. Wipe every step and the railing from the bottom to step 205. Wipe it all so well that I can serve you supper right upon it. Make it shine. I will clean the last 12 steps myself. Do you understand?"

"Yes, sir."

"And after you have cleaned the stairs and the railing, you will head outside and tend to the garden. Make sure all the plants and vegetables are watered, all the weeds pulled. Don't leave a single weed in that ground. Do you understand?"

"Yes, sir. Sweep the entrance, clean the stairs and railing and tend to the vegetable garden."

"Excellent. You may last 'til dawn yet. Surprising." The keeper turns and moves back to his position, looking out at the sea.

Thomas does just as instructed. He sweeps. He wipes down every step and the railing as if they were the bed he rested his head upon. He tends to the garden. He completes all these tasks and then does it again the next night; and the next night; and the next. The keeper has Thomas wipe down every step, clean the railing from bottom to near the top and tend to the garden every night. That of course happened only after he carried seven buckets, not six, but seven buckets full of oil from the vestibule house all the way to step number 205. He never got near the first-order high-powered Fresnel lens, the powerful source of the tower's light or the watch room up top. He got just below and did as he was told. For a full month Thomas did just as he was told and nothing more.

AS THOMAS tends to the garden and the sun is starting to rise, a familiar voice visits him.

"Hey," Zander's solemn, apologetic tone speaks greatly of a defeated man.

"Hey," Thomas rises, excited to see his friend.

"You've been working like a dog. I've seen it," he points out.

"Yeah. He's got me working pretty hard."

"He as mean as they say?" Zander asks.

"Pretty much," Thomas gasps and looks over his shoulder, seeing if the keeper is listening.

"He got ears out here too?" Zander chuckles as he asks the question.

"You'd be surprised. That old guy hears everything!"

The two men laugh together.

"What's the keeper's name?"

Thomas smiles and shakes his head.

"What?" Zander asks, curious what is so funny.

"I have no idea. He hasn't told me."

"You haven't asked?"

"I have. I have to call him *keeper*. That's it. No other name."

"No Bob or Ted or last name?"

"No idea," Thomas smiles back. "Each day, he tells me it will most likely be my last. Each day I carry buckets of oil, clean stairs and tend to this garden. He wants me to quit. He is seeing if I'll break."

"Why would he want you to break?"

"Because if I break for him, if I break doing this, then there's no way I can handle the job. That's all I can figure."

"Strange," Zander shakes his head.

"You head over to The Sunset yet?" Thomas asks his friend.

"I don't know. Maybe. I just…I don't know. It's not the Oceanic."

"But it's a job."

"Yeah. This is true." Zander agrees with Thomas.

"Go tomorrow. Go tomorrow and get a job."

"I will. I'll head over in the morning. I have my best outfit. It's all ready."

"Good," Thomas is happy for his friend.

They share a moment of silence and then Zander perks up.

"You get a night off?"

"In five days. He said I can have a night off if the weather holds."

"Then let's hang out. They got a new place down the road. Prohibition Act is coming so it's gonna be the last chance to get a few drops before they take it away."

"I can't drink off duty but I can head over with you."

Zander smiles and shakes his head. The two men continue to catch up.

The keeper is watching from inside the tower, looking down at the two men talking.

Nine

WHITMORE sits in the hallway waiting. He is dressed in his pressed officer uniform. A black eye patch hides his right eye. A scar runs from his right cheek, behind the eye patch and up to the beginning of his forehead. His perfectly shined black loafers remain still on the floor. He doesn't look comfortable sitting and waiting, but he also doesn't give away any nerves. His posture is perfect as he stares forward with his one good eye and a stoic expression.

The bronze plate on the door behind him reads: New Jersey Department of Corrections. The door opens and Warden Goodfried steps through. He is dressed in his best suit but the nice digs do not hide the bitter taste in his mouth. He groans as he exits the board room and immediately pulls out a cigarette. Goodfried is balding, tall and has a robust belly. His hair is combed over and inching up off his head as he appears as if he just got put through the ringer.

Whitmore respectfully rises for his superior.

"It's a shit show in there. They want heads for this, Whitmore. Now I have to go to Martin's family and finally confirm he is dead. A hunter found his body rotting in the woods, eaten by animals. They couldn't even tell what his face looked like. Found his identification card. That's all they had to go on—that and his uniform." Goodfried blows smoke and shakes his head.

"Sir, what do you mean *they want heads?*" Whitmore is concerned by his boss's tone.

"Three men escaped. They escaped under our care. They escaped under *your* care."

Whitmore nods, now knowing what this is about. He is being sold up the river for the flood, for the accident and the subsequent escape. He smirks and shakes his head, looking down, his one good eye peering up and away, attempting to figure out a new strategy for himself.

"It was a flood. It is a miracle I'm alive," Whitmore raises his head and replies.

"You and Bullocks. The only two we know survived."

"Bullocks? How do you know? I hadn't heard."

"He transferred over to the lighthouse division. He is working as a keeper's assistant or something. I don't know. He got out clean. He is the lucky one." Goodfried once again blows smoke.

"And what about me, sir?"

"Mr. Whitmore!" an annoyed voice calls from inside the board room.

Whitmore glances over toward the door, an ominous look on his face. He peers back over at Warden Goodfried for one last time.

"I got a write-up; a warning. I'm sorry, Whitmore."

Goodfried drops his cigarette and angrily smashes it underneath his black loafer. He turns and storms away, marching down the hallway.

Whitmore turns back to the door, a man on an island. He feels the weight of impending scrutiny lowering upon his shoulders. His chest stiffens, nerves trying to creep into the impenetrable man. He takes one deep breath, wiping weakness away from his thoughts, sticks his chest up, raises his chin and enters inside the board room.

"Close the door behind you!" a member of the three-person panel orders. It is a different voice than the first that called him in; but the tone is just as abrasive.

Whitmore closes the door and sees a single chair in the center of the room. The panel is sitting behind a long table on a raised platform. They look down upon the unfortunate person in the hot seat; a single slim-back wooden chair. Right now, that is going to be Whitmore.

"Take a seat," another one of the voices says, this time raspy and bothered. Now they have all spoken.

Whitmore slowly takes a seat, straightening out his uniform as he rests in the chair.

"It has come to our attention that you have been mistreating inmates for some time," the old gentleman in the middle states. He is anchored on either side by equally old faces. They all have grey hair and are near carbon copies of one another; old, judgmental white men in suits, their skin weathered by time, tan and wrinkled. They sit tall like judges, quietly sifting through documents they have spread before them. They confer with one another and make the process all the more intimidating for their victims; in this case, Whitmore.

"I don't know what you mean," Whitmore replies.

"You used a whip on prisoners?" the man flanked to the right asks. He is looking down at a document through his reading glasses as he speaks. Then he peers up over his spectacles to look at Whitmore and analyze the defendant's answer.

"I used only the issued materials mandated by the state of New Jersey." Whitmore recites an official answer that seems all too prepared.

"Recite it," the man on the left gargles, almost too angry to even look at Whitmore.

"What's that sir?"

"I want to hear you say it. Recite it perfectly, Officer Whitmore."

Whitmore bulks up his chest further as three sets of judgmental eyes all fall upon him in one challenging wave of tension. "The mission of the New Jersey Department of Corrections is to protect the inmates by operating safe, secure and humane correctional facilities. The mission is realized through effective supervision, proper classification, appropriate treatment of offenders and by providing services that promote successful re-entry into society; *sirs*."

"Safe, secure and humane," the gentlemen on the left preaches.

Whitmore remains silent and squints, his one good eye trying to figure out what exactly the panel is getting at.

"We will cut to the chase, Officer Whitmore," the man in the middle begins. "We have a letter from one of your fellow officers who sites you as a *major* concern."

"Bullocks," Whitmore bitterly states under his breath.

"It details a pattern of abuse, including and not limited to: using a bullwhip as punishment on numerous inmates—striking them like animals with ten lashes at a time, shackling them to bars and repeatedly kicking them and burning men with the ends of cigarettes. This is all cruel and unusual punishment. There was also mention of food withholdings, extensive time in solitary confinement for reasons unknown to fellow officers, and all under your guidance and command. There are disgusting details like food tossed in dirty puddles of urine on the floor; you directing officers to spit on inmate's food in front of them, etc., etc. I really don't see a need to go on. Warden Goodfried stood tall for you. He recommended strongly you receive a severance of some kind on your way out. But we have discussed all the facts before us and we see no reason to give you a cent. You have sullied the good name of the NJDOC and I will not have it sullied anymore. You are hereby terminated, effective immediately, officer Whitmore. If you were a citizen and committed these atrocities in the public eye, you would be in jail. You are lucky you leave free of handcuffs. Good day, Mr. Whitmore. I hope these proceedings have humbled you in some way."

The panel stares angrily at Whitmore.

Prideful as always, the terminated officer rises to his feet, chest and chin held high. His lips pull tightly together, hiding the anger building inside him. He half nods to the panel in a showcase of respect. He turns and whips around, marching out of the room.

THOMAS is fast asleep. He slowly comes to and awakes to the keeper standing in the corner of the room, staring out the window. Thomas jumps up, at first disoriented and not knowing who is there. He then realizes it is the keeper and calms himself.

"You scared the daylights out of me!" Thomas catches his breath, rubbing his tired eyes.

"They say there is a land in this world where men hunt lions for sport. They go there and they move through some of the most dangerous terrain on earth and they have only a rifle to protect themselves. They are outmanned, outnumbered and at any moment, death could be upon their doorstep. Without that rifle, that man in the African grasslands becomes extinct. He created a tool and that tool enabled him to live longer and survive. Today I'm going to show you a tool. Today you will learn how to survive in a great storm. If you dive into the cold waters as you did before, I am quite certain you will never return. You were very brave on that day, but it will cost you if you challenge *her* again. The ocean is fickle and chaotic. Don't challenge her, son."

"You think I got lucky?"

"I think every day we live above ground we are lucky, son." The keeper pauses, showing a chink in his tough exterior. He gazes out the window at the sunlight, pausing, as if dramatically reminiscing with deep rooted sincerity. It is a moment that Thomas recognizes, and sees for the very first time, the human side of the keeper.

"If you challenge her again, you will die. I know that much. The ocean is the most beautiful monster in the world. Don't challenge her again."

"Okay. Yes, sir."

"All right. Let's see if you'll earn your job today. We got work to do," the keeper states and quickly exits Thomas's room.

A BEACH cart is set by the water with the Lyle gun set atop it. The small short-barreled cannon has a line attached to the end of it. Both Thomas and the keeper have thick working gloves on.

"This here is a Lyle gun," the keeper starts to explain. He picks the long rolled tightly wrapped line into the palm of his hand. "This is not a rope. It is a waterproof braided linen line. It is crucial to be accurate with your first shot. If you miss, you must manually pull the line back in and once you have managed that, you must reset and reload the gun. This cannon has quite a quick. It can fire back as much as ten feet; so never stand behind her. She is tough and not easy to use," Henry pats the side of the small cannon. "It also prevents you from having to go into the water. I personally like the boats more; getting into the sea myself. But this is a good tool."

"How much gunpowder do we load in?"

"Good question. Too much and you may lose half your face. Too little and it won't fire properly. Forty-five grams is plenty. The measuring cup and powder is on the top shelf—in the vestibule house."

Thomas looks out to sea at the small motor boat bobbing just beyond the waves. Inside rests a very nervous passenger. "You doing okay?!" Thomas asks, shouting at the boat.

Only Zander's thumb pops up to show he is all right. His body clings to the bottom of the boat.

"We're not gonna hurt Zander, are we?" Thomas asks, his eyes flashing out toward the ocean.

"Hey, guys! I'm pretty cold and I'm floating away!!!" Zander pops his head up out of the small motor boat. He's wearing a life jacket and his swim trunks. He looks scared as can be and barely pokes his head up, like a turtle sneaking a peek out of his shell. Just one hundred yards off the coastline, his motor boat is slowly being pulled out to the sea in the soft kind current.

"He'll be fine," Henry mutters.

"We're about to fire!" Thomas shouts to Zander.

"I'm not sure if that's a good or bad thing," Zander mutters to himself, looking as if he is getting sicker by the second in the boat.

Thomas studies the cannon and then looks out at Zander's small motor boat.

"We're trying to shoot just over the boat," Thomas confirms with a statement that is really meant to be a question.

"Yes. We want to hook the line and give them support. This way they have something they can hold onto and guide them into shore. If they don't have vests, it buys us time to paddle out to them."

"Okay. Let's do it." Thomas has a gleam in his eye.

The keeper nods and carefully loads the Lyle gun with Thomas keeping a close eye.

"This isn't gonna hurt—right?!" Zander nervously asks.

"Just don't let it hit you!" the keeper shouts.

"Oh, God," Zander ducks down, placing his hands over his head.

"I placed 25 grams in. He is awfully close to shore. Normally, you will put a little more in."

"Aim small," Thomas says.

The keeper and Thomas are lining up their shot, making a last minute adjustment to the angle of the cannon.

"Yes, always aim small." The keeper's cheeks rise up, showcasing a rare smile, developing a liking to Thomas. He strikes a match and lights the Lyle gun. "Step back and hold your ears," the keeper advises.

The Lyle gun fires and its metal tip and linen line go soaring through the air.

Zander is curled up in a ball, sick and scared.

"Watch over me lord," he prays to himself.

The metal line flies just over the boat. The keeper and Thomas quickly move to the line and pull it back, the metal tip pulling up against the side of the boat.

"Grab the line!" Thomas shouts to Zander.

"Am I alive?" Zander nervously asks and pokes his head back up again. He sees the line stretched from the far side of his motor boat all the way to shore. He takes a hold of it as Thomas and the keeper pull the line in, the gloves on their hands protecting them from the coarse linen line. Thomas can't help but have an excited smile on his face through the grimace and strain of pulling Zander and the boat in. The keeper glances over and sees Thomas's face and lets out a brief smile of his own.

When Zander is close to shore, Thomas jogs over to the water wearing high water boots. He helps pull the boat aground. Zander is plastered to the bottom of the boat, scared to even move.

"Hey, buddy," Thomas smiles, looking down at his friend.

"Sure. Send the guy who doesn't know how to swim out in the middle of the ocean."

"Hey, it worked! We didn't kill you!" Thomas jokes.

"Ha-ha," Zander finds little humor in Thomas's joke.

"Get Sally out of the boat," the keeper sarcastically states.

Thomas helps the woozy Zander out of the boat and pats him on the back.

THOMAS is fast asleep in his bed, getting a few more minutes of shut-eye before dusk arrives when the keeper wakes him up. It's not a tap on the shoulder or the creaking of the floorboards. It's the sound of a man crying in his sleep. It's a whimpering, an odd sound Thomas has never heard before. Thomas curiously rises out of bed, thinking at first there is a dying animal in his midst. He listens and hears the wailing once again. It is coming from down the hallway. He rises up off the bed and slowly peaks his head into the hall to grab a listen. After a moment, he hears it again, just a bedroom away. Thomas moves slowly through the hallway and gently pushes the door open to the keeper's room. It is the first time he has stepped inside or looked into the room since the first day he was invited upstairs.

The whimpering is coming from the bed. The keeper is having a terrible nightmare, sweating profusely and shaking in his sleep. Thomas watches as the keeper whines and moans uncontrollably, the sandman taking him for a dark turn in his slumber.

Thomas looks around and sees a framed piece of paper from the military hanging on the wall encased in glass; an official notice of honorable discharge made out to Henry "Hank" Jones. Below the framed document hanging on hooks is a Krag-Jorgensen repeating bolt action rifle.

The US military-issued rifle has a few scrapes on it, but is as clean as a whistle; polished and proudly mounted.

Thomas moves carefully into the room and sees the keeper curled up in a ball. He is cringing and shaking.

"No," he mumbles. And then, "No," he breathlessly mutters again.

Thomas stares at the man and senses his pain. He doesn't know quite what to do. The keeper rolls over and seemingly begins to break free of his nightmare. He twitches and his eyes appear as though they may open. Thomas quietly backs out of the room like a cat burglar, not wanting to get caught spying on his boss as he sleeps.

Thomas quietly exits the bedroom and thinks to himself, reminded of his own nightmares.

Ten

THE sky rumbles. The cloudy evening in the suburbs of Philadelphia is marked by strong cool winds and the recipe for chaotic weather. The air is damp and moist, the heat and humidity colliding with an oncoming cold front.

"Make sure the car is put away in the barn!" a woman's voice shouts.

The front door is yanked open and an annoyed man appears; Warden Goodfried.

"Yeah-yeah," he mutters back. He has a cigar in his mouth and a glass of whisky in his hand. He steps outside onto his porch and closes the front door behind him.

"Stop slamming the door!" the woman distantly nags.

"It's the hinge!" Goodfried mutters through his clinched teeth, his cigar bobbing between his lips. He shakes his head, annoyed at his wife. Dressed in a white T-shirt, suspenders and black pants, Goodfried is looking over the stormy night. He takes a big puff of his cigar as thunder rolls in the sky, ominously predicting a stormy night to come.

He looks over at his car and shakes his head, tired and annoyed. He slowly moves through the strong head wind, darkness all around. Thunder grumbles again and a lightning strike causes Goodfried to hesitate. He looks around, feeling something amiss; the atmosphere as a whole growing into a horror scene. He scans his eyes through the surrounding dark tree lines, paranoid that a set of eyes are fixated upon him. He looks over toward his barn, the latched door shaking in the wind, sending out more sounds of horror. He waits just a second longer and continues to the car, his head and eyes on a swivel of paranoia. He reaches the car and goes to pull the door open. Before he can, a bullwhip snaps around his neck. Goodfried's head bends back, his cigar flying out of his mouth. He drops his whisky, the glass shattering on the ground beside his feet. With the wind blowing, the sound of glass is white noise in the chaos brewing outside. He reaches up with both hands, clinching around his neck. He tries to turn and see what is happening, the rain starting to fall from the sky. Thunder rolls and a lightning strike fires down, momentarily lighting up the dark world. Standing, holding the other end of the whip, is Whitmore. Goodfried struggles to look over his shoulder and sees in the momentary flash of light his former head officer. He's standing drenched in the rain with an eye patch and a crazed face; the desperate look of a desperate man. More wind, more rain and again thunder followed by a flash of lightning.

"Whitmore!" Goodfried angrily growls.

Whitmore yanks on the whip as if it were a leash, choking off any sounds Goodfried could make. The warden struggles to speak, making a few stuttered gargled noises; attempting to speak and breathe at the same time, neither of which is working.

Whitmore leads Goodfried over to his small barn, using the whip to force his feet to stumble along.

"On your knees!" Whitmore demands.

Goodfried obliges and lowers himself to his knees, all the while trying to loosen the whip's firm grip on his shredding neck.

"I…ca-ca-can't…breee…athe," Goodfried struggles. Whitmore takes out a pistol and releases his grip around Goodfried's neck. He unravels his whip back and aims the pistol at the man gasping for air on his knees.

"You ordered me to be hard on them. You asked me to rule with an iron fist," Whitmore begins.

"I'm sorry. It wasn't my choice. They were going to fire me too."

"So, I'm the fall guy! I'm the one that gets punished and you walk away clean?"

"I got a final warning," Goodfried attempts to defend himself.

"This is your final warning!" Whitmore belts out, thunder crackling above as if on cue.

"What do you want?"

"Where is Bullocks?" Whitmore looks possessed.

"What?"

"You heard me. You said he was a keeper at a lighthouse. Which one?" Whitmore demands.

"I don't know. How would I know?" Goodfried shakes his head, his hands held out away from his body in a submissive manner.

"You know he survived the accident. You know he works at a lighthouse."

"I heard. Yes. His name was registered with the state and I got a call. They asked if he worked at the prison. I figure he got spooked by the whole accident and flash flood. Maybe he was scared and needed a change. I don't know. I didn't talk to him."

"You're going to find out where he is stationed. If you don't, I will bury you and take your wife as my own," Whitmore sadistically threatens Goodfried.

"Easy-easy. I can make some calls. In the morning, I will make some calls. It may take some time."

"All right. Let's go inside. I would love to introduce myself to your wife."

"You will burn for this, Whitmore," Goodfried states with anger.

"You first, warden," the man filled with vengeful venom sadistically says.

THE wind is blowing but the weather is much better by the Barnegat Lighthouse. There isn't a cloud in the sky.

205 steps of cleaning. As Thomas nears the top step of his nightly duty, the keeper looks down.

"Thomas, why don't you come up here tonight?" The offer is an extraordinary occurrence as Thomas has only seen the bottom ninety percent of the lighthouse.

"Yeah," Thomas can barely contain his excitement and hurries up to the top steps. He rises and gazes around with a dopey entranced smile on his face. He begins to see the surrounding bay and landscape around the tower. It is a magnificent view as the light bursts out of the Fresnel lens across the dark waters of the sea. Thomas's mouth hangs open as he gazes across the Atlantic and looks back around toward the mainland. Sparse distant lights flicker in the night's wind as if they were hidden lights on a Christmas tree. It *is* Christmas to Thomas. He finally got to the top of the lighthouse. After two months of dedicated work, he reached the top.

"It's magnificent, isn't it?" the keeper asks.

"Yes, sir. It sure is," Thomas gawks like a child in a candy shop, a stupid smile struck across his awed face.

"Do you know why you are here?" the keeper begins.

"To be your assistant."

"Son, I could have found an assistant through the inspector. I could have searched the bay for a man who had the qualifications to be standing atop this tower. But I see myself in you. I see grit and determination in you. I see a stubborn sonovabitch who will never quit."

Thomas chuckles and nods. "That's me."

"I'm Henry Jones but my friends call me Hank. You can call me Hank." Henry extends his hand, the keeper finally letting Thomas in.

Thomas gladly shakes his hand. But when he goes to pull his hand back, Henry holds onto it.

Thomas's face goes from elated to confused, his furrowed brows and mouth dropping open.

"Tell me your name, son. Your given name."

"Thomas." He begins and then realizes what Henry is asking him. "You know," he states with a hint of uncertainty.

Henry turns Thomas's hand over, exposing his wrist. Scars from chains and ropes have dug lines that have healed over time. He is marked and Henry knows exactly what it is from.

"How long have you known?" Thomas asks.

"I knew the moment I saw you."

Thomas looks down, upset. He doesn't know what to say. "Are you firing me?" Thomas asks.

"Do you think you should be fired?" Henry poses.

"No. No, I do not, sir," Thomas stands proud and tall. He recalibrates his expression and pushes his chest forward, sticks his chin up into the air.

"Then why would I fire you?"

Thomas nods, relaxing, a small amount of relief comes over him. But he still is unsure of where this line of questioning will lead.

"You have a story," Henry begins. "We have exactly forty-nine minutes before we have to wind the mechanism again. Can you tell me the story in that time?"

"Yes."

"So tell me about yourself, Thomas. Tell me everything."

"I was a prisoner. I deserved to be in jail. Ironically, not for the crime they convicted me of. I got caught up with a bad man. He did bad things I knew nothing about. He killed men. And we both paid for his crimes. I made the mistake of sitting in a car. It was the worst decision I ever made. But I didn't live without sin. I too killed a man. We fought and we both were hopped up on moonshine and bad attitudes. I killed him defending myself and I killed him as an aggressor. Not a day goes by I don't think about writing to his family. See, he had a wife and a child. I made them fatherless—for better or for worse."

"It takes two to brawl," Henry gives Thomas some support.

"I ended up where I belonged. And then there was a storm. We were being transported up the state to Trenton. I was going to spend a long time in a small cell. The storm came. I survived a terrible flood. Others didn't. I took the identity of officer Bullocks. That's where I got my identification from. He was killed in the flood. I buried him proper out in the pines. It was a long twisted road to get here."

"It's all right, son. So what's your God given name?"

"I'm Thomas Dent. I was a petty thief growing up and I became an even worse man."

"It is very nice to meet you, Thomas Dent."

Henry gives Thomas a nod.

"I lived a past filled with deception. I stole and I lied. I have been a dishonest man most of my life," Thomas admits.

"You seem pretty honest to me, son," Henry states.

"I want to be a better man. I wish I was a better man, sir."

"Thomas, don't be the man you think you are. Be the man you want to be. You say you killed a man in a fight?"

"Yes, sir."

"Then you save ten innocent men to make up for that one life. It could have been you that died in the fight, but it was him. So, you save ten men. Once you save ten men, you've met your penance. You saved one already. Be the man you want to be, son. Be the man you're becoming, not the man you think you were. The past is gone."

Henry turns and looks out at the night. The wind is whipping around the tower, whistling proudly. It is a beautiful view as the light skips across the ocean's dark waters, cutting far out into the darkness.

"Look at where you stand now," he says.

Thomas stands next to Henry and looks out at the night with him. The glorious view is something to behold, a brisk beautiful evening with stars shining brightly in the sky.

"It's amazing," Thomas agrees.

"You've earned this view. This is yours. You are a keeper. I will make you the best damn keeper on all the shores." Henry is silent for a moment and then wags his finger at Thomas. "No mistakes. We can't afford any mistakes. We must be perfect each and every day. You hear me?"

"Yes, sir."

"Good." Henry moves over toward the Fresnel lens. "Come take a look at her."

Thomas moves next to Henry to look over the powerful lens over.

"We are 172 feet above sea level. The tower itself is 50 meters tall, or, 162 feet. This is the Fresnel lens," Henry points to the beautiful powerful, shining prism. "This puppy shines over twenty miles out to sea to help guide boats through the waters. She flashes once every ten seconds. This lighthouse is a directional guide for the lost; hope for the hopeless. We must keep her lit and shining at maximum strength at all times. The portholes all around must be adjusted to steady the flame. Keeping an eye on the flame is a key part of our job." Henry reaches down and holds up a large notebook. "In this log we write the passing of every vessel. If there is an accident, we log it. If we think we see a ship, we log it. Every storm is logged. The currents and tides are logged. Cleanings are logged. These notes are invaluable. They must be kept daily to perfection."

"Yes, sir," Thomas nods. Thomas stares at Henry with a curious look on his face.

"What?" Henry asks. "You don't understand something?"

"No. It's not that. I'm just wondering."

"Spit it out, son," Henry prompts.

"How many men usually run this lighthouse?"

"Old Barney, here? One keeper and two assistants."

"Well," Thomas smiles and looks around. "I got here and it was just you. What happened to everyone else?"

"I buried a good man shortly before you arrived. I hadn't gotten word to the inspector, Gus Philips. I saw you arrive and had a feeling."

"Still leaves you one short."

"I've been one short for a good time now. We can manage with two. I had a wife and she used to help. She was amazing, my Felicia. But that is a story for a different day." Henry pauses, the subject hitting an emotional chord. "We can do this job with two good men," he returns back on track. Thomas nods in silent agreement.

Dawn's light starts to arrive in the distance.

"Here she comes," Henry stares out at the light starting to arrive in the dark skies.

"It's something else being here. It's paradise," Thomas romanticizes.

"*It is*. It's paradise…and it's also a graveyard to many brave men and women. It's a complicated place—the ocean. The Atlantic is tough. But you know this. You know the waters. You know the skies. I can tell. You read them like words on a page."

"My father was a man of the sea. I grew up under the stars and I learned to read the weather. I did so for a while…until I didn't." Thomas also shares a tough memory.

"Perhaps a story for another day as well," Henry states, sensing Thomas's hesitation.

"How about I show you how to clean the prism," Henry offers.

"Okay."

"Every morning we do this. We use a special cloth and a duster. At dawn we clean her—every day."

Thomas nods and Henry shows him how to clean the precious lens.

THOMAS and Henry head into town on the train. They both are dressed in their full uniforms, a proud display as they walk around town. Everyone respectfully nods and shakes their hands as they move from the rail station in Barnegat City to the streets of Barnegat on the mainland. Using a horse drawn wagon, they move deep into town. The wagon is made available for Henry weekly for his supply runs. It is provided by the city, but *only* once a week. If he misses using the wagon on that particular day, he may fall short of supplies on that given week.

They need a variety of items and head to the General Store first.

"Stay out by the wagon. I'm going to head inside," Henry tells Thomas.

"Sure. You got it, Hank."

"I don't want them damn horses running off. Did that once after a car popped a tire."

Thomas smiles and sits tight as Henry heads into the store. He is casually relaxing, the streets busier, bustling, as summer is in full swing. The temperatures are approaching 80 degrees now.

"I know you," the kind female voice states.

Thomas curiously looks over his shoulder and sees Sarah standing there. She is wearing a nice summer dress with Jackson by her side. Thomas has a dopey smile on his face as he is surprised to see them.

"You don't remember us?" Sarah asks with a smirk and a grin.

"Sarah Jones and this is Jackson. I remember."

"He doesn't let go of that badge you gave him. That was very kind of you."

"Not a problem at all, ma'am."

"Please. Call me Sarah. You say, *ma'am*, and I look for my mother."

"Okay, Sarah."

"Sarah?!" Henry's voice calls in surprise.

Sarah's smile quickly flees and she slowly turns around. "Hello, father."

"Father?!" Thomas crows in confusion.

"Yes, Thomas. This is my daughter, Sarah."

Thomas nods, not sure what to think.

Everyone remains frozen in time for a few moments. Then Henry breaks the silence.

"I'm hungry. Let's eat."

Thomas's eyes pan back and forth over the scene, looking at Sarah and then back at Henry. There are no words, just silent agreement.

Eleven

AT THE keeper's house, Henry, Thomas, Sarah, Jackson and Zander are all seated at the dining room table. They have bowls of steaming hot beef stew in front of them with buttered bread on the side. It is quiet. There is no talking—only the sounds of eating, slurping and chewing.

Zander keeps his head buried in his food, unsure of why there is so much tension in the room. But he doesn't dare say a word as a guest in the keeper's home. Henry also quietly eats away. He has a near-scowl on his face as he digests his food. The look is normal for him, but at this tense environment, it can be construed in many ways.

"Your manners, Jackson," Sarah places Jackson's napkin on his lap, her soft voice breaking the silent room.

Thomas's eyes flash around, he is too uncertain of what to say. He is smitten with Sarah, but upon learning she is Henry's daughter, circumstances have changed.

"This is great beef stew," Zander finds the need to throw out a compliment.

Henry peers up from his food with a stern look. He subtly nods to Zander and continues on eating.

Zander glances over at Thomas. Thomas subtly nods and smiles at Zander, the two men both uncomfortably drowning in the awkwardness.

"Are you going to talk to me, father?" Sarah asks.

Both Zander and Thomas's eyes flare wide open and they direct looks across the table to Henry to gage his response. The sounds of slurping and chewing give way to complete silence. Everyone waits as Henry slowly sets his spoon down inside his bowl. His face is tipped down. He composes himself, uncertain of what to say.

"I invited you to supper, didn't I?" he states without looking up from his bowl.

"And you haven't said a word since. You were silent on the train ride over. You have been silent since we sat at the table. You buried yourself in preparing the stew." Sarah lists her many reasons of frustration.

"Thomas has trouble seeing when the stew is fully cooked. So, on beef stew night, I cook."

"It's true, I do," Thomas admits.

Both Sarah and Henry shoot looks over at Thomas and he gets quiet and looks away from their intense glares. He dips his head back down to his bowl and hides behind his meal.

Sarah turns back to Henry and continues. "Walls. Giant walls everywhere. You still haven't changed."

"Who is that?" Henry looks at Jackson.

"That's Jackson."

"I saw you with the boy last time." Henry states.

"Don't talk above him as if he doesn't know what you're saying."

"He doesn't speak. How would I know if he understands me?" Henry grows argumentative.

"Actually, he does…" Thomas chimes in and again gets angry glares from Sarah and Henry. He quietly finishes his sentence. "…speak," his voice trails off.

Sarah again refocuses on Henry. "What did I do?"

Henry goes back to his stew and stirs it around with his spoon, growing uncomfortable with this trip down memory lane.

"Maybe I should go," Zander cautiously rises from the table.

"Sit!" Henry, Sarah and Thomas all state in unison to Zander.

"I'll stay." Zander humbly sits back down.

"Dad? What did I do?" Sarah asks again.

"You didn't do…it's complicated. It's not you. I can't…" Henry lacks the words to finish his thought.

"I know you're upset I wasn't here when mom died. And I know you blame yourself for Henry Jr.. I know things haven't always been easy. I know the war was hard on you."

"What do you know about war?!" Henry slams his hand down on the table and shouts. The glassware clanks with a couple of glasses toppling over from the force of Henry's hand. Henry's uncharacteristic outburst is followed by a surprised look of humility as he quickly quells his temper. The world has stopped inside the keeper's dining room as everyone waits on Henry for what he will say or do next. All eyes are cast upon him in anticipation of *something*.

"I am…" Henry starts. "I am going to excuse myself for a moment. Sorry. Excuse me," Henry respectfully stands and softly places his cloth napkin down on the table. He exits the dining room and heads through the kitchen to the back door and disappears outside.

Sarah runs her hands through Jackson's hair, thinking deeply about her relationship issues with her father.

Thomas doesn't know quite what to say.

"This goes back a long way. I'm sorry I imposed upon your supper," Sarah regrettably states. "Come on, Jackson. Let's go." Sarah ushers Jackson out of his chair and they move toward the front door.

Thomas and Zander share looks of confusion over what to do next.

"You should—," Zander begins a sentence.

"Yeah," Thomas finishes Zander's thought, the two on the same page. Thomas jumps up and heads after Sarah. She is by the front door putting Jackson's winter coat around his shoulders.

"Put your arm through, sweetie," she says to him.

"Wait. Sarah. Just, wait." Thomas moves between Sarah and the door.

"I'm sorry, Thomas. A lot of this is from the past. It has nothing to do with—,"

"I know, Sarah. *I know*. But listen, I don't pretend to know your father as well as you. In all honesty, I'm just getting used to him. But I can tell you I know the man well enough to know that he cares about you. You get to him. You're his daughter and he isn't very good with words— *trust* me. He has put me through the ringer. But I can tell he has a lot to talk to you about. It's just going to take time."

"Time is something I've afforded my father before."

"Give him another chance. He's been different lately. He's been…," Thomas looks around, not wanting anyone to hear. "…he's been pretty nice," he whispers.

Sarah chuckles, amused. Thomas follows suit and the ice has been broken.

"Why are you fighting for us?" she asks with a glow in her eyes.

"Because your father fought for me when no one else would."

Sarah thinks about Thomas's heartfelt plea. She smiles and nods.

"All right," Sarah gives in.

"I know if you stayed here, he'd be happy—very happy."

"Okay. I'll stay—for now. And we'll go from there."

"Good," Thomas happily helps both Sarah and Jackson take their coats back off and he hangs them up. "We can fetch the rest of your things in the morning."

Sarah thankfully nods and smiles.

"Jackson, go ahead and sit back at the table, honey." Sarah sends Jackson off.

Thomas takes a step toward the dining room when—

"Thomas," Sarah calls out.

Thomas stops in his tracks and looks back at Sarah. "Yeah?"

"Did Jackson really speak to you?" she asks with curiosity.

"Yeah. He did. Why?"

"He doesn't talk to people. He will talk to me in private, but that's it. He doesn't talk to anyone."

"He spoke clear as day to me," Thomas casually confirms once again.

"That's interesting." Sarah thinks to herself and fights her desire to smile at Thomas by biting her upper lip. Her eyes twinkle as she looks upon him. Just as he had gazed upon her with a glazed look of countless possibilities when they first met, she now, too, has that same gleam in her eyes.

"Why don't you go check on your father. I'll take care of Jackson," he offers.

"Okay. Thanks." Sarah watches Thomas head into the dining room. She digests her feelings for just a moment longer, the smile emerging on her face. She breaks her trance and heads outside to speak with her father.

Standing on the back deck looking out at the ocean, Henry thinks to himself. The solitude is a safe place for him. The wind blows through his thinning hair as he stares off at the Atlantic.

"Dad," Sarah softly begins. Her tone is conciliatory, attempting to bridge a divide between them.

"I really miss her," Henry begins in a solemn tone, his eyes flashing to the ground and then back out to sea.

Sarah's eyes immediately well up and a tear rolls down the side of her cheek. She wipes the tear away. "I know, Dad. I know you do."

"She used to make the most amazing baked rolls. I'm certain in any oven they would bake the same. I'm certain, in any kitchen they'd be buttered with the same butter. But when your mother made those baked rolls, I just couldn't resist. And fresh—oh, goodness; her fresh rolls were something to behold. And her pies—the sweet scent of apple pie sweeping up to the top of the lighthouse. I would smell the cinnamon baking in the middle of the night and know she was awake—that she was thinking of me. I miss her awful," Henry turns to Sarah with his eyes welling, showcasing a few rare tears.

Sarah places her hand on Henry's back. "I've never heard you speak like this, Dad. I've never heard you talk this way about Mom."

"When you were young I did."

"Before the war," Sarah nods, understanding.

"I just wish I could have given your mother better years. I wish I could have given her more of myself after I came back. I *should* have given her more."

"It's not your fault she died." Sarah's eyes flash towards the dark waters of the Atlantic.

"No. It's yours," Henry turns to Sarah.

Sarah's face drops in shock. Fresh off of breaching one wall, another is hoisted up between them.

"What?" she asks.

"You left. You left us both. It was hard for us. It was hard on your mother. You broke your mother's heart when you walked out on us."

"I left to pursue my own life. I left to go chase my dreams," Sarah starts to get upset, the conversation taking a darker turn.

"You left us," Henry continues on his own train of thought, not listening to a word Sarah is saying. "You went off and gained someone else's child and lost your mother."

"Jackson has nothing to do with this. I am only taking care of him until his father comes back from Europe."

"His father is long gone, Sarah. He went and fought in the Great War and he is gone. He is lost like thousands of other men. He will never be seen again."

"He's not dead. And he's not like you. He will come back. Physically you may be here, Dad, but mentally, you got a long way to go." Sarah unloads a little of her own ammunition on her father.

Henry continues to stare out at the ocean, a deep look of hopelessness overcoming his face. It is a blank stare with lost eyes and a long face gazing out at nothing in particular.

"Just when I think you've come back, you run so far away," Sarah bitterly shakes her head.

"There's always tomorrow," his eyes flash to the side, his head tilting slightly down, acknowledging his shortcomings. His head then lifts back up and he refocuses on the dark abyss.

"It *is* tomorrow, Dad. It's been tomorrow for a long time." Sarah turns and walks away, heading back toward the house.

Henry remains focused on the deep dark ocean. Sarah's marching steps are filled with anger and the desire to run away. It is a common pace she takes walking away from her father. But as opposed to marching right into the house and continuing on out the front door, she stops. She pauses by the back door and slowly turns around.

"No. Not this time. This time I'm staying." Sarah's declaration seems to float out to nowhere for a moment, her words marinating in the cool ocean breeze with no destination in sight. Then Henry slightly turns his head.

"You are always welcome here, darling." Those are Henry's only words and he looks back at the ocean.

Sarah nods, accepting the olive branch. She pushes down her anger toward her father, swallowing years of frustration and hateful words. She accepts the invitation with a quiet subtle nod and no more. She turns and heads inside.

Sarah arrives back at the dining room table. Jackson is happily eating, giggling beside Thomas who shifted next to the boy to comfort him. Thomas is laughing as Zander smiles at the two as he finishes up his bowl. Sarah shows a brave face, hiding her frustration toward her father with a masking smile. Thomas picks up Sarah's sadness and frustration; her mask all-too-thin for him.

"Jackson and I were just making funny pictures in the beef stew. I made a boat and he made what we believe is an elephant—but the jury is still out," Thomas playfully states.

Jackson has a big smile as he goes back to eating and that brings a big wave of comfort to Sarah's face. She looks at the two bonding and can't help but feel good about it. Sarah bends down on the other side of Jackson as he sips his stew.

"I think we're going to stay here for the summer, Jackson. Would you like that?"

Jackson smiles and nods.

"What happened to his grandparents?" Thomas asks.

Sarah bends around Jackson and whispers. "Well, they are having some health issues right now. A young boy around wouldn't be a good fit, ya know?"

"Definitely. I think it's great you'll be staying here." Thomas replies in a calmed tone, but inside he is very excited.

Zander shoots a smile over at Thomas, knowing exactly why he will be excited Sarah is staying for the summer. The crush he has on her isn't hidden very well from his good friend. Sarah nods but doesn't say anything. She really doesn't know if it will be a good choice to stay at her father's home. But she sits down and eats. She eats while her father remains outside by the ocean; alone—as always.

"Well, I gotta head back home and get ready to go to work," Zander states as he rises from the table.

"How is The Sunset doing?" Thomas asks.

"Oh, she's getting herself busy. Folks are slowly filing in. It's a little slow, but we are seeing some of them fishermen coming through and staying. The catch is good which means the fishermen will come," Zander tries to speak in an optimistic tone, but his words are laced with apprehension and uncertainty.

Thomas nods and shows a supportive smile for his friend. "That's great, Zander. It's a start!"

"It sure is somethin'. Thank you all for this." Zander starts to grab his bowl and plate when Sarah comes charging over.

"Don't you dare. You are a guest here. I'll take those," Sarah takes the glassware from Zander.

"Mighty kind of ya, ma'am."

"Sarah. Only Sarah. No ma'am here," she smiles.

"Thank you...*Sarah*," Zander respectfully nods.

"I'll see you soon, buddy," Thomas shouts.

"Not if I see you first," Zander sarcastically states. He heads out the front door.

"He works right at The Sunset Hotel?" Sarah asks.

"Yeah. Right across the way."

"Where does he sleep? Where's his home?" she probes further.

"He sleeps in the Oceanic," Thomas states, knowing where Sarah is heading.

"The abandoned hotel? He sleeps there?" she says in disgust.

"Henry—your father, said he can't stay here. I offered to pay room and board with my salary for Zander to stay here."

"We'll see about that!" Sarah drops Zander's dishes off in the kitchen and marches back outside.

"Oh, boy," Thomas shakes his head and looks at Jackson.

"She is *not* happy," Jackson states with a smirk on his face.

"No, definitely not," Thomas agrees.

Sarah marches back outside with determined pounding feet.

"You've come for more?" Henry, sounding like a tired old man, asks, recognizing the firm strides as a distinct warning to a swelling argument.

"Well, since you brought it up, yes, I have."

"What now?"

"Zander should stay here. Thomas offered to pay his way," Sarah presents her case like an attorney dictating facts to the court.

Henry slowly turns and faces his daughter. "Now listen here, I am the keeper. This is my job and my house. You are my family and can stay here. Thomas works as my assistant and he can stay here. But homeless men aren't allowed to shack up here. This isn't a hotel. This is a house of business," Henry lays out the rules clearly, pushing back hard at Sarah.

"Is it because he's black?"

Henry shakes his head and turns away from Sarah.

"It is, isn't it? You always blamed Freddy for me leaving town! Freddy was just a friend. We traveled together. That was all!" Sarah attacks back.

"No!" Henry turns and shouts back at Sarah. "Just, you know the rules. I don't make them. Zander can't stay here. That's it." Henry turns and marches away in a huff, hurling a hand up into the air in frustration.

Sarah lets out an angry grunt and marches back inside the house. Thomas pretends to not have heard their argument, but anyone within twenty yards heard them clear as day. Jackson is staring up at Sarah, wondering why she is so angry. Thomas palms his head and points Jackson's face down at his food, not wanting to make the situation any more uncomfortable than it already is.

"It's how we communicate," Sarah explains to Thomas, trying to justify her complicated relationship with her father.

"I don't know what you're talking about. It's none of my business."

"It's going to be. Because you're gonna be hearing a lot about it each and every day." Sarah states. "I'm going to head upstairs for a nap," Sarah runs her hand through her hair. "Jackson, you want to come lie down with me or stay with Thomas?"

Jackson points to Thomas.

"Okay. Is that all right? Do you have time?" Sarah asks Thomas.

"Yeah. We'll be fine. I have nearly two hours before we have to head over to the tower."

"Thanks." Sarah's one word is filled with a great deal of gratitude.

"No problem," he willingly accommodates.

She nods and heads upstairs to have some time to herself.

"All right, Jackson. Let's make some dinosaurs out of this stew!" Thomas tries to get the young boy excited. They both smile and giggle and play with their bowls of food.

Twelve

DRESSED in their yellow protective work jackets, both Thomas and Henry each carry a bucket of oil up the long spiral staircase heading north inside Old Barney. As they make their way up the steps, Thomas's eyes flash down to the ground and up again. His mouth quivers with the desire to speak but no noise comes out. He wants to talk to Henry but is unsure of how to broach a serious conversation. He opens his mouth as if he is going to speak and then stops again. He is staring at the back of Henry's head. He silently starts and stops three times before finding a word that successfully leaks out of his mouth.

"Whaaat?" he awkwardly says and stops after the one word.

Henry stops walking and peeks over his shoulder, looking back at Thomas.

"What was that?" he asks with a stern grumpy tone. Henry is not in the mood for any nonsense.

"I…nothing. I was going to sneeze and then stopped." Thomas shakes his head at his own lame excuse. Henry shrugs and continues up the stairs, passing the question off as a strange noise. Thomas follows behind, subtly shaking his head in disappointment.

An hour passes and the men are side by side, wiping down the outer windows, making sure they are perfectly clear. As Thomas carefully cleans with his cloth, he continuously glances over at Henry. Again his mouth quivers with the intention of initiating a conversation. At first, Henry doesn't notice. But the glances continue and Henry finally gets annoyed, sensing Thomas wants to say something.

"What already?!" Henry blurts out.

"What's that?" Thomas plays dumb.

"You have glanced over at me at least ten times. Either I look very pretty or you have something to say to me. Which is it?" Henry continues to clean, not wanting to fall behind with gossip.

Thomas stops and turns to Henry, wanting to say something.

"Is your hand broke?" Henry asks, preempting anything Thomas is about to say.

"What?" Thomas replies, confused.

"In school, could you walk and chew gun at the same time?" Henry poses another strange question.

"I certainly hope so."

"Then you can wipe that glass and talk at the same time. We don't stop for unnecessary chit-chat in *this* tower. We work." Henry leaves no room for negotiation and demands perfect time management.

Thomas nods and starts to wipe the glass.

"Go on. Come out with it," Henry prompts Thomas again.

"It's about Sarah."

Henry stops wiping the glass, shaking his head. He lets out an annoyed grunt and continues to wipe. "Okay," he states, gritting his teeth.

"Maybe I shouldn't…" Thomas backpedals away from the subject.

"You already have," Henry turns and stares directly at his assistant. "So out with it," he demands.

Thomas nods, all too familiar with this tone from his grumpy boss. "Why don't you talk to your daughter?" he fires the question like a musket shot right between the eyes of Henry.

"You getting personal with me, Thomas? Is that it, son? You want to know about my feelings and my emotions? You want to bond over my pain and my past? You feel the need to learn more about me? Is this what you want? Is that the man you think I am? Do you think I share my inner-most struggles with others?" He rapidly fires question after question back in response.

"Am I supposed to answer all of those?" Thomas asks, overwhelmed by Henry's response.

"Am I supposed to answer your one question?" Henry hurls back.

"Okay." Thomas nods and goes back to wiping the window.

Henry shakes off the annoyance like a fly that was buzzing around his head. But the silence and their cleaning start to get to him. The buzzing in his head grows louder and he feels the need to respond to Thomas further.

"It's complicated!" Henry bellows out.

Thomas, who thought the conversation had ended, curiously glances over as he cleans. "I can imagine."

"She is stubborn. She is just like me in that way. Sometimes, though, she can be a little difficult to deal with. She loses her *place*." Henry pauses for a moment, reminiscing fondly. "She is strong and smart like her mother. I love that about her."

"Every journey begins with a single step. Right?" Thomas gently offers up Henry's own words as food for thought.

"Are you always going to be this much of a pain in my ass?" Henry asks of Thomas, his words dipped in a thick batter of sarcasm and playfulness.

"Heck, yeah, sir," Thomas proudly replies.

"I was afraid of that," Henry mutters.

The two men go back to wiping the windows. Thomas smiles to himself, a personal victory penetrating Henry's high walls of solitude.

A BAD summer storm is firmly digging in. Rain, wind, thunder and lightning are all on tap for a long night of bad weather. It is an ominous dusk skyline, the dark skies make it seem as though nightfall has come early, a sinister pall bestowing upon the world.

Thomas is looking through the telescope, staring out at the chaotic waves and the deep grey filling the landscape. Across the reef the surf thunders, channeling the fury of the oncoming storm. The helpless shoreline absorbs strike after strike, the waves curling fiercely against the sand particles; chewing away with each bite.

"I think I see it! Two o'clock—out ahead!" he shouts.

Henry hits the horn and attempts to manually adjust the light in Thomas's sightline. Thomas's obscured view is made difficult through the poor weather conditions. He tries to focus through the storm and see the small bobbing dot in the water. He saw it once before, a shadow. The sail and flag were visible just for a moment in the rolling waves. He continues to scan across the water. And then he sees it clear as day. The ship emerges, rising up to the water's crest for a moment before disappearing below, once again hiding amongst the rolling waves.

"I saw her again! Sail was definitely torn!" Thomas shouts.

"Stay on her," Henry orders. "Your eye stays on that glass. If we lose her, she may be lost forever."

"I got it!" Thomas excitedly shouts.

The ship helplessly rides up on an ocean's swell. Then it dips down below again. The ship is at the mercy of the rolling waves. With a torn sail and unknown damage, the ship could be a dead duck.

"What's the range?" Henry asks.

"Three hundred yards—maybe," Thomas guesses.

"Is it or isn't it?!" Henry barks.

"It is! Three hundred—and shortening. It's heading towards us, northwest."

"Can we catch it as it goes? Can we fire the cannon and try to save her?" Henry asks. He then sounds the horn again, alerting the ship, trying to give them an extra taste of hope.

"I don't know yet," Thomas ominously states.

"Stay on it. I'm going to head down and set up the cannon. When she is close enough, you come down and we'll take our shot!"

"Okay-okay. I got you!" Thomas confirms Henry's order.

Henry rushes down the stairs. As he gets near the bottom of the stairs he rolls his right ankle, falling to the ground. It is a painful twist, relegating him in extreme discomfort, writhing around on the ground.

"Dammit!" he grimaces in pain. He tries to stand but can barely muster getting to his feet. He growls, forcing himself up, fighting the pain.

As Thomas stares through the telescope, he hears the floating voice of Henry moving through the wind. It sounds like a distant wail of pain. It sounds like something may be wrong. But Thomas isn't certain of it and must remain at his post as instructed. He cannot remove his eye from the telescope and risk losing sight of the vessel. He hears another distant faded grunt floating through the air.

Henry steps outside, his face struck by wind and rain. Agony is plastered across his sunken pained face. Like the tough hearty man he is, he ignores the injury and limps, dragging his swelling ankle behind him. He moves to the Lyle gun. It is tucked away on the side of the lighthouse. He sizes up the wooden cart, its two wheels sunken in the sand. He dips below the wooden handles, painstakingly lifts up and pushes the two-wheeled cart along.

"Ah!!!" he screams in agony, the pain of his ankle nearing the worse extremes possible. The veins on his neck are pushing through his skin, extending it out to their limits. His face is beet red, the mental and physical battle of extreme fighting inside his body. He pushes the cart forward a step; and then another. He is channeling everything inside him as the storm rages around him. He knows what he must do and there are no other alternatives. Another slow, difficult push forward. "Ah!!!" Henry once again grits his teeth, the pain escaping his body through chaotic sounds out of his mouth. Another step. Then another. It is slow going as his own injured ankle prevents him from pushing the two wheels across the wet sand.

The thunder crackles above and bursts of lightning further highlight Henry's struggles with pain stricken across his face. His ankle swells worse and worse, the throbbing causing him to pause. Painful tears are squeezed out of the corners of his stubborn eyes, but they are immediately rinsed away by the teaming raindrops. The wind seems almost insurmountable and it blows into Henry's face. The ground is like thick quicksand, each driving step is like pushing a car stuck in the mud. He moves through the molasses with his one healthy leg; determined and focused. He takes another step, his ankle cracking. Was it a break? He doesn't know. The pain is undeniable. He pushes on. He pushes on with pride carrying him through his pain.

"Dad!" Sarah shouts.

She comes rushing over with a rain coat on. He looks up, peering over the small cannon, his face pushed to incredible extremes. Sarah's mouth is drawn open, awed, as she looks at her father's pulsating veins, signs of his pain stricken across his face. He is shaking from the physical alarms sounding off throughout his entire body.

"I got this," she says, stepping forward to help.

"It's too heavy for you!" he shouts through the storm.

"Your foot—what did you do?!" Sarah can see Henry clearly favoring his injured ankle.

"It's fine!" He barks at her.

"Then we'll do it together!" she yells back, equally defiant as her father. She isn't going anywhere. Sarah steps forward and ducks under one of the wood arms. She places it atop her shoulder and Henry moves to the other side. Now focused on just one wooden arm a piece, they dig in and push forward, one step at a time. It isn't easy, but they are able to sledge ahead at a quicker pace than before. With Sarah helping, Henry is able to redistribute his weight, moving it to his left foot.

Thomas comes rushing out of the lighthouse. He sees the two bodies moving the Lyle gun. He knows one is Henry, but can't see the hidden face and body of the other person. He runs over to the wood cart and sees it's Sarah.

"Sarah?" he says, surprised.

"Get the other side!" she shouts, ordering Thomas to step in for Henry.

"We aren't there yet!" Henry, as stubborn as ever, refuses to budge.

"He hurt his right leg—bad." Sarah stares intensely at Thomas.

Thomas moves over to Henry. "I'm not budging!" Henry continues to be defiant despite being in extreme pain.

"If you don't move, the men on that ship will die. What's more important, your stubbornness or their lives?" Thomas states his case as rain and wind pound his face. And Henry can hardly argue. He sees Thomas's logic and subtly nods, limping back out of the way.

"Get the powder. They are at a hundred and fifty feet," Thomas instructs.

Henry carefully dips away from the Lyle gun cart, his ankle injury causing a severe limp. Despite the pain, he moves rather quickly across the wet sand, dragging his leg over to the lighthouse to retrieve the gun powder.

Thomas steps in and he and Sarah move the Lyle gun into place.

"What does this do?" Sarah asks.

"It fires a line! Gives them a fighting chance!" Thomas shouts over the storm, his tone ominous.

Sarah nods. They move forward and get the small cannon into position.

"Come my way just a step more!" Thomas instructs Sarah. They set the two-wheeled wagon down. He pulls out the spyglass and looks out at the water once again. He tries to focus through his telescope to find the ship. He can't see it at first. Thomas grows anxious. Then it appears, bobbing up and down in the water, its sails torn to shreds. The ship is bending and looks as if the ocean is going to snap its hull in half like a twig.

Henry comes limping over.

"It's time!" Thomas urgently says.

Henry has the gunpowder and pours it carefully in, readying the Lyle gun as quickly as he can.

As he does, there is an explosion out at sea. Thomas, Sarah and Henry momentarily duck down, unsure of what just happened. They look up and see the boat is now on fire. The fishing vessel is now easily visible from shore, fire burning brightly despite the dark driving storm.

"Hurry!" Thomas shouts.

Henry looks down the front of the cannon and pulls out a match. He makes sure the aim is right. "Sarah, back away!" he shouts.

"I'm fine," Sarah states as she stands beside the gun, her stubborn streak shining once again.

"I'm not askin'. That's an order," Henry grits his teeth.

Sarah takes two steps back, staring out toward the burning ship.

"One shot," Thomas says to Henry.

"One shot," Henry confirms.

Thomas looks through the spyglass once again. He has the burning ship in sight. "Now!"

Henry lights the cannon and steps aside. The Lyle gun fires, the kick causing the small cannon to fly back eight feet, nearly clipping the slow moving Henry in the process. Henry dives to the ground to avoid the kick.

"Dad!" Sarah yells and rushes over to her father. She reaches down and helps him off the ground, all the while, Henry's hopeful eyes staring out at the burning vessel.

Thomas stares through the telescope, hoping his spyglass will reveal the start of a heroic event.

"Come on. Come on!" Thomas beckons.

"The gloves! Get the gloves!" Henry shouts.

"Where are they, Dad?" Sarah asks.

"In the vestibule house, on the shelf," he replies with a strained voice.

Sarah nods and rushes back over to the lighthouse. Henry struggles to his feet, staring out, breathless. Thomas looks on, watching as the line disappears beyond the ship. Sarah comes rushing back out with two sets of gloves.

"You and me," Thomas says to Sarah.

She turns to Henry for approval. He reluctantly nods in agreement.

Thomas and Sarah start to pull the line in. Together they pull with all their might.

"Come on! Firm up!" Thomas begs.

Henry comes over by Thomas, his face grim. He watches the rope getting pulled back with too much ease. He knows it hasn't caught on the ship. He knows they didn't see the line. His face tells a sad tale.

"No! Come on!" Thomas pulls faster. They pull and pull. They are straining as they drag the heavy hook and line back in. It takes nearly twenty straining minutes, but they get the entire line back.

"Again!" Thomas, exhausted, states. Standing beside him, equally exhausted and out of breath, is Sarah. She looks over at Henry, already knowing the bad news.

Henry is looking through the telescope, staring hopelessly out to sea.

"The ship is sunk," he states with dramatic certainty.

Thomas looks out at the water and sees the glimmer of a few flames. "The fire still burns! There is wood. If there's wood there could be men clinging to it!" Thomas shouts.

Henry looks through the spyglass once again. "I don't see anyone, Thomas. They're gone, son."

Thomas is running toward the jon boat.

"Stop him, Sarah! It's suicide!" Henry yells at Sarah.

Thomas gets behind the boat and is about to push it into the water when Sarah comes up.

"No!" she yells.

"There could be men out there! I can save them!" Thomas screams to Sarah.

Henry comes limping down the sand, charging the best he can to get to Thomas.

Thomas pauses, seeing Sarah's concerned face. She doesn't want him out at sea. Not on this night. Henry steps up, grimacing in pain.

"You need to go inside!" Thomas shouts at Henry.

Henry steps forward and grabs Thomas' shoulders. "They're gone!"

"How do you know?!" Thomas shouts.

"That sea is unforgiving! Those waves are dead man's waves! You head out in this boat and you won't come back! You need to stay alive in order to save others, son! I'm not losing you! I'm not losing you!" Henry emphatically shakes Thomas's shoulders and yells at him with an impassioned tone.

Sarah's mouth hangs open, shocked by Henry's show of emotion. She fixates her eyes on her father, looking closely at the concern written across his rain-soaked face. Thomas is frozen, caught between his heart wanting to risk everything and the people he cares about begging him not to. He looks out at the water, the waves are striking hard, the storm raging, the wind blowing heavy cold water drops across their faces.

"It's over," Henry says with a mouthful of sadness and regret. "It's over," he solemnly repeats.

Thomas looks out at the storm and gives in. He nods and looks down to the ground.

THE remaining wreckage at sea flames out. The pieces of the vessel never make it to shore. They are swallowed into the ocean and are pushed further north by the unforgiving current. No bodies are recovered. Henry climbs the 217 steps on his terribly injured ankle. He will listen to no one. Thomas can't fathom Henry's pain and tries to aid him up the stairs. But he sends Thomas ahead to the top. Someone must be up there at all times. Henry climbs one step at a time. He climbs the 217 steps slowly. He climbs to the top and logs in the wreck. He finishes his shift and then, as the dawn arrives, heads back to the keeper's house for treatment on his ankle. The men on the unknown fishing vessel are presumed dead at sea; more casualties of the unforgiving cold waters of the stormy Atlantic.

Thirteen

THE jungle is hot and sticky. The line of troops slowly move through, a permanent layer of sweat glazed upon their skin with the thickness of a heavy maple syrup. The night provides some opportunity for slow movement. The US soldiers quietly move through the foreign terrain. They are looking everywhere, their faces covered with fear.

"Hold it," the loud whispered call of Sergeant Henry Jones halts the troop movement. He senses something wrong. The men all freeze, looking around, wondering what he sees.

"Sir?" the private beside Henry asks.

"Sh!" Henry replies, listening closely to the jungle. He listens with his eyes bulging out of his head. He listens as if the plants are speaking to him; communicating on some level no one else knows. He waits for a response—for the jungle to give him his answer.

Within a few seconds, he gets it. Guerilla fighters from the Philippines come pouring out of the jungle, ambushing the line of US troops. They yell as they charge forward in no real pattern. They come with knives and start firing off rifles.

"Attack! Attack at will!" Henry shouts to his troops.

A warrior comes flying at Henry, jumping on him like a wild animal. Other men around him are also engaged. The private, who just moments prior had tried to speak to Henry, is getting stabbed repeatedly in the chest by a relentless warrior. The warrior stabs and stabs, his knife making tens of wounds in the now dead soldier; his eyes vacantly open, staring nowhere.

Henry has his own problems. He fights with all his might to keep a knife blade from penetrating his skull. The Philippine warrior, his face painted black and his slightly slanted widened eyes, fights to kill the American sergeant with all his will. He looks down upon Henry as if he is defending his family's life. Henry's two hands and arms are all that prevent the knife from plunging into his skin. Explosions sound, grenades going off all along the fighting lines. Men are screaming; men are dying.

Henry does all he can to prevent the blade from penetrating his skin and then evasively shifts to his right and pulls down, the knife just missing his ear. The blade plunges into the soft jungle terrain. Henry whips the back of his left arm and slams his triceps and elbow into the warrior's face. Henry breaks his nose immediately, the wounded Philippine soldier flying back onto the ground, holding his bloodied face. It is in that split second, that one moment of opportunity, that Henry reaches for the knife blade in the ground and grabs it, lunging forward into the wounded warrior. The knife blade plunges into his chest, the man's eyes flaring open in shock and sadness, the angst of his failure plastered all over his face. He immediately succumbs to the realization he is defeated. Henry lands on top of him, their faces an inch apart. Henry pushes the knife as deep into the warrior as possible. Blood splatters up onto the side of Henry's face. The Philippine soldier fruitlessly tries to push Henry back, to wiggle free, but he is trapped and the life has already begun to leave his body. The blood seeps out all over the soldier's chest, no longer spraying into the air. Henry pushes harder, his head bowed in determination. There is no more resistance. Henry looks up, another soldier's blood splattered across his face and sees the Philippine man's life leave his eyes.

Satisfied he is dead, Henry lifts up and hears the sounds of war. Grunts, screams, gunfire and explosions combine for a cacophony or horrors as men desperately engage in hand-to-hand combat. Henry pulls out his rifle and fires. He fires again. One by one he starts to pick off the insurgents as their guerilla attack is now backfiring on them. The US military, with superior forces and weaponry, start to push them back.

There is shouting in another language. Soon, the rogue warriors who ambushed the US forces start to flee. As they flee, a few of them are picked off by more gunfire. The short battle is over nearly as quickly as it began. There are casualties on both sides but far more of the Philippine fighters lay dead on the ground.

Henry moves over to the private who has too many stab wounds to count. He rips his dog tags off his neck and sadly gazes upon him. He takes a moment to mourn the loss of a fellow soldier. He reaches forward and closes his vacant eyes.

In the backdrop men are screaming in pain and agony. "Help me!" "I'm dying!" random shouts are heard through the battle lines.

"What in God's name are we doing here, sir?" a staff-sergeant, his face covered with other men's blood, his weapons stained with death, asks.

Henry sadly rises up to his feet and stares dead into the eyes of his staff-sergeant. "Our jobs," he says in a stern tone. "Get the men ready to move. Sergeant major gave us orders."

"Yes, sir," the staff-sergeant replies. He turns and shouts, "Get the tags and help the wounded. We're moving out!"

Henry rises to his feet, looking over the piles of dead bodies from the fight. He knows one of them could very easily have been him.

AS DAWN breaks, the squad comes to a clearing. The sergeant-major is standing beside Henry. He is Henry's elder at nearly 45 years of age. He stares intensely across a clearing up ahead. It looks like a poor village. The people are moving about the village in a very casual manner, not prepared for war of any kind. They are gathering plants and carrying baskets. They are wearing funny wide straw hats, this foreign group of farmers.

"They came from here," the confident sergeant major states as he lights a cigar.

"How do you know?" Henry asks.

"I don't," he replies and blows smoke into the air. Henry awaits orders from his commanding officer.

"Are we moving around the village?" Henry asks, optimistically wanting to skirt the village. He has no interest in killing innocent farmers.

"We don't know who they are. There can be fighters here as well. We have a local and he says there are fighters here. I don't want to lose any more men. Do you, sergeant?"

"No, sir," Henry responds.

"Then we destroy the village. Every single one of them. We burn it to the ground."

Henry stands in shock at the command. He is frozen for a moment.

"Do you have a hearing problem, sergeant?" his commanding officer asks.

"No, sir. I wasn't sure if that was an order," Henry replies.

"Consider it an order," the sergeant major makes it clear.

143

HENRY, asleep in his bedroom, is tossing and turning. His dreams haunt his slumber. His thick curtains are drawn to keep his room dark. He mutters over and over again.

"No. No. I'm so sorry. No." He repeats again and again. His face looks anguished. He is in his own private hell, asleep and a victim to his nightmares. After a few more moments, he suddenly rises up, the top half of his body thrusting forward, his hands out before him ready to fight. Sweat is dripping off of his face and he is breathing heavily. The nightmare has ended; for now. His breaths are quickened and begin to slow as he reacquaints himself to his surroundings.

"Is it the war?" Sarah, sitting in a dark corner of the room, asks. She has been watching her father sleep, his nightmares haunting him. Her front row seat has given her an insight into a small piece of her father's pain.

"It's just a bad dream," he once again denies his daughter *real* answers.

"I think we both know it's quite a bit more than that," she plainly states.

"It's my burden to carry. Not yours." He shifts in bed, his ankle killing him.

"Does it hurt?" she asks.

"My ankle will heal."

"I wasn't asking about your ankle, Dad." Sarah continues to stare at her father, wondering if he will ever open up to her.

"I know you weren't," he looks down and to the side, not wanting to make eye contact.

"You can't move forward in the present if you're stuck in the past," she again spouts wisdom at her father.

"It's not that easy," he states.

"Why isn't it? Why do *you* alone have to carry the burden?"

"Because it's awful. It's a terrible thing—a terrible thing. I would never share or want you to see the things I've seen."

"I don't have to see them. I just want you to unload that burden off your shoulders. Maybe we could have helped? Mom could have helped? I can still help," she pleads.

"How are you going to help my burden? How are you going to remove the image of burning innocent children? I still can smell their flesh charring—it's something that I smell each and every day. I watched innocent people beg for their lives—beg for their children's lives. How are you going to help that? There are no answers for that. You don't have table conversation over that! You can't possibly understand that!" Henry unloads a bit of himself to his daughter.

Sarah slowly rises to her feet. She gets up, tears in her eyes. She moves to her father's bed side and has a seat.

"It's okay, Dad. It's okay," she states in a forgiving tone.

"It's fine," he turns away, attempting to swallow the emotional turmoil bustling inside him. Everything is stirring inside his core, buried dark secrets of war rising up out of him. Tears well in his eyes as Sarah runs her hand across his face.

"It's okay. It's behind us," she says forgivingly again. "Let it go. Just let it all go. We all forgive you. I forgive you," she states.

Henry bobs his head down, his entire face overcome with emotion. He painfully makes one last attempt to hold back his tears; but it's futile. His pained look of regret and anguish boils over and the hardened man bursts into tears, exploding with emotion. Sarah pulls her father's head to her shoulder and runs her fingers through his hair. He cries like a child, the emotion exploding out of him. He releases years of pent up nightmares, letting them go for the very first time. His self-torture has come to an end in one grand moment of forgiveness brought about by his daughter.

Henry cries and cries in Sarah's arms. He cries for twenty minutes straight.

THOMAS, dressed in his keeper's uniform, is standing outside, ready to head over to the lighthouse. The sun is descending in the sky, but still a while from sunset. He looks around, wondering where the normally prompt Henry is.

Sarah steps out onto the deck dressed as if she is ready for some work. She has overalls on, a sweatshirt underneath and one of her father's old outdoor work hats.

"What's this?" Thomas asks with a smirk.

"I'm your assistant today," she says with a playful smile. She walks by Thomas and heads over to the lighthouse, leading the way.

Thomas does a double-take, looking back for Henry with a perplexed look on his face. He then jogs over to catch up with Sarah.

"Where's Hank?" he asks, chasing after Sarah.

"I benched him," she states. "You got me today. The tower is yours."

Thomas is shocked as he walks next to Sarah, marching over to the lighthouse. This is the first time Thomas will run the lighthouse at dusk by himself, a position Henry helmed up to this day. Thomas stares up at the tall tower, clouds quickly sprinting by in the sky above. He is awed and intimidated as he stares up. *The tower is mine.* He lets out a deep breath, exhaling some of his nerves away.

Sarah notices the butterflies in Thomas's belly. "You do know how to do this job?" she asks with a playful grin of Thomas; feeding off a momentary bout of insecurity.

"I think I got this," he returns with a half-cocked smile, showing a braver front.

They approach the lighthouse. Thomas looks down at the pad lock on the door and freezes. Sarah extends her hand with the key inside. She extends her hand to Thomas. It is his duty to unlock the door. Thomas happily accepts, an excited look for an excited young man. He bites his lip and smiles at her. She is happy for him and returns the smile. He unlocks the door and they enter.

They stand in the vestibule house, filling three buckets of oil.

"Why only three?" Sarah asks.

"I've gotten used to carrying two. I figured you can carry one."

"You carry two—I carry two," she states with intense purpose.

Thomas smiles and shakes his head. "You really are your father, you know that?" he says with an unstoppable grin.

"Stubborn as an ox," she agrees.

Thomas grabs an extra bucket and begins filling the fourth.

"How did you get that man to stay in bed?" Thomas wants answers to a mystery he cannot fathom.

"My father is a stubborn man. I know. He's tough; *real* tough. But even the toughest know they will only hurt themselves and others if they test bounds far beyond their control. He can't crawl, let alone walk, on that foot right now. He could never live with sacrificing other men's lives over his own pride."

"He's a good man," Thomas chimes in. He sticks up for Henry despite how hard his boss can be. He sticks up for him to Sarah, trying to show that there is goodness beyond the thick exterior.

"Yeah. I know. That's why I stayed. I'm trying. I swore I'd never come back to this place. But I'm trying." She shows great concern in her ongoing emotional battle with her father and the difficulty they have building a relationship together.

"What happened? Why did you leave in the first place? It's beautiful here."

"My father came back from the war a changed man, Thomas. For the first year, he woke up violently screaming during the nights. He slept-walked one night and took a blade to my mother's neck. He nearly slit her throat until he woke up with us screaming at him. He was a tortured man. And somehow, someway, they found it in them to have a son, my brother, Henry Jr.. Through the chaos they had this blessing. The doctor had said my mother could no longer conceive. They were so excited. It brought my father out of that fog just for a little while. It was his lighthouse. It steered him away from the darkness. Then my brother, one morning, was dead in his crib. There were no reasons. He just didn't make it. The doctor thought maybe it was because of my mother's age. They fought constantly after that. They were never the same. She helped with the garden and tending to some details, but as he slept during the day she worked on the grounds. When he awoke at night, they ate supper in silence. Then he went to the lighthouse and she went to sleep. Every day this happened. Every day they grew further and further apart. They were the ships in the fog. Their love was lost forever. It died with my brother and my father slipped back into his personal hell. I'm not sure if he blamed my mother more or himself. He just was angry and didn't want to talk. The lighthouse was his salvation. It kept him alive all these years. It gave him a purpose. His thoughts torture him but the lighthouse has always given him hope; just as it gives lost souls at sea hope."

"Maybe he'll find his way past the fog."

"He already has. He's close to the shore now. You changed him. You have given him hope. I don't know how and I don't care. But he is a different man today than he was yesterday."

"We all are," Thomas floats three words that carry far more meaning than Sarah realizes.

"Thank you for bringing him back. He may not be the man he was before he left for the war, but you have given him *something*. I still don't know what it is. Maybe he sees Henry Jr. in you, if that's even possible. Maybe he sees himself in you. Either way, you have made him nearly whole again. You have made it possible for me to see my father. I can't thank you enough." Sarah's words penetrate deep into Thomas's core. He starts to talk, but no words come out. He wants to share the truths about himself; his own past. He wants to be open with Sarah as she has been with him. However, he feels compelled to hide in silence; to keep to the shadows. He, like his mentor, Henry, sits alone atop their personal towers not knowing when they can come down and rejoin the rest of the world.

"Were you going to say something?" she asks, recognizing his internal strife.

"No. I mean…yes. We have to get these buckets up there," Thomas deflects away from his own feelings. He forges ahead with his job first, his personal feelings inconsequential.

Sarah nods, but knows Thomas had much more to say to her. She accepts the order and they carry the buckets up the 217 steps to the top of Old Barney. With one more trip, they prepare to light the great Fresnel lens.

12 feet and over two tons, the giant lens sits upon steel support beans. The massive prism is waiting to get fed

its light. Thomas dips under the giant lens and stares in awe as he prepares to light her for the first time ever. He has seen Henry do it a hundred times but he has never done it himself; and definitely, never alone.

"You've done this before, haven't you?" Sarah asks, sensing his slight hesitation.

"No. It's gonna be great though," Thomas smiles like a young school boy, excited he is about to light the greatest flame of his life. He takes out a wood box with supplies inside. He reaches in and pulls out a large match stick. He looks over at Sarah with joyful wide eyes. "You ready?"

"I guess," she replies, uncertain of exactly what to expect.

"Let there be light." Thomas strikes the match. He reaches out of sight from Sarah. She tries to see what he is doing but cannot. Then, all of a sudden, the light erupts inside the giant two ton lens. It blasts out into the early evening skyline, darkness almost completely upon the world. But now, Old Barney shines brightly, cutting into the dark waters, firing a light across the top of the sea.

Thomas steps back out and looks up at Sarah with a big smile on his face. "That was really cool."

Sarah shakes her head, amused by his boyish charm and that smile of his. "Boys," she musingly mutters.

IT IS the early morning hours. Sarah is bundled in a warm coat, seated in a chair. Thomas is looking out through his spyglass at the calm waters. He is surveying the area, seeing what is out there. He glances back and sees Sarah's exhausted face.

"Go to bed. I have this," he states as a gentleman.
"Not a chance."
"You are *really* stubborn."
"I prefer tough," she says with a smirk.

They have a moment of silence and then a thought comes to Sarah.

"My father is worried about the lighthouse," she begins.

"What about it?" Thomas continues to survey the Atlantic through the telescope.

"He said the lighthouse was in danger."

Thomas pulls away from the spyglass and turns to Sarah.

"What do you mean?" his brows furrow with confusion, his head tilted to the side. He shows great concern for Sarah and her loaded declaration.

"The storms. They're getting close. The Oceanic is in danger."

"It's abandoned though," he says.

"So is the keeper's house. You had to have seen the water during a storm. You've seen it."

Thomas subtly nods and looks down. It is a truth he didn't want to face. "Yes. You're right. The water is coming dangerously close."

"It's more than that. My father believes a bad storm could swallow Old Barney whole. He's been fighting to get a jetty built for years. That much I know."

"How do you know he thinks the lighthouse is in danger? He told you?" Thomas asks with curiosity, hearing all this information for the very first time.

Sarah thinks and shrugs, a strange half-cocked smile on her face. In one brief moment she comes to terms with a confession. "I've been listening to him sleep."

Thomas looks at Sarah with an implicating smile, surprised she is infringing upon his personal space. He doesn't say a word—he doesn't have to.

"Okay-okay, I know it's not right. But I have learned a lot about my father. He tends to talk in his sleep," she smirks, raising her eyebrows in hope of the excuse being acceptable.

"I've heard," Thomas acknowledges.

"Then you've heard the nightmares?"

"I have," he replies, nodding, his smile fleeing as their conversation takes a more serious turn.

"They're bad. He has bad dreams. He has lived through some rough times." Sarah shows rare empathy for her father.

"And he talked about the tower?"

"Yeah. He is worried. Unless the government helps and builds a jetty, he thinks this side of the island is in big trouble."

"I guess you can get a lot from someone when they sleep," he smiles in response.

"More than *you* know," Sarah fires back with a big smile of her own.

Thomas tilts his head and gives her a squinty playful look, amusingly paranoid Sarah's been watching him sleep at nights. He shakes his head and looks through his spyglass once again.

There's a thud on the lighthouse tower. Thomas continues to stare through the telescope, scanning the waters. Sarah is curiously looking around, wondering if Thomas heard the noise. There's another thud; and another. Sarah rises to her feet, looking around with concern.

"What is that?"

"What's what?" Thomas casually replies.

"That thud? You don't hear it?" she asks.

Sarah stands by the lookout glass and stares outside. A bird flies right into the glass and she nearly tumbles backward. "Oh, my gosh!" she yells.

Thomas chuckles at her.

"Was that a bird?!" she shouts in shock.

"I sure hope so or bats are getting a heck of a lot bigger!" he jokes.

"Why did it do that?" she asks, shocked and horrified.

"They're attracted to the light. They sometimes crash into the side of the tower."

"That's normal?!" she wails in a high-pitched tone.

"It happens," he regrettably admits.

"Do they die?"

"If you fly into a solid tower at fifty miles an hour, you'd be in pretty bad shape."

"It's not funny. They're birds!" Sarah smiles, trying to remain serious despite Thomas's sarcasm.

"I know. But they do that. They don't know better. They're drawn to the light."

Sarah thinks for a moment, pondering Thomas's statement. She smiles, a thought crossing her mind.

"What?" he asks, recognizing she may have something to say.

"So were you. You were drawn to the light."

"Yes. Yes, I was."

Thomas nods in agreement and goes back to looking through the telescope. Sarah smiles, happily taking in Thomas's company at the top of the tower.

MORNING comes and they exit the lighthouse. The ground is riddled with dead birds; nearly a dozen. Sarah stares across the sad sight as the sun rises.

"You head inside," he tells her. "We have to do this from time to time."

"Can you bury them?" Sarah asks. "Please?"

"Yes. I'll bury them. I'll bury every last one."

She respectfully nods to Thomas, giving him a sweet smile. She turns and walks toward the keeper's house. He gazes at her longingly as she walks away. *What a night.*

A shade is opened in the keeper's house. Henry watches through binoculars from a distance. He sees Thomas staring at his daughter as she walks away. He looks down and sees Sarah's face. She is smiling, full of the same joy Thomas is exhibiting. The old keeper knows these looks. Henry looks seriously upon the scene, his own mind racing away with thoughts.

As Sarah gets closer, she looks up toward the house. She looks up by her father's bedroom window. The shades are now drawn. He is nowhere to be seen. She continues on to the house as Thomas cleans up the beach. He gets a shovel and buries every last one of the birds just as Sarah had asked.

Fourteen

IT IS a beautiful afternoon. Henry is standing next to Jackson as the young boy tries to cast his fishing line out to the water. The pole is long and adult sized, so Jackson is a bit overmatched. He is persistent though.

"Good," Henry compliments him. "Now reach back and flick that wrist as you come forward."

Jackson does as he is told and casts his line nicely out into the water. He has a big smile on his face, looking up at Henry for approval.

"There you go! Well done," Henry once again is supportive.

Henry and Jackson each hold their lines, standing side by side on a few rocks. Henry glances over a few times at the silent Jackson. The young man is quietly enjoying his fishing.

"You don't talk much, do you?" Henry asks, already knowing the answer to the question.

Jackson looks over at Henry and then back at the water, acknowledging the question only with his eyes.

"That's okay. I don't much like talking to people either."

Henry peeks at Jackson. The boy is curious as to why and glances over a couple of times at the old keeper, wondering what his thoughts are. Henry knows the young boy is curious and draws out the moment with silence.

"You want to know why?

Jackson's eyes again peer over at Henry. He has a curious look on his face.

"Okay. I'll tell you," he acknowledges the young boy's unspoken words, not pulling his teeth further. "I can be a bit difficult." Henry smiles and chuckles, amused by himself as he attempts to describe his personality to a boy he barely knows and who he has never uttered a single word to him.

"And…I tend to draw away from other people. I like to be alone. I guess some people think I'm mean. I probably am sometimes."

Henry looks over at Jackson to make sure he is still listening. And he is. His eyes are focused on Henry, his cheeks raised up into a partial smile, listening to his every word. So, Henry goes back to talking.

"It's okay to not want to be friends with everyone. Sometimes it's good to only have a few. I guess that's where I need to grow a little. Right?" Henry smirks, posing the question to Jackson.

They both go back to fishing for a few minutes. Then it happens.

"Sarah says it's cause you went to war." Jackson's words are shocking to Henry. He is dumbfounded by the noise coming from the boy's mouth. Henry gathers himself and nods, jumping into the conversation quickly but carefully.

"Yes. That's probably true. War can be hard on a man. It's ugly—the worst kind of ugly there is in the world—the worst kind of ugly there can be." Henry shares with Jackson on a very personal level. He doesn't want to fool with the boy. He has him talking.

Jackson has thoughts rolling around in his brain. His shyness is always an obstacle to speak. But Henry has him on the hook and patiently waits, wanting so badly to continue the conversation. However, he is careful not to pressure the boy. This conversation is on Jackson's dime and Henry will wait.

"My dad went to war," Jackson shares.

"Yes. Sarah told me."

"You think he got messed up?" The young boy looks up with innocent eyes. He wants to be comforted. He has so much hope behind his stare.

"I don't know, son," he states with honesty. "I know it's not easy on anyone. No matter how much fighting you do. It's never easy."

Jackson nods and again looks down. The answer isn't comforting and it wasn't what he was hoping to hear. But respecting Henry's honesty, he continues on with the rare conversation.

"You think he's gonna come back?" Again Jackson's eyes sag with hope but are plagued by the realities he faces.

"I don't know," Henry replies, knowing as little as Jackson knows about the situation.

Jackson accepts the response, but again is left unfulfilled. This time, Henry comes back to prop the young boy up a bit.

"Listen, it's not you. It's not anything you have done. Your father fought in a hard war. He served his country with honor. You should be proud of him. I know it stings that he hasn't been able to come home. To be honest, I don't know if he ever will, son. But there is one thing I do know. Your father fought proudly for his country and that's something you will never forget. You make sure you tell your children about him. You make sure you share with your grandchildren someday that he fought for his country. You tell others about his great memory. You carry that torch for him. He did you proud."

Jackson nods, a dash of pride and hope getting sprinkled upon him changes his facial expression. His long face lightens up and he goes back to fishing with the biggest of smiles on his face. He has a prideful gleam behind his eyes. Henry smirks, the exchange providing him with a wave of paternal invigoration. They continue to stand side by side, fishing, like a grandfather would with his grandson, quietly casting out into the ocean.

AS DUSK rolls around, Sarah has her work clothes on and is once again prepared to help Thomas out. Thomas sees her appear on the back porch. They smile at one another, a dopey glazed look of a budding romance.

"So…you're coming back out tonight," Thomas states the obvious.

"I figured you could use a hand." She smiles back at him.

"Definitely." The two stand before one another as if they are about to head out on their first date. Their moment together is disrupted by a stern tone and an annoyed voice.

"Seven full buckets," Henry barks, limping out onto the deck, using a wooden cane to aid his injured ankle.

"Always," Thomas respectfully perks up. "Yes, sir."

"And you're adjusting the portholes? You have to keep the light shining as far as it can go!" he barks.

"I know. Yes, sir."

Sarah squints a little, attempting to ascertain the meaning behind her father's intense tone. He is standing there wanting to be forceful but has little substance to his words. He is a bee without a stinger.

"Yes, well, no distractions up there! You better be focused at all times." Henry's point is now clear. This is about Sarah and Thomas.

"Dad, I think we—,"

"You are not the keeper!" he interrupts her with a forceful shout. Henry shows little patience and struggles to find the right words to convey his thoughts. "This job is important, Thomas. You need to focus on the job—you *must* focus on this job." His outburst is unchallenged as Sarah and Thomas wait.

Henry thinks to himself. "Have you filled the logs?"

"Yes. Every day."

"Every ship you see!" Henry's finger goes up in the air.

"We've been writing them down, Dad!" Sarah is getting a little annoyed with this spontaneous inquisition.

Henry slowly turns to her. He stares angrily into her eyes. "You dear, shouldn't even be up in that tower. You are not the keeper. You are not an assistant. Carry a bucket, sure. But you shouldn't be up there. Not all night. You shouldn't be distracting him with this grab ass!" Henry acts as a protective misguided father, throwing his right hand up in disgust.

"Sir, she is helping and I am focused. I promise you that." Thomas steps forward to reassure Henry.

Henry looks at Sarah and then back at Thomas. He is uncomfortable and doesn't know exactly what to say. "Ah!" Henry throws his hands up at the situation, annoyed. He starts to limp away and then turns back, angrily glaring at Thomas. He points with his right finger. "I thought you had something! I thought you could do this job! What a fool I was! What a fool I always am!" Henry limps quickly back into the house, storming away as quickly as his injured ankle will allow him.

Thomas shakes his head, trying to get a better read on why Henry all of a sudden is acting so strangely.

"Come on. Let's set up," Sarah says to Thomas. She is used to this kind of erratic behavior from her father.

Thomas and Sarah carry the oil up the cast iron stairs and light Old Barney. The light shoots out over the sea as darkness falls upon all of Barnegat and the Jersey Shore.

Thomas stares out at the ocean, the clear evening providing a beautiful display of stars painted all across the sky. Sarah comes up the steps with a brown bag and a thermos. She pours two cups of coffee and hands Thomas one of the two sandwiches she prepared. They drink and eat.

"I heard something strange," Thomas begins.

"About what?"

"Call it a rumor I guess. About your father."

"Oh, gosh. I've heard them all. Let me guess, he killed a man up here?"

"Yeah," he smiles and nods. "What is that?"

"There was a man. He broke into the lighthouse. He got almost to the lens, to Old Barney's heart. I don't know what he was doing or why he did it. But my father got to him before he could reach the lens. He didn't kill him. The guy was drunk as a skunk. He fell down the stairs on his way out; broke his arm, his leg, fractured his ribs. He was a mess and people told tall tales about my father. Never did another person even look at Barney the wrong way." Sarah and Thomas chuckle, having a good laugh over the story.

"Glad to hear he doesn't slaughter visitors," Thomas jokes.

"No. And it's funny. For someone who doesn't like people, he loves when they come and visit the tower. Look," Sarah grabs the visitor log. "While we slept yesterday he took eight people up the tower. I saw him take a couple up here when I woke up in the middle of the day to check on Jackson."

Thomas looks through the log. "Wow. I can't believe he walked up and down all the stairs on that ankle."

"He does it for the people. He loves this tower. He loves this city. It's his home—the only home he has ever wanted.

"I saw him with Jackson today," he says.

"Yeah?" Sarah asks, perking up.

"They were fishing."

"Yeah. My dad said he was going to try and show him a few things."

"He did. They talked. I heard a little of it. I had come downstairs and they talked about Jackson's father."

"I bet you're wondering what's going on with that?" She smiles.

"I have had a thought or two."

"I'm raising Jackson. He was my best friend's son. She died while her husband went to war. We have no idea what happened to him. There isn't a record of him dying in the trenches. There is no record of him returning home. He is just gone; one of the many that disappear in war. Maybe he's lost like my father. Maybe he is dead and buried. I don't know. I don't think we'll ever get that answer," Sarah sadly predicts.

"Probably not," Thomas realistically forecasts.

They eat a bit more and sip their coffee, sharing silence for a few moments.

"Have you adopted him? Legally that is?"

"Yes. I did. He doesn't know. He still holds out hope his father will return. But I have taken him as my own."

Thomas nods. "That's good. He needs family. He needs someone."

"You're the only one that knows. I haven't told a soul. It was his mother that insisted right before she died."

"What if he comes back?" Thomas asks an intriguing question.

"We know that his battalion went into battle. We know that not one of the men from his battalion came home. The government won't tell us anything else. They're all gone—every last one of them. So if Jackson's father survived, I'm guessing he had an angel on his shoulder. Even so, he would have returned by now. It's been three years since we heard from him last. Not a word since."

Thomas nods. There is a moment of silence as they both are resigned to their own silent thoughts.

Instinctively, Thomas picks up his telescope and looks out to sea. He is casual about it at first and then steps forward as if seeing something. He has a peculiar look on his face; his eyebrows pulled in, his mouth slightly hanging open.

"What is it?" Sarah asks.

"I think...I think I see something," he is trying to focus. Then the light slightly turns and shines upon something in the water. "Someone's down there!" Thomas shouts.

Sarah rises up to her feet, the situation firing adrenaline through both their veins.

"I need to get to the boat!" Thomas shouts.

They both go storming down the stairs, heading to the ground. Thomas hands Sarah the spyglass and rushes to the jon boat. She looks through the telescope and tries to locate what Thomas saw.

"I don't see anything!" Sarah states with concern. She looks over at Thomas with angst on her face, not wanting him to risk his safety for nothing.

"I saw something. I know I did. Keep looking."

Sarah reluctantly goes back to looking as the wind picks up. She scans the waters but can't see anything. She looks over and sees Thomas rushing out with the jon boat, paddling into the waves and out to sea.

"No, wait! Thomas!" she yells, not seeing anything out in the water. The wind and waves cause her voice to become white noise as he is well-out into the water, furiously paddling. He paddles and paddles as she watches nervously from shore. The wind is causing choppiness out in the dark waters. The light cast out into the open water provides some illumination, but Thomas is paddling out into darkness, the most dangerous of all of the keeper's duties. His jon boat is skimming successfully over the restless waters of the Atlantic. He paddles further and further. Water smacks against the boat and whips into his face. The sea is growing in anger, the water becoming more chaotic and making it difficult for Thomas to paddle. He looks behind him and grabs a life jacket in the boat, forgetting himself. He throws it quickly around his neck as the boat is slammed by a wave, knocking him back. He falls backwards, his head hitting the back of the boat. Thomas, bobbing along with the boat up and down in the chaotic waters, shakes off the fall. He feels the back of his head. Some blood appears on his hand. It is a jarring wound, but isn't serious enough to stop him. He gets back up, grabs the paddle and rows again. He searches around, hoping the light from Old Barney will shine upon the lost soul. He continues to search with fervor.

From shore, Sarah is looking desperate. Her mouth is dropped in concern as she stares through the rising waves attempting to find Thomas. He appears for a moment and then disappears again. The water is rising as the tide builds. The wind is kicking ocean spray violently up into the air and making it difficult to see. "Come on, Thomas," she begs for his safety. She continues to stare through the lens but finds nothing in her sightline. He has disappeared in the darkness. "Dammit!" she hollers to herself. She is becoming restless wondering where he has gone. "Oh, God, please," she begs. "Not Thomas. You can't take him. You can't take him!" she repeats, speaking out loudly.

Thick fog is rolling in, making matters worse. The skies are thickening above and like a light switch that has been flipped, the world is growing much darker. Sarah looks up and sees the ghostly view of thick billowing clouds swamping the entire island. Even the tower is falling victim to the sudden change in weather. The light out to sea is dulled due to the deepening fog.

A few minutes of silence and darkness pass. Sarah's worst fears are becoming realized. She nervously scans her eyes toward the keeper's house. She has thoughts of racing over there and awakening her father. This is a matter greater than she can deal with. Her nerves are starting to unravel, thinking the worst. She helplessly scans again through the spyglass. The telescope is giving her nothing but deep fog and the light from Old Barney reflecting worthlessly off the ghastly scene.

Sarah is shaking with nerves. She gives it one last scan and then gives up. She turns to charge to the house.

"Sarah!" the faint voice yells through the wind.

She stops and turns around. She sees Thomas, exhausted and wet, steering the jon boat to shore.

She sprints at him like a lost lover that just returned. She runs to the boat and helps pull it up safely on the sand. Thomas is exhausted and struggles out of the boat. He holds the back of his head. Before he can say a word, she rushes up to him and wraps her arms around him. She squeezes him tightly, pulling him in, thankful he is alive.

"I thought I lost you!" she says, hugging him with all her might.

Thomas is surprised by her sudden show of emotion. He thinks to himself, stunned for a moment. Then a comforting smile emerges on his face. He reaches around with one hand and hugs her. Their faces and lips are just an inch apart. Thomas's hand slides up to the side of Sarah's face. They are each looking down and then their heads tilt up, their eyes engaging with one another. They stare, breathless. It's an agonizing of uncertainty.

Sarah's eyes pan to the ground. She slowly backs away from him, realizing herself.

"I'm sorry," she subtly pulls back but remains close to him. She looks up, her hair blowing in the wind. He looks down at her, his hand moving the hair off her face. They stare at one another, their moment has come. Their eyes are interlocked, their souls becoming entangled upon one another. Their heartbeats skip and they both want so badly to move closer to the other. They stare as the wind blows until something catches Sarah's eye. She breaks their trance and grows concerned.

"What is that?" she asks.

"What?" he replies, confused.

"On your head," she steps to the side of Thomas and inspects. "You're bleeding!" she grows concerned.

"I'm all right."

"You could have been hurt," she admonishes him. "There was nothing out there. You can't just go risking everything for nothing!" she scolds.

Thomas looks toward the boat. "It wasn't nothing," he solemnly states.

She curiously follows his eyes over to the jon boat. There, resting lifeless, is a decaying dead body. She backs away, horrified. "Oh, my God!" she covers her mouth.

"Can you get me the gloves, Sarah? I need to bury him."

Sarah's eyes flash to the side of Thomas's head and his wound.

"After," he concedes. He knows he needs some treatment.

"Okay." She nods. The moment now takes on a new life as Thomas fulfills his duty and buries the dead man from the sea.

Fifteen

THOMAS, Henry, Jackson and Sarah all share a meal at dusk together. It is breakfast for Thomas and Sarah. It is supper for Jackson and Henry.

"I'll be back tomorrow," Henry blurts out, breaking the silence at the table.

Thomas nods. "Sounds good," he states. He tries to hide his disappointment, enjoying his moments together with Sarah.

Henry's eyes wander over to Sarah, seeking her reaction. She remains locked down on her food, not wanting to show her own disappointment over the news. She too has truly enjoyed her time with Thomas.

"You got it alone tonight," Henry states in an order-like manner.

Thomas and Sarah both look up from their food with curious looks on their faces.

"Okay," Thomas agreeably states without hesitation. He accepts Henry's order. He glances over at Sarah who has an angered look upon her face.

"Why should he have to?" she asks. "I slept during the day. I can help him."

"Because…'cause I said so." Henry isn't certain of his reasoning just yet.

"Really? Cause you said so?" she hurls his words back at him, displeased.

"I'm not a fill-in father. You should be with Jackson. You're his…his…his keeper," he stumbles through his sentence. "I'm no babysitter. And Thomas has to learn the job. It is a lonely job. It isn't a job where you socialize and have friends with you. It's a job where you stand alone atop a tower and you make sure the world sails forward as safely as possible. That is the job of the keeper. He will do that job tonight; and he will do it alone." Henry makes his proclamation known.

"He has been doing that job!" Sarah sticks up for him with annoyance.

"I got it, Sarah," Thomas holds up his hand. He wants to speak for himself.

Sarah, annoyed by it all, tosses her napkin down on the table. "If you will all excuse me," she turns, marching out of the dining room.

Jackson quietly continues eating, an unwitting audience member to this show.

Henry stabs bitterly at his food, something is bothering him inside. He wants to unleash his anger but there isn't a determined direction just yet.

Thomas eats, seeking to change the subject and see if he can bring Henry out of his funk.

"The tide is getting high," he begins.

"It does that. It's the ocean. Tide comes in and the tide goes back." Henry is unwilling to meet Thomas half-way just yet.

"Yes, but it's getting *really* high. I'm concerned. I think you are too."

"You fancy yourself a mind reader now?" Henry is argumentative and in no mood for an intelligent conversation. Thomas continues on anyway as they both pick at their food.

"No. I'm not. But I know tides and that tide is getting dangerous. If there's a bad storm…"

"That's true of any beach!" Henry cuts Thomas off. "You think you know these tides better than me? You think you know this tower better than me? Are you trying to take my job—my daughter?! Is this what you have come here for? Are you taking all that is mine?!" Henry slams his hands down on the table.

Jackson flinches and remains seated, scared. He doesn't say a word. There is silence in the room as Henry recalibrates his emotions and calms himself down. He starts to cough. The one cough grows into a long series of deep phlegmy gyrations.

"I, um, I need to get ready. If you will all excuse me." Thomas takes his plate of food, moves away from the table and walks into the kitchen. He rinses his dish and passes back through the dining room amidst a thick layer of uncomfortable silence and tension.

Henry closes his eyes, frustrated about many things. He takes a moment of self-reflection. He peers up and sees Jackson sitting quietly. Jackson is staring at Henry with his head tilted to the side and has a judgmental look on his face.

"I know-I know. You don't have to tell me," Henry says to Jackson, as if reading his mind. The young boy has successfully put the old dog in his place without a word spoken. "I know," Henry mutters again to himself, his tone reflective of a man who knows he has greatly overstepped his bounds.

ATOP the lighthouse, Thomas gazes out at the sea, silently thinking to himself. Down below, he hears the slow staggered steps of someone making their way up Old Barney. The pacing is slow and inconsistent. He knows

Henry is on his way up. Thomas takes a deep breath and looks around, making sure the top of the tower is neat and tidy.

Henry reaches the top and sees Thomas wiping off a ledge by the window, his final touch-up.

"It's fine. You've kept a good tower in my stead, Thomas. You've been doing a fine job, son," Henry commends.

"Thank you, sir," Thomas states.

Henry moves over to the glass and stares out at the Atlantic, taking a moment. "I've checked every day," he casually states.

Thomas smiles and nods, not surprised.

"I have to. You have to be perfect. This will all be yours soon enough. You will be the keeper of this tower if I have my say. You will be in charge of protecting her, taking care of her needs, making sure Old Barney shines as brightly through the dark as she must. You understand I must be hard. I must make sure you know the right way so you can teach others; so you can pass on this sacred legacy."

"Yes, sir. I do understand."

Henry lets out a breath of air, thankful to get those words off his chest. "And, from time to time, I am a stubborn mean old ass. I know that," he admits his faults. Then he reaches into his coat pocket and pulls out a large stack of letters. He hands them to Thomas. Thomas curiously looks through the letters. He sees responses from the mayor and the local government.

We are sorry to inform you that there are no funds available at this time to further secure your lighthouse. Please use all means to do the best possible job at keeping your tower safe. You have our full support. Thank you for your inquiry.

Letter after letter shows denials over the request for funds.

"She is dying; slowly, each and every day. She is dying," Henry pats the side of the inner wall of the tower. He gazes upon his lighthouse with great pride and sadness. "One terrible storm could wash her away. Without a new jetty, she is doomed. And then what? Then what will they do in the storms and in the foggy nights? The low tide swallows ships whole here. It will be a graveyard of lost souls spread throughout our bay and our shores. Then what will they say when it's too late?" Henry asks rhetorical questions, his frustration over the subject abundantly obvious.

"So you've been trying for years to get help?" Thomas asks.

"Yes. Many, many years. We've begged and pleaded. The storms are getting worse. The tide is getting closer. Soon my home is going to disappear along with this great beacon of hope. It's painful to watch this happen. It's painful to see that occur right before your eyes."

"I can imagine," Thomas paces, thinking to himself.

"If they just appropriated a small amount of funds for a jetty. The sand could build back up by the shore and keep the water from eating away at the beach like a starving animal. It eats and eats and we are left with nothing. We need to save this shore, Thomas. We need to save the homes. We need to save Old Barney."

"What if we built our own jetty?" Thomas asks with optimism, an idea brewing.

"What do you mean?"

"Well, if they won't pay to build a proper jetty, what if we get all the junk we can and make our own? It won't be as good, it won't be as secure, but it will be something. It gives us a chance. It gives us a fighting chance!" Thomas bursts with optimism.

Henry smiles and nods. "Tomorrow I'll see the mayor. We are going to build our own jetty," he smiles with renewed optimism. Henry goes to walk back down the stairs when he stops. "Sarah is a good girl, Thomas. She is strong. She is much stronger and smarter than her old man. You are a good man. If you would like to speak with her on a level beyond friendship, I may not like it, but I support it." Henry offers a fatherly olive branch to Thomas.

"Thank you, sir. Respectfully...thank you."

Henry nods and heads down the stairs.

A FEW days later, Barnegat City is abuzz. The mayor, loving the idea brought to him by Henry, has spread the word. The townspeople all adore Old Barney. They all support the proud structure and start to pitch in. Broken down cars, large hauled stones, bags of sand, everything and anything is brought over to the shore. Men are lining up by the dozens to begin to assemble what is a manmade jetty of garbage and large solid structures. Car after car, hunkers and drivable vehicles, are being ushered into the water. Fishing vessels on either side are bobbing out in the sea attempting to help the people form the jetty. Another line of men are using push carts and getting heavy rocks to toss into the sea. Multiple horse draw wagons bring more rocks and metal scrap over. The community effort to build a proper jetty is on. The residents happily work as Henry watches, barking orders and making sure the construction goes as planned.

As the people continue their work, Sarah heads to the house to help Jackson get something to eat. She is making him a sandwich and glances up out the kitchen window and sees Zander crouched down, carefully sneaking back over to the Oceanic Hotel. He appears paranoid as he sneaks into the abandoned structure. Sarah finds his actions curious and finishes making Jackson's food. She sets Jackson up with a ham and cheese sandwich and curiously is drawn outside, staring at the Oceanic.

The abandoned Oceanic whistles in the wind as the distant sounds of construction and men hollering flutter in the wind. Sarah walks to the back deck of the Oceanic and slowly looks around. She curiously steps inside, her eyes scanning the dark empty building. These are her first steps in the abandoned hotel since it was opened long ago. She gazes upon the decaying remains of the once vibrant establishment. She hears music playing in the background, a bustling of people moving through the halls. She can remember the jovial atmosphere of laughing and children rushing to the shore. The Oceanic was a grand dream that crumbled into this empty abyss. Sarah was young when she stepped through these doors last. *So much changed over time. So many things are no longer the same.*

Sarah walks through the first floor and looks to the walls. Grand paintings used to dawn the walkway as you moved through the first floor. Now, it is peeling wallpaper, darkened by the plague of empty time and salt eating away at the once mighty structure. Sarah's focus is broken by the distant sound of piano keys playing a sweet Southern melody. The Blues echoes through the abandoned walls, a beautiful melody drawing Sarah closer. She smiles as she follows the perfectly played musical notes, heading up a flight of stairs to the second story and over to the ballroom. She enters the ballroom with a smile on her face. She watches as Zander plays away at the piano. He is off in another place; his own special world. He relishes his solitude and plays and plays. She leans against the wall and listens, a silent spectator as Zander finishes up his private set. The song comes to a slow soulful finale and he lives through the music, all the way through to the very last note.

Sarah begins clapping. Zander snaps his head over, surprised he had an audience.

"Oh, I'm sorry," she apologizes for surprising him.

Zander smiles and shakes his head. "It's all right. I was just surprised is all. Usually I only allow payin' customers in to hear the Blues," he jokes with his half-cocked smile.

"You're quite good," she compliments.

"I've played a little," he bunches his lips with a prideful smile.

"You just left for work in that uniform and now you're back. What happened?"

"They sent me on home. Slow day," Zander makes an excuse he knows is false, his head dropping, his eyes flashing up to see if his lie played.

"You don't work there, do you Zander?" she asks a direct question.

"I don't know what you're…" he starts to make an excuse when Sarah cuts him off.

"You never worked there. Your heart has always stayed here."

Zander gives up his charade. He looks down to the ground, embarrassed and upset. He nods and a grin overcomes his face.

"I went there. I did apply. And I would have been great. But the manager said they already had filled the colored positions for the season. Meanwhile, some other man comes through the door with less experience, looking like he fell off a farm wagon and hit the ground a hundred times. And *he* gets hired?! I heard the manager say they were *desperate* for help. But all the *colored positions* had been filled. That smarted me a bit."

"I'm sorry."

"I just didn't want Thomas to know. He was pushin' me *real* hard for the job. He wanted me to find my second chance just as he found his. And the folks over there were very nice at The Sunset. Don't get me wrong. I just didn't fill the available position they had."

Sarah nods. "You play a hell of a piano. They know that?"

"If I ain't good enough to carry a bag over there, I'm not going to give them the satisfaction of hearing my tunes." He sticks a pride stubborn foot in the ground, his chin rising high into the air.

"I can't blame you there. But you are good. *Real* good."

"Thank you, Sarah. Much appreciate it."

"No. Thank you, Zander."

Sarah starts to head back out.

"Oh, Sarah…," he calls out.

She turns and answers him before he can even ask the question. "Your secret's safe with me."

"Thank you, kindly."

Sarah nods and heads out. Zander looks his piano over and closes his eyes, slowly falling back into his moment. His fingers strike the piano keys gracefully and he plays for the empty abandoned ballroom. He plays as if he has a full house listening just to him. He starts into a jazzy tune and his foot bangs the ground. His head wobbles backward as if on a swivel, his eyes pinched tightly as if he were a blind musical magician. He plays and plays, letting out a few *heys and yeahs*. He drives life into the lifeless building.

HENRY and Thomas look over the manmade jetty as the townspeople continue to build. Their efforts are coming to a close. There is a visible barrier reaching nearly fifty yards out into the ocean. The newly built jetty gives the lighthouse a fighting chance against brutal storms.

"I hope this works," Thomas says.

"You've given her a chance. The stormy season is coming soon and you gave her a chance. A chance is all we can ask for; wouldn't you agree?"

"Yes, sir," Thomas states.

"Give Sarah that same chance. Give her a chance to know who you are—who you *really* are. Give her the chance you asked me for. You can't have a relationship built on lies, son. I may have to accept my own shortcomings and face my past, but so do you. Don't you think it's about that time?"

"That's not easy to answer."

"It's life, son. It was never meant to be easy."

"It's funny how we build walls. We build walls to keep enemies away. We build walls to keep loved ones from getting too close. We even build a wall to stop the ocean. We build walls everywhere around us. Sometimes, we don't realize how high those walls truly are."

"Aren't some things better left unsaid? Isn't the past in the past?"

"That's not for me to answer, Thomas. It's your reflection that you must face in the mirror each day. I stare at my ugly mug and that's enough for me. This is your fight—your choice."

Henry pats Thomas on the shoulder and walks away. Thomas is left to ponder what Henry said.

THOMAS enters the keeper's house and sees Sarah washing dishes in the kitchen. He takes a deep breath and walks over to her. He is determined, sporting a serious concentrated face.

Jackson is sitting at the dining room table working on a model boat he was gluing together. Henry is nearby and recognizes the look behind Thomas's eyes. Without saying a word, he turns to Jackson.

"Hey, kiddo, why don't you come upstairs and I'll show you a real rifle," Henry offers.

"Dad!" Sarah barks.

"It's not loaded. The boy can hold it. You did!"

"Fine," she reluctantly gives in.

Jackson excitedly gets up and dashes toward the stairs. Henry tips an imaginary cap to Thomas, yielding the floor to the budding lovebirds. Thomas nods and smiles, appreciating the privacy.

"You need some help?" Thomas searches for a way to begin a difficult conversation.

"I don't. But you can dry," she happily welcomes the extra hand from Thomas.

He grabs a dish towel off the counter and begins to dry dishes one at a time as Sarah hands them to him.

"Jackson's a really great kid," he compliments.

"Thanks. He's incredible. I love him to death. I know I can never replace his mother, but he is mine and I have a big responsibility."

Thomas nods in agreement. "Yeah, that's great."

They continue with the dishes. Then, Sarah all of a sudden turns to Thomas, staring right at him. It's an aggressive move that surprises Thomas. He is drying a fork and drops it to the ground.

"Oh, I'm sorry."

He bends down to pick it up at the same time she does. They both are down by the fork, staring into one another's eyes. Sarah places her hand on the side of Thomas's face and they lean in and kiss. It is a soft perfect kiss, their lips gently pressing against each other's. They start to slowly open their mouths, the tips of their tongues just touching. The romantic moment seems to last forever as they kiss and kiss. They continue until water starts to splash upon them, sprinkling from the sink above. Then more water starts to overflow and they abruptly pull back, looking up at a waterfall coming from the sink.

"Oh, gosh!" Sarah turns the water off and unclogs the sink from the bowl that got caught by the drain.

They look at one another and laugh as the water in the sink starts to slowly recede.

"I'll um...I'll get towels," Thomas states with a school boy smirk on his face.

"Thank you," she replies with the same silly smile.

Thomas dashes off to go get the towels. Sarah watches Thomas as he jogs away. She smiles, her heart warmed.

Sixteen

A STORM batters the jungle palms of the Bahamas;
the palms bending halfway over appearing as though they
may snap in half from the force of the wind. Lights are on
in a local bar, the patrons inside listening to music and
laughing the night away.

The doors are kicked open and Pratt stumbles out,
drunk, one arm around a beautiful local and the other
gripping a bottle of rum. They both laugh as they stumble
along. They walk through the driving rain and wind as if it
were nothing. They move through the chaotic weather over
to a small hotel next door. Pratt leads her all the way to his
room. He pulls out the key and tries to unlock the door. He
drops the key and they both chuckle, the evening full of
alcohol and laughs.

Pratt aggressively pulls her head back and starts to
kiss her, shoving his tongue down her throat, his free hand
groping her chest and pressing up against her breast. She
pulls away, caught off guard by his aggressive maneuver.
He opens the door and holds it open for her. She is
reluctant, but enters. They stumble inside and Pratt attempts
to locate his lantern.

"Where is that damn light?" he growls. He stumbles and searches around. Finally he finds it. "Here it is." Pratt lights a match and lights the lantern. He holds the light to his scruffy face and turns with a devious smile. "You're gonna have the time of your life, baby." Pratt's smile quickly flees as he stares in awe of someone. His mouth drops and concern emerges, his lips quivering to speak words that have escaped his breath.

"What are you doing?" a dark figure asks, his words laced with a Jamaican accent. The whites of his big eyes glow in the darkness as he glares at Pratt. He is wearing an opened buttoned down shirt and white pants. He has a hemp necklace hanging with multiple shark teeth attached, dangling down on his broad black chest. He is a tall intimidating man with a shaved head and dark intentions.

"Just having some fun, Del," Pratt spouts, his words laced with liquor and sarcasm.

"The fun will be over when the shipment is delivered." The man's tone is stern and he has little patience. He sharply stares at the local girl in the room. She recognizes the large Jamaican man and takes the hint. She respectfully backs away, leaving Pratt's room.

Pratt slams his hand on a nearby table, shaking his head. "Are you kidding me?!"

The Jamaican rushes Pratt and takes him by the throat, walking him back up against the wall. The bottle of rum falls out of Pratt's hand and it spills all over the floor.

"Do I look like I am kidding, duppy?" The Jamaican stares intensely with the whites of his eyes bulging out of his skull. Pratt stares with anger and bitterness right back at the Jamaican.

"Oh, you think you a bwoy," he challenges Pratt, raising a hunting knife up to Pratt's throat.

"I am da bad bwoy," Pratt imitates the Jamaican's accent and smirks.

The Jamaican laughs and slowly releases Pratt's neck. "I like you, duppy. You one crazy bwoy. You a bad man." The Jamaican slowly steps back from Pratt. "We leavin' early, man. At dawn we sail north."

"Bring some girls aboard."

"What you mean, duppy? You didn't have enough this last week?"

"Bring some girls. Some dark skinned types; with them accents. Bring them with us. They will sell the booze all on their own."

The Jamaican paces around in the room. He thinks, tapping his large hunting knife against the side of his face. "How?"

"They will sell; the way they talk, their accents, their looks. The booze and the girls go hand in hand in America. Only juices the pot for us."

"You believe they will like them that much?"

"I do," Pratt projects his evil smile.

The Jamaican again smiles, quietly thinking things over. "You a good businessman, duppy. Very good. Why not? We'll bring a few girls."

"And they will make us more money."

"Ah. *Us.* I will see what you do with my rum, duppy. There is no *us* until I see American dollars. Then we talk *us.*"

The Jamaican walks away, exiting Pratt's hotel room, leaving the door open. Pratt stares angrily toward the door, a bitter taste left in his mouth. He moves over to the floor and picks up his mostly empty bottle of rum. He brings it to his lips and takes a swig. His eyes linger at the door with evil thoughts brewing in his mind.

A FIVE-masted schooner sits in the aqua clear blue Caribbean waters. The sun is just rising as Pratt drags himself down the dock toward the boat. The last of the barrels of alcohol are being loaded onto the ship. The tall

Jamaican is standing with a military man. The Jamaican military official is angrily barking at Pratt's business partner as he holds a smoking cigar. His partner is barking back. Pratt watches closely as the heated discussion comes to an end.

The large Jamaican walks toward the ship and sees Pratt staring down at him.

"What is it?" he asks in an annoyed tone.

"We having some problems?" Pratt asks.

"Nothing I can't handle, duppy."

"All right, Delmar. I trust you." Pratt sarcastically states.

Delmar shakes his head, laughing, taking a puff of his cigar and blowing the smoke up into the air in Pratt's direction. He stares directly at Pratt through the smoke, his smile morphing to a cocky glare. "You have no choice, bwoy."

Pratt's smile flees as Delmar makes his way to the ship.

"Let's go! We are late!" Delmar shouts to his crew of five men working to gather supplies and complete the loading of the heavy rum-filled barrels. "Duppy. Come here!" Delmar calls to Pratt. Pratt, annoyed he is being beckoned, walks over to Delmar.

"Come with me." Delmar smokes his cigar and leads Pratt below deck to the cabin. He walks down and finds five scantily dressed young Jamaican girls in T-shirts lined up side by side like a cattle call. They are not wearing bras and have on only underwear. "Is this acceptable?" Delmar asks.

Pratt looks the women over, very impressed. A dopey smile overcomes his face.

"I am guessing, yes?" Delmar asks with a confident tone.

"Oh, yeah," Pratt has numerous carnal thoughts as he looks the women over.

"You can do as you wish until Florida. After that, the girls are off limits."

"Yeah?" Pratt is surprised he is receiving such an offer.

"It is business, man." Delmar takes another puff of his cigar, taking great pleasure in releasing the smoke into the air. "How can you sell the goods if you have not had a taste yourself? Yes?"

"Yeah. I'd definitely have to agree with that logic."

"All right. Enjoy." Delmar heads back up on top of the ship's deck.

Pratt looks the five women over, all of whom are smiling and willing participants. "Yeah, rum running is good," Pratt jokes to himself.

"YOU playin' us, duppy?" Ja says. Ja is Delmar's close friend. He is short with dreadlocks and a scruffy inconsistent beard. His skin is just as dark as Delmar's, the whites of his eyes popping on this evening. He is smoking a joint as he stares Pratt down. The ship is sailing through the dark waters where the Caribbean kisses the Atlantic.

"What does that mean-duppy? You both always call me that," Pratt asks with a smirk.

"It means ghost. Da *white* bwoy we do not trust."

Pratt smiles and nods. "Well, I'm going to make us all rich men. You can retire and have as many coconuts as you want and I can find my own island."

"You may have Delmar convinced, but not me. No-no-no." Ja comes around and sits right in front of Pratt. The two are uncomfortably close.

"I guess you heathens don't do personal space."

Ja laughs and shakes his head at Pratt in disgust, annoyed he needs to be a part of anything having to do with this white criminal. "I know men like you. I've met others. They think they are so fine with what they do. They think they know all that there is to know. But they talk big. Big talk, duppy. They lie. You lie."

Pratt takes the joint right out of Ja's hand and takes a puff himself. He savors it and then blows the smoke up into the air. "This is good," Pratt compliments. "What do you call this again?"

Ja wants his joint back from Pratt. "Mine, duppy."

Pratt smiles and nods. "All right." Pratt pauses and then, "What did I ever do to you, Ja? How did I piss you off?"

"Why aren't you cocking it up down there? Da women not good enough for ya, duppy?" Ja ignores Pratt's question.

"I needed a break."

Ja stares at Pratt, not believing him. "You come all dis way. You far from home, duppy. And now you come and make business with my bredda. You make a deal. You talk all kinds of big money."

"I know people in Philadelphia and New York. This is all set up because of me." Pratt becomes defensive.

"Yes. You say, dis. You say it a lot. We will see, duppy." Ja blows smoke in Pratt's face. "We will see if it is just smoke or you come through." Ja gets up and walks away.

Pratt watches Ja walk away. "Oh, you'll see," he promises in an ominous tone to himself. Pratt takes out a knife and picks up a small piece of wood he had hidden by his feet the entire time. He sharpens the tip of the wood to pass time; wood he has been sharpening for some time now.

DOWN in the cabin, Delmar is lying with one of the Jamaican women. She is naked, pressed up against his body with a thin blanket hanging off them. He is topless with his pants on, asleep. Ja comes quietly walking into the room and Delmar shoots up from a dead sleep, pulling out a pistol, aiming it at Ja.

"Easy, bredda!" Ja places his hands up in the air.

"Ah! Ja, I sleepin', man." Delmar shakes his head and sits up. The woman next to him starts to awake. "Let's go! Let's go, woman!" Delmar wakes her up with a soft slap to the face. She gets up and quickly rises out of bed, naked. He smacks her in the ass as she trots out of the room.

"You think they necessary, bredda?"

"Ja, we here to make money. We come to America to make money. This is what we want, yes?"

"I don't trust the duppy, Delmar. I don't trust him at all."

"Look. We have the girls and we have the rum. If we don't like the way things turn out, we throw the duppy in the ocean on the way home and we keep all da money for ourselves. How dat sound?"

Ja smiles, nodding in agreement. "Bredda, dat sound good."

Delmar smiles. He gets up and pats Ja on the shoulder. "It's all gonna be *good*, bredda," he says back to his smaller close friend. Ja smiles, Delmar making him happy with this new plan.

"Land!" a distant voice calls from up top.

Delmar smiles, excited. "Here we go!" He grabs a button down shirt and throws it on. Ja quickly heads up onto the deck. The ship is approaching land.

The ship sails toward port. Upon arrival the ship docks and ties up.

There are multiple trucks waiting by the docks with men holding guns. Pratt is staring out at the scene with a smile on his face. "Now I make some real money," he smiles, mumbling to himself.

"Come on!" Ja shouts as the girls come parading out from the lower deck. They are escorted out onto the docks.

Pratt and Delmar walk over to a heavy set man in an all-white suit. He has a mustache and a cocky smile.

"Mr. Batone," Delmar respectfully states. He follows his greeting with a head bow, uncertain how to greet an American businessman.

Batone smiles, amused by Delmar's attempts.

"Mr. Batone," Pratt extends his hand and the two shake. Delmar flashes an angry embarrassed glare over at Pratt.

Batone shakes hands with Pratt and then he and Delmar connect on a handshake of their own.

"I'm sorry. I am new to these parts," Delmar states, trying to sound professional and save face.

"No, shit," Batone jokes back, his tone laced with disrespect. Delmar stares stoically straight forward, annoyed. "What is with these exotic women?"

"They're for you and your men. Tonight, we celebrate!" Pratt states.

"Very nice. Rolling out the red carpet for me. Thanks, boys!" Batone nods, a big smile on his face.

"Hey, man! Get off that!" Ja shouts at one of the men. Batone's other men grow nervous and aim their guns toward Ja. The other Jamaican men on the boat take out guns of their own and aim them at Batone's men.

"Hey!" Batone shouts, annoyed.

"Easy!" Pratt also shouts, not wanting a shootout.

"Put them down," Delmar steps forward, shouting. "What is this?" he calls out to Ja.

"They want to open the barrels." Ja is standing guard by the six barrels they rolled off the boat.

"Let them! They want to try, let them try. They are paying for it all anyway!" Delmar shouts.

The man beside Ja steps in and continues to open the barrel, chuckling at Ja. Ja steps back, shaking his head.

"I have rooms for you and your men," Batone states to Pratt.

"His men?" Delmar flashes angry insulted eyes at Pratt.

"For *all* of you. You can stay the night," Batone restates to include Delmar.

"That's great, Mr. Batone. We really appreciate it." Pratt plays nice with the businessman.

"We need to go. We have other business to attend to," Delmar steps in, making it clear who is in charge.

"All right. Suit yourselves."

"I shall," Delmar asserts.

Batone goes to hand an envelope full of money over to Pratt and then hesitates. He turns and sees Delmar's hand slowly extend out. He hands the money to Delmar.

"Good day, gentlemen," Delmar tips his hat and walks away. "Let's get going, boys!" he shouts to his men.

Delmar opens the envelope and counts the money. He turns to Pratt and stares angrily at him. "Go get the girls, duppy. We leavin' this place," Delmar turns, annoyed and walks back to the ship. "Prepare the ship! We sail!" he shouts orders to the rest of the men.

Pratt stares angrily at Delmar as he walks away. He shakes his head and turns. Standing in front of him is Ja.

"You got somethin' to say, duppy?" Ja recognizes Pratt's annoyed expression.

"Yeah. Delmar wants you to go round up the girls, errand boy. *Pratt-man.*"

Delmar and Ja are just a few inches away from one another's faces, having a brief stare-off. After a few moments, Ja breaks and laughs. He raises his right hand and softly pats the side of Pratt's cheek. He turns to go get the girls, just as Pratt said. Pratt's eyes are narrowed, his expression sinister. He has many evil thoughts swirling in his head.

Seventeen

THE clouds are moving over the five-masted fishing vessel turned rum-running ship. It is growing much colder. Pratt bundles up as the ship sails through the waters of the Atlantic heading up the northeast coast.

"Why are we so far from shore?" Pratt barks.

"So da white men don't steal our rum, duppy!" Ja barks back, his hands steering the ship.

"Easy, bredda," Delmar says to Ja. "Our business partner already made us some money. Let's not get feisty."

Ja goes back to steering the ship, shaking his head. He mumbles angrily under his breath, staring at Pratt as bitter unrecognizable sounds tumble quietly out of his mouth.

"He is just jealous," Delmar intimates to Pratt. Delmar has a map he is reviewing to ascertain their exact location. "Where you think we are?" he asks, Pratt. Pratt walks over and looks the map over. He glances up at Delmar briefly, his eyes flashing with hesitancy. He stares at the map and then looks up toward the sky as if he were attempting to read where he was. He surveys the ocean, staring out in all directions. Delmar watches him with a bit of confusion, wondering what Pratt is doing. Ja shakes his head from the ship's wheel, watching as Pratt stumbles along with no seafaring intuition.

"He don't know!" Ja shouts and laughs.

"Ja! Shut-up!" Delmar barks.

Ja throws his hand up into the air and shakes his head. Pratt wanders back to the map and looks it over. He sees Atlantic City marked and runs his finger down the map to the coast of North Carolina. He slides his finger up slightly to Virginia.

"We should be just off the coast of Virginia. By nightfall we'll be in Atlantic City."

"You think we *that* close?" Delmar isn't certain of Pratt's seafaring knowledge. He himself doesn't believe they are near their target.

"Yeah. Right here," Pratt points to the map. "I'm never wrong," Pratt confidently looks up and states.

"Okay, duppy."

THE ship sails on into nightfall.

"There!" Ja points to shore. He sees a light in the distance. "The shore! Is that it?" he asks.

Pratt and Delmar step forward on the bow of the ship. Delmar pulls out a rusted old bronze spyglass and stares through it. "I'm not sure," he states with confusion.

"A lighthouse?" Pratt asks.

"Perhaps." Delmar isn't convinced. "By your calculations, this could be our stop. But I do not see Atlantic City. I do not see anything like you described."

"Shall I pull closer, Del?" Ja asks.

"Yes. I need to see better, bredda."

Ja steers the ship and they turn toward the shoreline. The men on board remain quiet, attempting to see where they are. Pratt reaches in his pocket for his pistol, sensing something is wrong. He has led them blindly through these waters. His eyes push forward, his hand reaches slowly into his coat where he pulls out a pistol. He holds the gun out, remaining still and quiet. There is almost no noise except the ocean water dancing up against the sides of the ship. With little wind to speak of, it is as silent as ever.

Delmar looks over at Pratt, seeing the pistol in his hand. Delmar's eyes squint, his brows furrow, fixating on the drawn pistol. He is confused as to what Pratt is preparing for. He pulls the spyglass back up and looks through it. He stares toward the beach in the direction of the light. However, he sees no light. He sees a small tower with a flame burning on top of it. He looks confused and pans his view over with the spyglass, searching the surrounding beach. Two cannons with men dressed like scoundrels are simultaneously lighting the cannons to fire. A moment later, the cannon blasts cut right through the tense silence. The cannon balls fly through the night's sky.

"Down!" Delmar shouts.

Everyone hits the deck as one cannon strikes a mast, carrying pieces of wood and part of the sail into the water behind them. The other cannon blast strikes the bow of the ship, taking a chunk with it. Delmar quickly jumps to his feet.

"Ja! Turn the ship!" He shouts.

Ja reaches for the wheel and sees pirates climbing up onto the ship. It is too late. There are a few gun blasts from the pirates coming aboard, keeping the Jamaican's at bay for a moment. The pirates climb aboard, eight of them, charging forward with pistols drawn. Ja takes out a pistol of his own and fires, racing towards the ragged scoundrels.

Pratt looks around, ducking back into a corner as the Jamaicans and the thieves fight. The pirates have knives and pistols, just as the Jamaicans do. After a few wild gunshots, the exchange of gun fire seizes as hand-to-hand combat is engaged all over the ship. Pratt keeps his gun out in front of him when a pirate jumps onto his arm, knocking his pistol away. Pratt is struck across the face and the thief is on top of him, pulling out a knife. Pratt's eyes flare open as the pirate reaches up with his knife to plunge it into Pratt. Just before he does, the thief is shot by Ja's gun. Ja stands over the pirate, his gun still smoking. He angrily stares, for just a single moment at Pratt, his gun pointed in his direction. Pratt isn't certain if he will be next, his body pinned under the dead man's carcass. The two men share a dark stare, showing their outward disgust for one another. Pratt is the lesser of two evils and Ja reluctantly leaves him alive, rushing off to continue fighting. Pratt rolls the pirate's dead body off of him. He looks his shoulder over; a flesh wound from Ja's bullet that grazed him. He grabs the pirate's gun and knife and searches him for anything else. He pulls a silver plated pocket watch off of him and looks up, readying for any other attackers.

Yells and screams sound on the boat as men are dying. A pirate is tossed overboard by Delmar. He finishes killing one man and looks for more. He is shot in the shoulder and the force bends him back, nearly over the side of the boat. He looks and sees the pirate trying to reload his gun. Delmar yells, an angry roar and charges at the man. The pirate gets the bullets in and closes the chamber. He wants to raise the gun but Delmar gets to him first, knocking the gun away. He lifts the man up off the deck by his throat with just his left hand, showcasing his incredible strength. He reaches and pulls out his large hunting knife with his right hand, shoving it into the sternum of the pirate. He carries the man over to side of the ship and pulls his knife out of his gut, tossing his lifeless body over the edge of the ship. The fighting behind him begins to calm down and Delmar looks for more, blood trickling down his arm from the gunshot wound.

Pratt stands up, holding a wound of his own. Ja comes around the corner. "You see any more, duppy?" he intensely asks.

"One had gotten past me. I think he went down into the cabins!" Pratt shouts, a lie to distract his arch enemy on the ship. Ja races past him and before Ja knows it, a knife is stuck into his back. Pratt's hand is holding an ivory handle blade, the same blade from the pirate Ja killed moments before. Pratt pulls out his small wood spike he had been sharpening and plunges it into Ja's neck.

"I made this for you," Pratt, staring at his wooden stake, states.

Ja's anguished face tilts just slightly, his eyes peeling to the edges to get one last sad glimpse of his killer. He barely sees Pratt, and wants to speak. But too much blood is filling his lungs for words to form and the blood spills from his mouth.

With the job done, Pratt quickly hides his hand-made wood weapon. Ja's head slumps slightly, in shock over Pratt's sneak attack. He falls to his knees, futilely holding his neck as blood pours from it. Pratt is staring down at him with no sympathy, happily watching as his arch rival slowly dies. Ja's body falls limp to the ground, the knife sticking up out of his back.

Pratt turns, wincing in pain from his shoulder and moves to the side of the ship. He quickly dumps the bloodied wood stake into the ocean. It is the only evidence left of him puncturing Ja's neck; the death blow.

"What are you doing, duppy?" Delmar barks, looking strangely at Pratt who is leaning over the edge of the ship. Delmar's shirt is blood stained from the gunshot wound by his shoulder. His shirt contains some of the pirate's blood splattered across it like a Pollock painting.

Pratt's eyes bulge open and he pulls his pistol out. He aims it toward Delmar. Delmar's eyes flare open in shock as Pratt fires. The bullet whizzes right over Delmar's shoulder and hits a charging pirate in the chest. The pirate drops his knife just a few feet away from Delmar. Delmar looks at the dead man on the ground and then back at Pratt with the pistol still smoking in his hand. His mouth is hanging open in shock, surprised he was almost killed and equally surprised it is Pratt who saved him. Delmar subtly nods to Pratt and turns back to the main deck to continue whatever fight remains.

Pratt lets out a breath of air, relieved he wasn't found out. He also shakes his head, shocked he just saved Delmar's life.

The fight gives way. The remaining bodies of the pirates are dumped overboard. One Jamaican crew is tossed and Delmar sadly carries Ja, his best friend's dead body, to the side of the boat. The remaining four Jamaican crew hold their heads down in respect of Ja. Pratt stands beside them, doing the same for appearances. His face is bland, indifferent.

"You were a good bredda, ma. Da best. I will see you on the otha' side." Delmar regretfully dumps Ja's lifeless body overboard, into the ocean water below. His body floats for a moment before dipping down and getting swallowed by the ocean. "Da best, bredda." Delmar gives his good friend one last look.

IN THE cabin below, Delmar enters and sees Pratt wincing from pouring some rum onto his wound.

"Da whisky does betta," Delmar states. He pulls his shirt off and reaches into a high cupboard. He grabs whisky and removes the cork with his teeth. He pours some whisky on Pratt's wound. Pratt winces in pain. Delmar then does the same to his own wound, but shows no signs of feeling the alcohol burn into his exposed bleeding flesh. He grabs a towel and presses it up against his wound. Next, Delmar spits the cork out of his mouth onto the counter and takes a swig of the stiff alcohol. He savors it for a moment, squinting at Pratt—looking at him with a curious expression.

"What?" Pratt asks, confused by Delmar's look.

Delmar offers Pratt a sip of his whisky. Pratt happily accepts.

"Thank you," he nods to Delmar.

"It is funny. I thought you would kill me in my sleep," Delmar half-jokes.

Pratt coughs as if he were a 15-year old taking his first swig, Delmar's comment and the whisky simultaneously catching him off guard, burning his throat. He coughs a couple more times as Delmar takes the bottle back.

"It is strong, yes?" Delmar laughs, amused by Pratt. He takes another swig.

Pratt clears his throat, gathering himself. "We do what we have to, right?"

"You saved my life. You surprise me, duppy. You a bredda now; partner. *Pratt da man.*" Delmar again offers Pratt the bottle.

Pratt happily accepts and takes another swig, this time a bit more cautious and conservative. After the burn dissipates in his throat he looks back up at Delmar. "Partner," he nods, handing the bottle of whisky back. The two men drink together, bonding over their wounds from the unexpected battle.

"We caught one. He is alive," Delmar states.

"What are you going to do with him?" Pratt, asks.

"We are going to question the man, bredda. You and me."

Pratt nods.

IN ONE of the cabins, a single thief rests, cut, bruised and beaten. Blood is stained across the scoundrels torn dirty clothing. His face is unshaved, his torso average in size. He isn't much without his weapons as he sits quietly with an annoyed smirk on his face. That is when Delmar and Pratt enter the cabin.

"What is this?" the lone remaining pirate asks.

"This?" Delmar sadistically responds. His eyes are glazed with hate and vengeance as he pulls out his bloodied hunting knife. The dried blood of one of the pirates still remains on it. "These are your last rights, man. You tell me what I need to know and you die quick. You waste my time and I make it slow."

"This negro rules you?" the dirty scoundrel looks at Pratt.

Pratt whips his hand around and slaps the man across the face. "Do you taste that?" Pratt asks.

The thief spits a mouthful of blood out onto the floor. "Taste what?"

"The taste of your own blood," Delmar steps forward with a sadistic smile, excited to jump in. "Get used to it," he promises.

"What do you want?" the man nervously and angrily asks. His head is tilted down, his eyes peering up. He is reluctant to talk but realizes he has no choice.

"Where are we?" Delmar asks with great curiosity.

Pratt is a little nervous, unsure how far off he was with his nautical estimations. The man smirks at Delmar and Pratt, his face frozen for a moment. He believes the question must be more complex than it appears on the surface. He searches with his feeble mind for other alternatives but comes up with none. "Where are we?" he asks back in return, confused over such a simplified question.

"Where?" Delmar grows louder, using a demanding tone and a drawn face, with exploding white pupils to further his point.

"Okay-okay. Easy. We call it Gingo on the island. Older folks call it Gingoteague."

"Where the hell is that?" Pratt steps forward with a perplexed look on his face, having no idea what the pirate is talking about.

"You in Carolina, North," the man spouts with his cheeks slightly raised in amusement. He is an amused reflection of the utter confusion and frustration taking place before him.

"Ah!" Delmar slams his hunting knife up against the cabin wall, it driving through the coarse wood. "Bredda..." he begins.

Pratt steps forward, hesitant and curious what Delmar has to say to him. Delmar now knows he has been steered wrong by Pratt who clearly has overstated his seafaring prowess. Delmar remains with his back turned to Pratt, trying to compose himself. He can't look his newly anointed partner in the eyes at the moment; too angered by their navigational missteps.

"You take care of 'dis man. Throw him in the ocean when you are done." Delmar waits for a moment, not looking behind him. He is too angry thinking about his good friend, Ja, and his unnecessary death. Delmar takes out his pistol and tosses it in the center of the room between Pratt and the tied up thief. Without a word, he leaves, slamming the cabin door shut behind him, letting the two men battle for their will to live.

Both Pratt and the thief stare at the pistol on the ground. Pratt's eyes are wide open and he reaches for his own gun, but it's not on him; his hand coming up empty.

Despite having his hands tied, the scoundrel is closer and dives right on top of the gun, trying to grab it with the back of his hands. Pratt looks to the wall where Delmar left his large hunting knife. He reaches for it, trying to yank it out of the wood. Delmar plunged the large blade deep into the door frame and Pratt fights to get it out. The thief rises and fires a stray bullet backwards, missing Pratt by a few feet. Pratt works harder, and using all his strength, finally dislodges the knife. Pratt falls backward after grabbing the knife. The scoundrel fires another wild shot and it strikes the ground beside Pratt's face, small shards of wood flying up.

"Jesus!" Pratt shouts. He swings the knife and strikes the pirate's hand, cutting off numerous fingers in the process.

"Ah!" The pirate screams in pain as blood splatters on Pratt and pours onto the floor. Pratt swings the blade again and again. He swings the blade numerous times, taking out his nerves and anger on the man. He butchers the pirate like an animal, striking him over and over with the large hunting knife. The cabin becomes a horror scene of splattered and poured blood, staining everything, everywhere.

DELMAR stands by the map, looking it over. A lantern is lit and provides him light in the dark night sky. He has a perplexed look on his face, plotting their course. Pratt steps up out of the cabin with the pirate's dead body. He struggles with the limp bloodied carcass. He moves to the side of the boat and uses all his might to toss the body overboard. The loud splash doesn't faze Delmar as he continues to study the map, knowing exactly where Pratt is. Pratt bitterly looks back at Delmar as he reaches into his pocket and tosses the stray chopped off fingers of the pirate, the last remaining parts of their prisoner. Pratt makes it across the darkness over to Delmar. He comes to Delmar and light shines further upon Pratt's appearance. He has blood everywhere. He is covered from his face down to his toes in splattered blood patterns. Pratt takes the large hunting knife and slams it into the corner of the map, sticking it into the wood. The bloody knife stands straight up into the air.

"If you don't mind, I'm going to keep the pirate's pistol. I seem to have lost mine."

"Yes, bredda. You can have that one," Delmar casually states with a smile. He glances over at Pratt, seeing the struggle that he had. He doesn't react to the blood soaked man standing beside him. "We are here. We need to get here," Delmar points to Atlantic City as their desired destination on the map. "You were wrong with the map before. Do not be wrong again." Delmar pulls his bloody hunting knife up out of the table and wipes it dry on his pants leg. He puts the knife back in its scabbard attached to the side of his pants leg. He walks away from the table, leaving the bloodied and angered Pratt to stew.

Eighteen

THE stars are sparkling in the sky above. The clear crisp autumn night is home to a beautiful spectacle of balls of fire shining brilliantly all across deep space.

"How do you know that's Pegasus?" Sarah asks.

Sarah and Thomas are lying on the beach with a blanket wrapped around them. They are close and cozy, staring up at the stars.

"You see that box of stars?" Thomas points, attempting to direct Sarah's eye line.

"Yeah."

"The top arc of stars is his head and the bottom is his leg. The main stars form a square. You see?"

"Yes," Sarah smiles.

The two star-crossed lovers share a moment, looking at one another. Thomas pauses, caught in Sarah's gaze. He then reminds himself of one glaring fact.

"Your father is probably looking down at us right now. Literally right now." Thomas's eyes flash up to the top of the light tower.

"Tell me more," Sarah smiles, refocusing back on the sky, bailing Thomas out of what could have been a sticky situation.

"The story goes that Pegasus was tamed by Neptune, the sea god. There's Cassiopeia, the Queen and the queen's daughter, Andromeda. Right there is Perseus." Thomas points out constellations with his finger, one after another. "When Cassiopeia boasted that her daughter, Andromeda, was more beautiful than any creature in the ocean, Neptune became furious. He had Andromeda chained to a rock as prey for a terrible sea monster. Just as the monster was going to destroy her, Perseus heroically arrived on his flying horse. Perseus had slayed Medusa, a horrible creature that could turn things to stone with one look from her evil eyes. Perseus showed this monster the head of Medusa. As the monster focused on the strange decapitated head, Medusa's eyes suddenly opened. The monster was immediately turned to stone and Andromeda was saved. Up in the sky, you can still see Perseus waving Medusa's head, one of her eyes fading and then getting stronger, like it's winking. It's the blinking star right there," Thomas leans in close and their cheeks nearly touch as he once again uses his finger to point things out to Sarah. They turn, their faces an inch apart. They share a smile and then Thomas pulls back to conclude his astronomical lesson. "That is the story of the autumn stars."

"Wow. That is *some* story. Do you believe in them—the stories?"

"They are tall tales. But I believe in the stars. I know if you believe in them, they will believe in you."

"I believe in you," Sarah rapidly returns with an intense stare.

Sarah and Thomas's eyes are intertwined with one another. They slowly lean in, drawn by passionate forces, and kiss.

Up in the lighthouse, Henry is coughing, holding his spyglass in his free hand. He coughs so hard, he can barely stay on his feet. He is holding a handkerchief by his mouth. When he stops coughing, he slowly pulls away the small white piece of cloth. There is fresh red blood upon it. Henry composes himself, stuffing the piece of cloth back into his pocket. He raises the spyglass and surveys the waters. He sees a ship out at sea, bobbing in the water not too far away from the coast. He squints and then sees a small skiff being rowed toward the shore with what appears to be two men inside. They are barely visible in the dark waters but Henry sees them. He is confused and then looks over at Sarah and Thomas on the beach. He grows paranoid and concerned over the strange visitors and their sudden appearance by his shoreline. His face fills with alarm, his eyebrows sagging down and his cheeks pulling in, twitching. Henry makes a decisive decision and moves over to a small locked box in the corner of the tower. He reaches into his pocket and takes out a small key. He unlocks the box, reaching inside. He pulls out a small revolver and opens the barrel. He makes certain it is loaded. Satisfied, he places the revolver in the back of his pants between his waistband and his skin. He looks up with an uneasy feeling.

Henry makes his way down the steps and over to the beach. Thomas and Sarah are laughing and are in the middle of a conversation.

"Up!" Henry shouts with urgency.

Thomas jumps up and Sarah turns, confused.

"Is it my shift, sir?" Thomas asks, hopeful he wasn't spotted kissing his boss's daughter.

"Dad, we weren't doing…"

Henry cuts off both their trailing thoughts. "A boat's coming." Henry hands the telescope over to Thomas. Thomas takes the looking glass and peers through it. He sees the boat anchored out at sea.

"I see. But she looks anchored out there."

"She is. Now look closer. A skiff is on its way." Henry prompts.

Thomas scours the water with the spyglass and comes across the small skiff being paddled toward shore.

The light is shining just enough to pick up their dark outlines as they make their way right toward the lighthouse.

"They're coming here." Thomas lowers the telescope and stares at Henry with the same look of concern.

"Yes. But who?" Henry queries out loud, a sinking tone to his voice. Both men are trying to ascertain who may be coming.

"Sarah, go inside," Henry orders.

"Dad, I'm fine."

Henry whips his head over to his daughter. "Sarah, for once in your life don't be as stubborn as me. Get my gun off my bedroom wall and you get Jackson up and ready to leave. If there is trouble, you take him and go and don't look back. You go get the law and bring them back here."

"These could just be lost fishermen? Maybe their boat is damaged?" Sarah tries to see the best in this scenario.

"They found us so they can't be *that* lost," Thomas chimes in. "He's right, Sarah."

"Oh, so the two of you are protecting the woman. I don't need it."

"But I do," Henry reaches and grabs her arm. "Please. Allow me to be paranoid and to know you are safe."

Sarah sees the seriousness behind her father's eyes. She nods and gives in. Sarah plunges into the sand, her feet digging slowly at first, as she walks away from the shoreline. Then she picks up to a jog, her steps quickening, rushing over to the keeper's house.

"Why do you think they're coming ashore like this?"

"They need something. They need something or they wouldn't be sailing the skiff over. I'm not sure what it could be."

The skiff approaches the beach. Thomas and Henry stand side by side as the skiff pulls up to the sand. The dark-skinned Jamaican gets out and pulls the skiff safely onto the sand. Delmar follows right behind his crewman and gets out of the boat.

"Hello," he says.

Thomas's eyes squint immediately recognizing the foreign accent. "You're Jamaican," Thomas says.

"Ya-man," Delmar smiles.

"What are you doing in New Jersey?" Thomas again takes the lead with questioning.

Henry's hand moves toward his back, his fingertips just an inch away from being able to pull out his gun. He is taking no chances as Thomas questions the strange man.

"We were looking for Atlantic City. But the ship is damaged and we are having trouble adjusting our sails. One of my masts was shattered and my sea captain is no longer on the ship."

"No longer on the ship? He jumped off?" Thomas jokes with Delmar.

"We were attacked by pirates, from the shores down south. They damaged my ship and killed two of my men."

"I'm sorry," Thomas apologetically looks down with regret.

"You did not know this. I am not great without the captain for directions. We need a quick fix of the ship. We have money to pay for some help."

There is a moment of silence as Henry and Thomas look at one another.

"Can you bring the ship closer?"

"That's why we took my skiff. I wanted to ask you first."

"Yes," Henry finally speaks up. "Bring the ship in. We'll help you out and get you back out to sea."

"All right. Thank you!" Delmar is relieved and smiles.

"You'll be stranded until high tide once you come closer. Does that work?" Henry asks.

"It be fine. As long as she sails. We can pay for some food—a meal for my people aboard? There be ten of us. Five females and five males."

"That's fine. Yes."

"Thank you, bredda," Delmar respectfully nods and turns to have a private conversation with his one crew member.

Thomas turns to Henry. Henry doesn't take his judgmental eyes off of Delmar. He is still reading him—watching his actions closely.

"I think they're all right," Thomas states.

"They are something, Thomas. But they definitely aren't all right." Henry's eyes are like a hawk, focused and penetrating. He starts to cough and turns away from Thomas. He coughs and coughs. He pulls out his white cloth and uses it to cover his mouth, hiding the action from Thomas. Henry walks away, heading back over to the lighthouse, coughing all the while. Thomas watches with concern, focused on Henry. His face sags just slightly, sensing something may be wrong with his mentor.

"He has consumption," Delmar surprises Thomas with an assertive statement. He is standing right beside him. Thomas peeks over his shoulder and can appreciate Delmar's massive size. He also sees a small smattering of a blood pattern on the side of his shirt.

Thomas's mind takes a moment to process Delmar's statement. "What's that?"

"Consumption. He sounds like he has it. It killed my sister's husband and my grandfather. Nasty game."

"I think it's just a cough." Thomas chooses to look at things from an idealistic point of view.

"Okay, bredda. Thank you for the help. It is much appreciated."

"Everybody needs help some time. Right?"

"You got dat right, man." Delmar smiles and turns away from Thomas.

Thomas's attention moves back over to Henry who slowly makes his way back into the lighthouse.

THOMAS steps into the keeper's house with Delmar. Sarah is holding the rifle with a confused look on her face. Jackson, half asleep, is standing behind her in his pajamas.

"You going to war, woman?" Delmar jokingly asks.

"They need some meals and we're gonna help them get their ship fixed. They were attacked at sea." Thomas finishes his explanation.

Sarah nods, not completely convinced. She turns to Jackson. "Jackson, go upstairs and get back in bed." Jackson silently agrees with a nod and heads upstairs. She turns back to Thomas with a squinted look, still trying to get a read on Delmar. "I'll be back down in a minute." Sarah heads upstairs, her disapproving eyes all the while remaining fixated on Delmar and Thomas.

Thomas lets out a breath of air, shaking his head.

"She none too happy with you, man," Delmar smirks, shaking his head. He moves toward the kitchen and looks around. "Dis a nice place," he compliments.

"Thank you. It's the keeper's home. We live here and work at the lighthouse."

"That's how da pirates got us. They pretended they were a lighthouse. Lit some wood on fire." Delmar smirks and thinks about the past incident. "Clever fellows," he states.

Thomas looks at Delmar wondering where the conversation is heading. He is only half-listening to the stranger in his home. He is more guarded over his presence. Delmar moves to the dining room table and has a seat.

The back door opens near the kitchen and closes. Footsteps approach. Delmar looks over and is unimpressed, his eyes rolling with annoyance.

"They got a bathroom in this place? I gotta take a piss," Pratt states as he clears the wall into the dining room.

Thomas is frozen as the dark ghost from his past reappears right before his eyes. Thomas is staring at him, his mouth hanging open in shock. He doesn't know what to say or do. His two feet might as well be stuck in thick cement.

"Hey, bredda-man, my partner needs a bathroom," Delmar looks over at Thomas. He immediately becomes intrigued by Thomas's change in demeanor. He sits up, curious why he is looking at Pratt as if he were a specter.

"Oh, well...um, yes." Pratt chuckles, he himself not knowing quite how to react. He moves over to Thomas and gets uncomfortably close to him. The two men are now just a foot apart from one another.

"You know dis man?" Delmar asks with a curious grin.

There is silence between Pratt and Thomas, a moment where both men are attempting to figure out how best to answer this question.

"How many am I cooking for?" Sarah's voice saves the day as she makes her way down the stairs. She moves over to Thomas, casually looking for an answer.

"There is a bathroom around the corner," Thomas keeps a blank stare and takes care of question number one. He waits, nervously with his stoic face, wondering if Pratt is going to call him out on their checkered past.

"Much obliged, sir," Pratt replies, his tone a convergence of respect and sarcasm.

Delmar is still curious and didn't get an answer to his question. Pratt walks away as if not knowing Thomas. Thomas doesn't look over his shoulder, not wanting to give anything away. His eyes flash up to the suspicious Delmar.

"You said for 10?" he asks.

"Yes, bredda. Please. We pay for the food. I insist." Delmar is respectful in his response but continues on his suspicious track. He bends his head just slightly to the side and looks closely at Thomas. Thomas doesn't bat an eyelash.

Zander breaks the silence by popping in through the kitchen door.

"Henry needs the black tool box," Zander says.

"Zander?" Thomas is surprised by his presence.

"I fix things. Fixed many a boat. Hank got me. Said I could earn a few extra."

Thomas nods. "All right."

"He wants you to stay inside." Zander's eyes flash over to Delmar, the insinuation being it is Thomas's job to keep an eye on the strangers and protect the house.

Thomas subtly nods. Delmar gets up and moves to the back door.

"I'm going to check on the ship," the large Jamaican says to Thomas. He gives Thomas one last suspicious glare, not feeling all that comfortable with the current situation. He senses something is wrong and he is right. Delmar disappears out the back door.

"I'll go get that for you," Thomas nods to Zander and walks into the living room. He nearly walks right into Pratt who is returning from the bathroom.

"Thomas Dent," Pratt says with a sadistic smile in a low tone.

"Pratt. I never thought I'd see *you* again."

"Because you left me for dead?"

"I just hoped I would never see you again," Thomas states, staring at Pratt with a sarcastic smile. Pratt sports his own smile, the evil-laced grin of a villain.

"You could have grabbed my hand, Dent," Pratt states.

"I go by Thomas Bullocks now. I'm respectable."

"Oh, you are?" Pratt chuckles and shakes his head. "Bullocks? As in Officer Bullocks?"

Thomas is quiet, not wanting to respond. He looks over his shoulder, making sure no one is hearing.

"Oh, you didn't," Pratt laughs, momentarily bending over at the waist. He brings his index finger to his lips, shaking his head. He is thoroughly amused. "Of all the things *we* have done—you and I together and apart, all those evil things, I've never come close to stealing a man's life as my own. You definitely one-up'd me, Dent." Pratt puts his hands up, "I mean, Bullocks." He cackles and shakes his head. "Well done."

"Why are you here?"

"Lost at sea, my friend. Wouldn't be here if I didn't need to be; back in New Jersey at the scene of my greatest achievements. Am I still wanted? They offering a reward?"

"Leave, Pratt. Leave this place and never return."

"Tommy?" Zander calls from the other room, wondering where he is.

"Yeah, *Tommy*. Get on going. Run your errand—errand boy," Pratt gives Thomas about as much sarcasm as he can with his words.

Thomas shakes his head and hesitates, wanting to bury Pratt where he stands. He grits his teeth behind his closed mouth, his cheeks pulsating just slightly. The moment passes and he thinks better of a confrontation in his own living room. He remembers himself and returns back to his new sanity.

"I need to get some tools for your ship, sir," Thomas respectfully states.

Pratt smiles and watches Thomas scurry away. Plans galore flash through his evil mind.

Nineteen

SEATED around the kitchen table are Pratt, Sarah and Thomas. There is a fourth place setting with hot mashed potatoes and beef. Thomas and Sarah are each picking at their food. Pratt is guzzling the meal down as if he hadn't eaten in days. He is almost giddy as he soaks in the awkwardness of the situation for Thomas.

"Sarah, I should go outside and help…" Thomas starts, wanting to leave the table as quickly as possible.

"I told you, eat first, Thomas. You need your strength. You're needed up in the tower." Thomas nods and reluctantly keeps on eating.

Pratt can't resist and chuckles, amused by Sarah pulling rank on Thomas.

"Is something funny…I'm sorry, what was your name again?" she asks.

"Just Pratt will do, ma'am."

"Mr. Pratt. Was there something amusing?" Sarah comes back and asks the question directly at the sinister man, wanting more answers from the stranger at her table.

"No, ma'am—just enjoying the fine meal. Thank you for your hospitality."

"You're paying for it." Sarah is cold in her response.

Delmar enters the kitchen through the back door.

"Thank you for the food. The men are gonna keep working on the ship and eat after. They have the food and the women chose to stay aboard the ship. They be more comfortable there. But they sure are liking your cookin', miss." Delmar goes out of his way to rain respect upon Sarah. He has a big smile as he sits by the open place setting of food.

"Thank you." Sarah is reluctant to even reply, but does so, respectfully returning Delmar's compliments. She sets her fork down as the three men eat. She sees Thomas shifting in his seat, an odd angry scowl on his face and the slight shaking in his right hand as he holds his fork. Then she catches his eyes flash at Pratt. These are eyes she has never seen before. They are the eyes of an angry man. Thomas's eyes flash back over to Sarah and he sees her staring at him. He buries his face back down into his food.

Delmar is playing the same game as Sarah. He is also looking upon Thomas and Pratt. He is trying to get a read on how exactly the two men are connected.

"I sure do appreciate this food, ma'am," Pratt states with a big smile on his face.

Everyone ignores Pratt. Sarah does a subtle head nod, but she does not like the man enough to verbally reply; even to a compliment.

"Mr. Delmar, right?" Sarah asks of the Jamaican man.

"Yes, ma'am?" he replies.

"How much longer until your ship is fit to sail?"

"Sarah, honey," Thomas starts but is cut off immediately by Sarah's hand. She is in no mood for games. Whatever dark cloud has been brought by these strange men, she wants it to blow back out to the ocean from where it came.

"How long?" She again asks.

"I think a couple of hours. The boys have the mast in a good spot. Shouldn't be long now," Delmar states. He looks the table over, sensing all the tension.

"Good," Sarah takes her fork and picks at the food as if she is sifting through sand. It's only a few moments before she gives up and looks up.

"How you two know each other?" Delmar asks again. He is looking at Thomas and Pratt, trying to piece things together as if he were Sherlock Holmes. His eyes are bouncing back and forth between the men.

"What do you mean?" Thomas asks.

"There is something about you two. Very, very strange." The Jamaican can't help himself.

"I agree," Sarah chimes in, intent on figuring things out herself.

Thomas's eyes flash over at Sarah, surprised she would pile on top of Delmar's accusations; true or not.

"We do know each other," Pratt starts.

Thomas snaps his head over at the villain. He can't reply to Pratt and give anything away and at the same time is anxiously waiting on his former partner's next words. Thomas's eyes beg for mercy as his face narrows in anger and hatred.

"Yes. You do. You do know each other, don't you, duppy?" Delmar sits back, waiting for Pratt to give an answer.

"Thomas was an officer. I was wrongfully accused of a crime and our paths crossed for just a moment in time," Pratt begins. Thomas watches the theatrics just as Delmar and Sarah do, unsure of what the serpent-tongued man will say next. "There was a gunrunner I ran with. He went mad and shot his competition dead. I had no idea what was happening. I was innocently seated in the car. He was supposedly making business for us; or so I thought. So, when the police came, they brought me in and threw the book at me; that is, until a few good witnesses came through and got me off. Now I'm here; moved on. And I see the good Officer Bullocks has moved on as well. Isn't that right, Tommy?"

Thomas takes one more long lasting stare at Pratt, trying to decipher his angle. He doesn't take too long, though. He jumps in to back up Pratt's story. "Our paths crossed in an eyelash of time; just for a moment. I thought that was you. I'm glad to see you're doing well. Things are going your way, now."

"Well, I don't want to be one to brag, but Del and I are doing pretty well. We hit a couple of speed bumps along the way up, but all seems good now," Pratt proudly boasts, his cocky endless smile projecting off his long villainous face. His jaw waggles down low with this smile, one that Thomas wishes he could punch right off Pratt's face.

"Sarah!" the distant call from Jackson is heard.

"Excuse me." Sarah gets up and rushes to the stairs, heading up toward Jackson's calls.

There is a knock at the door. One of the Jamaican crew pokes his head inside.

"Boss, the ship is almost ready. Want a look?"

"Excuse me, gentlemen," Delmar excuses himself as well. He heads out the back door.

Pratt and Thomas are left at the table. Pratt sits back with a victorious smile on his face.

"Well-well-well, I bet that surprised you."

"What is your game, Pratt?"

"Bygones be bygones. All water under the bridge. Maybe we can start a new partnership?" Pratt smiles, an evil strategy-session smile exposing a real truth. He interlocks his fingers and looks over his shoulder, making sure both he and Thomas are all alone. He leans forward, his elbows becoming stilts for his body on the dining room table as he gets as close as he can to Thomas. "We kill the big black man and we toss the crew. Hire a new bunch and we run rum from the Caribbean all the way to the doorsteps of the good folks in Philadelphia, Atlantic City and New York. I even have a contact in Florida now. It's all there. I could use a good partner."

"You could-could you?" Thomas sits back in his chair and shakes his head. "You're something."

"Oh, I know," Pratt sits back his chair, his arms placed upon the armrests as if he were a king. He glows with confidence and oozes evil.

"You come into my house and tell my story. You want me to go back to the world I left behind a long time ago. I don't want that life anymore."

"A long time ago? Tommy, boy…it was just a bit ago." Pratt glares, his eyes calling Thomas out for the man he was.

"Leave me alone, Pratt."

"I know you. Don't forget that. I know you have killed. I saw it with my own two eyes; you murdered a man. I've seen you steal. I've seen you beat men to the last strand of their lives just to steal a meal. Oh, I know you, Thomas Dent. I know you all too well."

"I'm not that man anymore," Thomas asserts.

"Looks like the same reflection to me."

Thomas leans forward, an intense look on his face. He has had enough of Pratt's games.

"If you ruin my life again, I'll bury you in that sand. I'll use both my hands and bury you as deep as I can go. Nobody will ever find you. You will disappear and nobody will know where you went. Nobody will even care."

Pratt's *royal* smile lowers, gravity forcing it into his more normal cocky grin. "Well, I can see you are no longer a businessman. You've gone on to playing house with a woman and her child."

Thomas angrily rises to his feet, standing up in an aggressive manner. He holds himself there, on the edge of insanity; his fists clinched, the veins in his neck pulsating with rage.

"There you are, Thomas. There you truly are," Pratt takes pleasure in bringing the worst out of Thomas.

"Go away."

"You could have set things up nicely here from the shore. The whole world is around you. You could have made a lot of money, Dent. But go ahead, you live your life and I'll live mine." Pratt rises from the table. "Nice knowing ya."

Thomas watches as Pratt exits out the back door. He starts to calm himself and turns, seeing Sarah by the bottom of the stairs. She is accusing Thomas of numerous atrocities with her incriminating glare. Her eyes speak a thousand unspoken words. She turns, whirling away, angrily storming back up the stairs.

Thomas dips his head back, knowing after Pratt's boat is repaired, he will have a lot of repairing to do himself.

HENRY is seated upon a sea of headstones. He sits upon the grass before the headstone of Felicia Jones. The headstone reads:

Loving Wife, Mother and Amazing Woman (1857-1917).

"Hello, my love," Henry begins. He coughs. He brings his white cloth to his mouth, the force of the cough pushing small amounts of blood upon it. He looks the blood over and smiles. The smile isn't over the cloth or the blood. It is an acceptance of fate; a calm setting in. The man who has fought all his life takes a breath and looks at the grass growing around him. He peers across the headstones to a line of pines, their leaves a fantastic blend of red, orange, yellows, and still a few greens, dancing in the wind.

"What a life. What a life we have lived, Felicia. What a time we had. You should see Sarah. She is so strong. She is just like you. She has my stubbornness as a kicker." Henry chuckles and sits back. He looks around and closes his eyes, sticking his chin up into the wind, absorbing the life around him, drinking it up like a man parched and desperate to consume water. He breathes in the life around him and then looks back down at the headstone. He runs his hand along the grass, as if feeling for her spirit.

"I won't be long." Henry smiles at the ground around his fingers, a few tears running down from his eyes, off his cheeks, escaping to the grass below.

THERE are two distinct halves to the fall season by the New Jersey shoreline. There is the beginning where the summer's grip tries to reach deep into September and withers away some time in October. And then there is winter's preview; a sneak showing of the frigid air that is set to come and the deepest darkest heartbeat of the cold which sends chills down people's spines. Fall is a season caught in a classic game of tug-of-war. And by November, winter always wins.

It is nearing Thanksgiving and the weather is turning colder and colder. The makeshift jetty has done its best, weathering a few small storms and preventing the bay from filling with too much sea sand. But those storms pale in comparison to the beasts of the cold season set to make appearances—one after another.

The change in weather has Thomas concerned for the safety of the tower and his new adopted family. Other items plague Thomas with even greater worry. As he stands atop the chilly tower, the wind whipping all around, coughing and more coughing fills the air like a sick symphony. The song is a depressing one, as Thomas knows Henry is succumbing to much more than a bad cold. He hasn't made his way up the steps to the top of the tower in two weeks. Thomas has worked the nights all by himself as Henry helps with small duties down below. But most of the time, Thomas sees Henry's body wilting in time right before his eyes. He has lost weight and the mighty proud man can no longer thrust his chest forward and power through his life. Age and health have become enemies to Henry. Thomas has a front-row view of it.

Thomas shakes his head, wanting the sad thoughts to leave. He moves downstairs and periodically hears the coughing as he makes his way to the bottom. He stops a few steps up, watching as Henry sweeps.

"You need to use the bathroom?" Henry asks.

Thomas sees the blood stained rag sticking out of Henry's pocket. It is common now and there is little need to hide it.

"I don't think the medicine that Doc Palmer gave you is helping. Can I fetch him and he can maybe try something else?"

"You stare at me as if I were already buried, boy. You stare at me with sad long eyes. Do I look that sad? Am I that pathetic to you?" Henry continues to sweep. He can't stop. He doesn't know how to hit a pause button. He works and works some more, glancing up with vigorous looks to challenge Thomas's deductions about his physical state.

"I can take care of this. You taught me to take care of this. We can get another assistant. We're supposed to have two—,"

"Enough!" Henry barks with a deeply congested chest cavity. His words are coated with raspiness and phlegm. He wipes his mouth and peers angrily up at Thomas, his head still tilted to the ground. He isn't certain how he appears, but straight on, he is weak and old. So he keeps his head tilted down, his eyes fighting up, the only look of strength he has left in him. He has a scowl spread across his face, an angry look of a defiant man nearing the end. His eyes continue the conversation in silence.

Thomas sees the lion in Henry roar. It is a tired, injured roar, one that is meant to scare away all aggressors. But the roar is done out of fear—fear for what others will think if the lion can no longer stand his ground. It is a prideful display, one Thomas knows all too well from Henry. He swallows his concerns and slowly makes his way back up the stairs, no more words exchanged between the two. Henry sweeps and sweeps. He coughs periodically as Thomas makes the charge up Old Barney's 217 steps. The sounds of suffering below are like daggers poking at Thomas's heart. He does his best to hold his own head up and do his job—just as Henry taught him to. Echoing sounds of disease flutter to the top of the tower by way of the wind and haunt Thomas every minute he works.

HENRY is sitting on a rock as Jackson casts his line into the water. There is only one pole—one line in the water today. Henry lacks the energy to stand and hold his pole. He can no longer cast out his line into the ocean like a mighty fisherman. Instead, he is a spectator.

Jackson holds his fishing line steady, just as he was taught. It's been out in the water for nearly ten minutes, and then something changes. Jackson feels a tug, his face dropping in nervousness and excitement. He looks around, not knowing what to do.

Henry's eyes are half-closed, enjoying the sun and the air.

Jackson's pole bends and Henry hears the line squealing. He perks up like he was injected with adrenaline. Henry rises, his bones creaking, his hands shaking. He barely lifts his feet as he drags forward like an aging boxer; expressionless and beaten by time. He stumbles over to Jackson who nervously is trying to hold his line steady.

Henry positions himself behind Jackson, the two working hand-in-hand to try and draw the line in. There is a pull and then some give; pull and some give. The fight wages on, both Jackson and Henry glowing with anticipatory smiles, relishing the action. Together they pull and pull, and then a fish flies up out of the ocean, flapping violently. The large fluke is hooked and is battling hard to wiggle free. Jackson looks up at Henry with a huge smile, the mighty fluke being his first ever catch. They reel and reel, pulling the fish closer toward them. They lean back and the fish flops up out of the water, landing on the sand before them. Henry is out of breath, Jackson electric with excitement. They are bubbling with victory. The nearly seventeen pound fluke rests on its side upon the dirt. Jackson holds the line in his hand and turns to Henry.

"Look how big he is, Grandpa!" Jackson shouts with jubilation.

Henry is choked up, Jackson calling him *grandpa* for the first time. Tears well in his eyes as he forces through a proud smile. He pats Jackson on the back.

"You did it, son," the old man bursts with joy. He leans down and kisses Jackson atop his head, indescribable happiness filling his insides.

Jackson continues to smile and hold onto the fishing line. Henry grabs his fishing glove and a bucket of water he had ready *just in case* they nabbed a fish. It's time to *bucket* their catch.

"YOU can't ignore me forever," Thomas's voice is like a decaying breeze for Sarah. She washes the dishes as he stands by a doorframe in the dining room, gazing fondly upon her. She doesn't react. He is white noise and is not a confrontation worth having at the moment. Her scars run deep. But Thomas isn't there for his own salvation. He has other plans in mind.

"I'm worried about Hank. He isn't well."

Sarah washes dish after dish, her hands infused with the anger swirling down to her fingertips. She is firm with the dishes and makes them clink so loudly, it pushes the china to their breaking point.

"Can I help you with that?" Thomas moves by the sink, looking to help Sarah.

"I got it."

"Here, I can dry," Thomas offers, picking up the drying towel.

Sarah stops washing the dishes and turns, facing Thomas with authority. She is annoyed and angry. Her hand moves to her hip, her head slightly shakes and the look of epic disapproval is showering down upon Thomas.

"I got it," she barks with an anger-filled glare.

Thomas nods, taking the hint.

"Listen, he's sick. He's really ill. If you don't want to talk to me, that's fine. But your dad is dying. I'm watching it happen. Every day that passes, a little bit of his life is chipped away. His eyes are more sunken. I can see his cheeks pushing against his skin. He's aged a lot. He's gained ten years when he should have only gained ten months. You don't see it? You don't—,"

"You don't think I see it?! You don't think I know?! I've spoken to the doctor. I've seen the blood on his handkerchief. There is no cure, Thomas. There is only the end!" Tears well in Sarah's increasingly glossy eyes. "There's only the end," she says more solemnly now. Sarah turns away, her emotions overwhelming her.

Thomas steps forward and opens his arms up. He starts to console Sarah, pulling her in close as she cries. She tries to push him away at first; a feeble attempt at best. She concedes her pain and wraps her arms around him with two clinched fists. She has a good cry and Thomas stands still, enduring the sadness, absorbing as much pain as he can from Sarah. After a few moments, she slowly leans back and sniffles.

Sarah steps back and pulls the small flowered drapes open in front of the sink. She looks out at the ocean, staring at Jackson casting into the water. Seated down on a large rock is Henry, his now normal position to watch the young man as he fishes alone. No longer is Henry casting out to sea. No longer is he standing, holding his pole with excitement and anticipation. He is a spectator for the event, his arms firmly wrapped inside his large comfortable wool jacket.

"He just watches now. He used to love to fish. My greatest memory of my father, the one that sticks out most, was when he taught me to fish. I must have been four or five at best. He went through it all—how to bait the line, why we were using pieces of raw meat. He showed me how to work the pole—how to cast out to *just* the right spot. He showed me how to hold the pole and he told me to never speak when the pole was out there. He said, *Sarah, you remember when you play telephone with your mother? When you put the plastic cup to your ears and all you had is one long string attached carrying that sound? That string on your pole will do the same thing. If you talk too much, your voice will carry out to sea and scare those fish away. So we only whisper. We talk low so we don't scare the fish away.* And we did. We would whisper to one another by the water's edge. I remember that like it was yesterday; my dad, young and strong. He hadn't disappeared in the far away land yet. He was still here and we whispered to one another every day. He was just an assistant then; learning the job here. He was funny like that. Maybe it's true, I don't know. But I remember him at sunrise casting into the ocean. He would delay the morning lens cleaning to cast with me. He always went back and finished his list that he had for the morning, though. He never skipped a step, even if it meant him getting less sleep. He *always* did the job."

"I know it well," Thomas jokes, his head tilting down to the ground, nodding with a smile on his face.

"He's like that. But he took the time at least once a week to show me how to fish. He looked so big and strong to me. He was such a figure out there; a force of a man. And now I look through the kitchen window and I see him sitting next to Jackson. He has been whittled away by life's cruel hand. He is leaving us one day at a time. He is leaving me right after I got to know him again." Sarah stops for a moment, thinking to herself. "And then there's you," she starts, turning her attention to Thomas. She is looking him square in the eyes, her demeanor changing from sadness to anger. "You lied. Does my father know you lied?"

"You father told me to be the man I wanted to be. The past didn't matter. I told him. He knows everything. He knows who I was. But I am not that man anymore, Sarah. I grew up. We all have to grow up some time. Your father helped me become a man. I'm not Thomas Dent, anymore. I'm Thomas Bullocks, a good man."

Sarah shakes her head as it drops slightly to her right shoulder. She looks off to the side at nothing in particular, digesting Thomas's pleas.

"He knows. But I don't?"

"I was scared. I'm still scared. It's not an excuse. I just have never been a stand-up kind of guy. I've never made good choices; until now. Up until I got here, I was nothing. Then something happened. Your father showed me what it was to be a man and hold a job. He showed me what it was to have respect for something greater than yourself. I believed in him and what he was doing. I believe in the tower. So I grew up. I learned to be a better version of myself and nothing I am is a lie except for a name. And your father taught me something about that too. He said, *it's not the name that makes the man, it's what that man does that makes his name.* I believe in that. And then I met you. All I've done is work hard and share with you who I am."

"Not your past!" Sarah calls Thomas out.

"You want to know that I've started and stopped writing a letter to a widow for a man I killed when I was sixteen? He had a child—they had a life. We fought and I killed him. I grew up the son of a sailor. My father became a captain. I often was on the ship since my mother passed away when I was young. I saw my father forcibly take women. I saw him kill men and women alike. I saw him steal. He was a bad man. He was a pirate; a common thief. When his crew held a mutiny and killed him, they spared me. They sent me ashore in Mississippi. I had nothing but the clothes on my back. I was a kid. I stole. I did what I had to do to survive. I was a street rat for a long time. I finally made my way up north after I killed that man. I was going to try to get into a new kind of business. That's when I met Pratt. I was waiting outside when he murdered men inside a drinking hole. The police came and took us both in. I had nothing to do with it. I didn't know what he had done. But I figured I was just paying for all my past sins. I could accept it. There was a storm. I survived and I made it here. I figured God was giving me a second chance. I finally had a path that I could touch. For the first time in my life, I felt inspired. If you want to hate me forever for my past, I can live with that. I hate myself for it. But every day I try to make up for who I was by being that much better. Maybe someday it will all even out."

Sarah consumes Thomas's every last word. She looks down and takes a step forward. She places her hand on the side of his face. She looks up into his eyes, the two staring longingly at the other.

"Thank you," she says in a whispered, exasperated tone. With those two perfectly stated words, Thomas feels a sense of vindication.

Jackson comes bursting into the room "Help me! It's Hank!"

Sarah looks out the window and sees Henry lying on his side, slumped over on the sand. Thomas races outside, followed by Sarah and Jackson. They run to Henry's side.

BED rest isn't a place for a strong man. However, when it's doctor's orders, you have no choice. Lying under the comfort of sheets day after day isn't the life someone chooses to live. Henry Jones, in all his past glories, a war hero, a lighthouse keeper who manned a tower by himself for long periods of time, a father, a husband, a fisherman, a man who has done so much in his life, isn't meant to lie helplessly in a bed slowly decaying away from the inside out. With the seeds of death planted, it isn't *if* Henry will pass on, it is *when*.

Days pass and winter comes. With the cold moving in, Henry has gone to allowing Zander to sleep in one of the spare bedrooms. He has caved with age and time against him; compassion is filling his soul. There was one catch: Thomas needed to teach him about the lighthouse and teach him to swim. Happily, Thomas started Zander on the same learning program Henry put him through with additional swimming lessons in frigid cold water. The two men worked tirelessly together.

CHRISTMAS arrives just as quickly as Thanksgiving passed. Henry barely makes it down the stairs for Christmas supper, picking at his food. His appetite is thinning as quickly as his frame. He is coughing and mucus and blood are filling cloths. He is weak and January is hard on him. Thomas spends a lot of his free time with Henry. He reads to him when he floats in and out of consciousness. He sits by his bedside sharing stories of the tower and his daily job duties. He reviews his logs with Henry as if he was still manning the tower himself. He shares nearly every minute of his life with Henry. And on one late January morning, Henry becomes more lucid. He awakens as Thomas is reviewing the logs.

"And then, I of course, wiped down the lens and feather dusted it perfect, just as you would. I showed Zander how to clean the lens today. He is picking everything up so fast. I had a good teacher." Thomas smiles to himself. He doesn't expect any exchange with Henry as the old man's words have lessened day by day. After a moment, Thomas continues. "I smell a storm in the air. The clouds are moving angrily, coming in from the south. I think we got a good storm ahead. Heavy snow I'm thinking."

"Thomas," Henry begins.

Thomas freezes, his eyes panning up to Henry with excitement and joy. It is a rare opportunity to hear him speak these days. It is even rarer to have the words mean something. And right now, Henry's eyes are wide open as if he turned back the clock for just a moment.

"Yes, Hank?" Thomas almost jumps out of his chair to continue the conversation with his idol.

"Thank you. I wanted to say thank you." Henry's eyes flutter as he stares at Thomas with a half-smile.

"It's no problem. I'm just doing my job." Thomas reaches forward and grabs one of Henry's thinned hands. His fingers are becoming brittle, death looming upon his doorstep. Thomas leans forward like an excited child at a carnival.

"No. Not that," Henry struggles to roll onto his side and coughs. He reaches for his handkerchief on the nearby table. His hand reaches slowly, little strength left in his shoulders to sustain his own body weight. Thomas quickly reaches for it and gives it to him, trying to hold it by his mouth. Henry, being the proud man, pushes Thomas's hand away. Henry takes the cloth into the palm of his own hand. He coughs and coughs. No blood comes out this time as he slowly removes the cloth away from his mouth. He is almost surprised as he inspects it with his half-closed eyes. He shifts onto his back and swallows, the coughing robbing him of his spit. He needs to gather himself once again so he can speak. He takes a moment and composes himself.

"Do you need some water?" Thomas asks.

Henry waves him off and gathers enough saliva to continue the conversation. "I want to tell you something. It is important to me. I want you to know this. *I give you my blessing,*" he states with increased vigor, his eyes bulging open for these five words.

Thomas's brows pull forward, his mouth hangs open, he stops all his train of thoughts to focus in on this moment.

"I give you my blessing with Sarah," he states with further clarification. "I don't know if you two will end up together, but if you do, you have my blessing." Henry reaches out and takes Thomas's hand in his own. He squeezes it tightly. "You are a good man, Thomas Dent." Henry grinds his teeth and uses his free hand to help himself lift up off the bed, leaning up toward Thomas. He stares intensely into his eyes. "Be the man you want to be—be the man you are, not the man you once were."

"Okay."

Henry clinches Thomas's hand just a bit tighter. "It's okay, Thomas."

"Yeah. I know. Thank you."

"No. The past. It's okay. Your father, it wasn't your fault. The things you had to do to survive, it made you the good man you are today. It's okay."

"I know. Thank you."

"NO!" Henry shouts, digging deep inside him for the gargled yell. "You are a good man. Say it."

"I know."

"No! Say it!"

"I'm a good man," Thomas says it in a melancholy tone, unsure of what Henry wants.

"Believe it. Believe it as I believe in you. Say it again."

"I'm a good man," again Thomas is bland.

"Say it again!"

"I'm a good man."

"Again!"

"I'm a good man!" Tears start to form in Thomas's eyes.

"Again!"

"I'm a good man!"

"Again!"

"I'm a good man!" a tear rolls down the side of Thomas's face.

"Now, come here." Henry opens up his arms.

Thomas leans in and hugs Henry. Henry wraps his arms around Thomas.

"You are the son I never saw grow up. I'm so proud of you, Thomas. I'm so very proud of you." Henry sniffles. "I'm so proud of you, son. You are a great man."

Thomas closes his eyes, clinching Henry, tears rolling down his cheeks. Thomas continues to hug tightly until he feels Henry's arms loosen around his back. They grow limp. Thomas slowly leans back, wiping the tears from his eyes. He looks Henry over, concerned he just spoke his last words. He leans down and listens for a heartbeat; he listens for a pulse. Deep grumbling sounds are faintly heard. It builds in strength. Thomas leans back with a smile on his face as Henry snores; his gargled congested chest causing the sound to be deep and bellowing. Thomas rises up from the side of the bed and tucks Henry in. He leans down and kisses him on the forehead.

"Sleep well, Hank," he whispers.

Thomas quietly leaves the room.

Twenty

SLEET and hail are falling from the sky. The dark clouds have converged into one big ominous storm. The wind is blowing and making visibility nearly impossible. Thomas is staring out from the top of the lighthouse trying to see through the wicked weather. He shakes his head, unable to see anything.

"This is terrible," he mutters.

Zander comes walking up the stairs, shivering, his keeper coat covered with stray pieces of ice. He is dressed in the uniform of the lighthouse keeper, just as Thomas is dressed.

"It's bad out there," he comments.

Thomas is still looking through the spyglass, trying to see anything out in the grey-washed ocean.

"Why didn't you tell me?" he asks.

"Tell you what?" Zander is confused and has a perplexed expression on his face.

"Why didn't you tell me about the job at The Sunset? You could have told me. We could have got you training here quicker."

"No. You couldn't have," Zander confidently states.

Thomas lowers the spyglass and turns to Zander. "You still think Hank is against you because of your skin?"

"Nah. He hates everyone pretty fairly. He's just stubborn and follows the rules; most of the time. When I helped rebuild that ship with those fellows that came ashore in the fall, that's when we got to talkin'. Once he knew what I knew, and saw my handiwork on fixing that vessel, he knew then. He made me wait as he is prone to do an extra month. But when he invited me into the house he already couldn't make it up these stairs. He didn't hire me for me. He hired me for you. He knew he wasn't feeling well. He was taking care of you, Thomas. He loves you like a son. I see how he looks at you. He sees himself in you. What he wants is for you to be the best man you can be."

Zander's words are striking and hit Thomas's emotional core. He nods, digesting all that his good friend has to say. It makes him sentimental and almost well up.

"Head back over to the house. Stay warm. It's probably going to be a very long night for us. The storm is only going to get worse."

"You sure?"

"Yeah. Head back. I'm good." Thomas goes back to looking through the telescope, surveying the rough sea waters.

Zander nods and heads down all 217 steps. He reaches the bottom and hears the roaring of the wind whistling inside the lighthouse. He hears the sleet and rain pounding the tower. The storm sounds awful and mad. Zander opens up the lighthouse door, his face immediately swamped by sleet and freezing rain blowing sideways. He struggles out into the chaos and closes the door behind him. He marches through sand covered snow and ice. The terrain isn't nearly as bad as the visibility. Zander can barely see in front of him, guarding his face from the flying pellets of hail being hurled down from the sky above. He stumbles along through the wind and makes his way over to the keeper's house. He struggles in through the backdoor and is almost out of breath from the short journey.

Sarah is standing by the dining room table.

"It's awful out there," Zander comments, covered in ice and a few snowflakes.

She is staring into the living room, her face drawn and her mouth open. She is breathless and not moving. Zander recognizes the odd expression.

"Sarah?" he asks with concern.

She doesn't say anything. She stares straight into the living room with the same frozen look on her face. She isn't moving. As Zander slowly walks forward, he clears the wall and his eyes search for whatever it is that is bothering Sarah. Then he sees it; he sees what's wrong. Pratt is standing, holding a knife to Jackson's throat. Pratt is wet and cold from outside, his clothing torn up and his face dirtied. A pool of water has formed around his feet. Two other thugs are standing behind him, men of similar ilk. The two roughnecks are both unshaven and look just as dangerous as Pratt.

"What are you doing here?" Zander asks, his eyes flared open with concern.

"I'm in a bit of a pickle. I'm gonna need your hands, black man," Pratt requests.

Zander and Sarah share a look of concern.

"All right. I'll help you. Just let the young man go. He ain't done nothin' to ya."

"You tryin' to negotiate with me, boy?"

"No, sir. Just tryin' to help you," Zander attempts to keep Pratt's nerves calm.

"Oh, *you* gonna help me, boy. You definitely gonna help me. But the kid here, he is gonna stay."

Zander lets out a nervous exhale.

THOMAS continues to look out at the raging sea. The water is pushing closer and closer to the coast. He finally sees a ship in the chaos.

"What in the world?" Thomas tries to focus through the spyglass. He sees a 5 masted ship bobbing in the chaotic waters.

From below, footsteps are coming up the tower stairs. One by one the footsteps are getting closer and closer.

"Zand, we got a boat out there!" Thomas continues to focus on the ship, calling back over his shoulder but staying focused out to sea. "I recognize that ship. I know that boat," he says out loud to himself. Thomas pans his view, something catching his eye. He sees a man that looks like Zander in the keeper's uniform down by the jon boat, pulling it out toward the water with two other men he doesn't recognize. "What the heck?" Thomas asks in a world of confusion. He then slowly pulls the spyglass away from his eye.

The footsteps stop behind Thomas and he slowly leans his head back, his mouth dropping open, wondering who is behind him if Zander is outside. He hears the ominous sound of water dripping on the floor below, pooling on the ground. Drip-drip-drip.

"Mr. Bullocks. Finally, I find you," the dark voice is oh-so-familiar to Thomas. It sends immediate chills down his spine. He slowly turns and sees the man responsible for the villainous tone. Just as surprised as Thomas is to see Whitmore, the evil man is equally surprised to see Thomas.

"Dent?" Whitmore states with confusion. He is sopping wet, marinated heavily in the storm. His eye patch and unshaven face make him look like a pirate. He is not the polished cruel officer he once was. Now he is a scruffy dark dirtied man of the night.

"I can't get away from this," Thomas mumbles to himself in utter awe of the man standing before him.

"You can't be a lighthouse keeper. This can't be you. You are a criminal. You are a criminal at large!" Whitmore grits his teeth in anger, his eyebrows arching, readying for a fight.

"I'm a different man now, Whitmore. What are you doing here?"

"I came to confront Bullocks," Whitmore says, taking out his favorite bullwhip. "I was going to kill him. But now I find you and I see a different path. Instead of vengeance I can become a hero again. I can get my job back," Whitmore details his new plan out loud, thinking to himself.

"You were fired?"

"Yes. Because of you. Because of Bullocks. Because of an unfortunate storm. All of this doesn't matter anymore, Dent. All that matters is I'm going to bring you to justice, dead or alive. The choice is yours." Whitmore talks big with an angered-filled smirk.

"Then I guess we'll see who's left standing." Thomas's eyes glance over to the wood box on the floor where Henry keeps the emergency gun.

"I was hoping you would say that," Whitmore has an excited villainous tone and snaps the whip in the air.

SARAH is sitting on the couch with Jackson by her side. One of the two thugs is standing beside her with a pistol drawn. He is pacing in the room, staring at Sarah as if she were a piece of meat.

"You're one fine, lady," the thug says.

Sarah turns away, disgusted. Jackson buries himself further into her arms, curling his body up into hers.

"This is a nice place you have here," the thug states.

There is a creak upstairs, the wood above their heads sounding an alarm that someone is moving about.

"Who's up there?" the thug asks, paranoid.

"No one," Sarah intensely stares back, not wanting to give away her dying father's position.

The man's eyes are flared open as he tries to look up the stairs and then back at Sarah and Jackson. He doesn't know what to do, torn between needing to watch them and wanting to see if anyone else is upstairs.

"We have a cat," she hurls out in hopes the lie will stick.

The thug isn't convinced as he glances back and forth. "Up. Both of you's. And over here." the thug says, using his gun to motion them to stand. Sarah and Jackson stand and tentatively move toward the man. "You lead the way. One false move and I start firing," he threatens. "Now move nice and slow," he states, breathing hot air onto Sarah's neck in a disgustingly seductive manner.

Sarah and Jackson slowly start to walk up the stairs ahead of the thug. She glances back, feeling his gun buried in her back.

The darkening house shakes, and sounds of the storm grow louder and stronger. The wind is whipping through and sleet is slamming against the sides of the house and the window. It is an eerie sound as the creaks of the stairs only add to the cacophony of horrifying early evening sounds.

Step by step they move slowly up the stairs. As they reach the second level, Sarah keeps Jackson right in front of her, holding his arms, steering him along.

"Stop," the thug states. It is dark atop the stairs, no lanterns to light the way. "We need some light. I can't see so well in the dark."

"They're downstairs," Sarah states. "The lanterns aren't up here."

"Then go get them. I'll watch the boy." The thug reaches out and grabs the silent Jackson by his shoulders, now holding on to Sarah's prize possession. He stares intensely at Sarah, showing he is capable of doing the worst things imaginable.

"If you hurt a hair on his body…" Sarah begins, letting her threat marinate in the darkening cold air.

"You should be worrying about your own body, miss," the thug looks Sarah up and down, once again insinuating carnal intentions with her.

Sarah crouches down and looks Jackson in the eyes. "Jackson, be brave. I'll be right back."

Jackson subtly nods, his face mostly stoic. His chin is dipping forward into his chest, his eyes pointing right at the ground, concealing deathly fear over the situation. Sarah hesitates just for a moment, not wanting to go. The thug raises his gun up into the air to add extra incentive.

"Quickly now," he urges.

Sarah nods and rushes down the stairs. She disappears into the darkness to go retrieve some light. The thug is left alone with Jackson.

"What's the matter boy, you don't speak much?" the thug asks, nervously holding his gun out, his eyes as open as they can be as he attempts to see in the dark. Dusk has come and gone, the storm already pushing the world into darkness well ahead of schedule. The house shutters and shakes and the creaking makes the thug nervous. He spins around, holding Jackson tightly against him and points his gun down the hall. He can't see anything but futilely tries. He clearly is unnerved by the situation. Another creak and he spins around. His hand is shaking as he holds the gun.

"I know you're here!" the thug shouts, frightened, with an itchy trigger finger.

Ice is pulverizing the roof of the keeper's house, causing the thug to look up. His face drags long, his mouth opened, his cheeks pulling in, the whites of his eyes popping in the dark. Another creak and he swings aground.

"Who's there, dammit?!" he shouts, seeing nothing.

Jackson acts, smacking the gun right out of the thug's hand.

"Hey!" the thug yells. Jackson takes off as the thug searches frantically in the dark on the floor for the gun. He can't find it at first, his hands combing the ground like a blind man searching for his cane. He searches and searches until he hears the cocking of a rifle behind him; the large hammer clicking back into a ready position.

The man slowly turns, seeing a shadowed figure standing with the large gun. Leaning against the wall, Henry, using all his strength to stand, has the rifle out before him. The thug slowly raises his hands and rises to his feet. Lightning strikes outside and the brief light shines upon Henry's diseased-looking face. His eyes are sunk, his cheeks pulled back as if purposely trying to highlight his bone structure. Dried blood has stained one side of his mouth as fresh blood drips down his lips to his chin. His grey thinned hair is tangled and frayed. He is wearing a white blood-stained T-shirt and his pajama pants. Henry himself, holding the rifle, is a horror movie, looking more like a crazed vampire than a man.

"Easy, old man," the thug nervously states. He doesn't quite know what to think of Henry.

"Easy this, you son of a bitch." Henry fires his rifle, the blast striking the thug, knocking him back down to the ground. The thug wails in pain, the bullet tearing through one of his shoulders. Henry takes a step forward, refocusing himself and then recocking the gun.

"Who are you, old man?" the injured thug holds his shoulder as he cowers on the ground. He puts his uninjured arm up before his face hoping it will act as a deterrent to a fatal blast.

"The last man who will ever hear the evil words drip from your serpent tongue." Henry, without hesitation, fires again. This blast ends the man's suffering and his life. Henry leans against the nearest wall, out of breath. His body slides down against the wall as if the gravity pull has increased. He helplessly shifts down to the ground. He reaches the floor and struggles to stay upright, coughing some more. More blood trickles out of his mouth and he slumps onto his side. Henry's eyes close, his body going unconscious.

SARAH races through the chaotic weather across the beach. She runs for her life, carrying Jackson in her arms. The wind and ice are furiously bringing all their might on this evening, nearly blowing her over. She struggles to maintain her balance as the waves thunder in the background, crashing wildly against the shore. She reaches the abandoned Oceanic Hotel and rushes to the back entrance. The ocean water strikes the deck right near her feet, causing Sarah to pause. She is out of breath and cold, staring nervously at the water as it has risen all the way to the deck and is threatening to encroach further. She looks around and realizes she has nowhere else to go. She will take her chances here. She races inside to get Jackson to safety and out of harm's way. They disappear into the confines of the abandoned structure.

THE jon boat struggles through the nasty storm and ocean's fury. Zander uses the paddles the best he can to steer them to the anchored five masted ship. The ship's masts are being ripped apart, the large boat struggling in the wild shallow waters. It is stuck on rocks and sea sand, the massive push of the storm piling the sand up at the ocean's bottom despite the efforts of the new jetty. The wind is blowing with such ferocity; pieces of wood are flying off the boat, the large structure being taken one small piece at a time. The shards of wood fly wildly through the air. With the boat stranded and breaking apart, Pratt is desperate.

A single man is on the ship awaiting Pratt, ducking down by the ship's edge. The ship creaks and snaps in the storm, the entire vessel sounding as if it is about to be ripped in half.

"We have to hurry, sir!" the man on the ship respectfully shouts to Pratt. He struggles to stand, tossing a rope ladder down. Pratt grabs on to the ladder with his hands.

"We have to get the rum barrels off the ship!" Pratt shouts. He looks back down at the jon boat and stares at Zander and his other thug.

"Shoot him if he moves," Pratt orders the thug.

"Happily," the thug smiles, relishing an opportunity to shoot someone. Pratt climbs up the ladder and aboard the broken down ship, helped by the man on the boat. Zander and the thug are left by themselves on the jon boat, bouncing up and down in the chaotic Atlantic. Each wave causes the jon boat to smack against the larger ship. Zander, holding the ores, is doing his best to keep the jon boat close but at a safe distance away from getting broken apart.

"We're all gonna drown!" Zander shouts to the man, struggling to remain safely seated inside the small skimmer boat.

"We'll see," the man flashes a sadistic smile, showcasing his missing and blackened teeth. "We have plans for you and your friends." The man takes great pleasure in issuing the veil threat.

There is the faint sound of Pratt shouting an order. Neither Zander nor the thug can make it out. The thug rises to his feet and looks up to see what is happening on the ship. Zander's eyes narrow as he suspiciously watches and listens. He is shivering as the storm ferociously rages with the continued pounding of near hurricane force wind and rain.

"Get rid of him!" Pratt shouts down, leaning over the edge of the ship. "We don't have room!"

Zander hears most of Pratt's orders and becomes alarmed. He looks left, then right, every which was to figure a way out of this.

The thugs smiles and turns to Zander, his chin up, his chest out, his arm extending out with his pistol. A huge gust of wind nearly blows the thug over as he struggles to just keep his balance. He holds on tight and then sees a splash. Zander is gone, diving down into the cold Atlantic. The thug moves over and searches the water and blindly fires once; then again. He looks all around the water and can't see anything but the cold dark unforgiving wavy Atlantic.

Under water, Zander swims as a couple of bullets whiz by. He can barely see under the churned up dark water. He looks and a large creature, a shark, passes right by his face, whizzing by him. Then it is gone. Zander freaks, trying to swim quickly away.

In the boat, the man continues to look for Zander, surveying the water with his pistol drawn. The jon boat is continuously smacking up against the side of the ship. The jon boat starts crack, the edges coming apart.

As the thug continues to survey the waters, a shark's fin appears and the thug becomes concerned.

"There are sharks down here!" he shouts in a panic.

He continues to look around and then hears the massive cracking of wood, like a tree snapping at its stump.

Pratt and the other man atop the boat shout. Suddenly, one of the large masts comes slamming down. The thug looks up and sees the mast fall right at him. He yells and dives off the ship. The huge piece of wood slams into the jon boat, destroying it on contact.

The thug nervously surveys the water as he bobs his head around. He sees the rope ladder and quickly swims toward it. He sees a distant shark fin and gets freaked out, swimming faster. He gets to the rope ladder and reaches up. He starts to go up when a large great white shark comes by and explodes out of the water, taking the thug and the rope ladder back down with him. He screams but the storm drowns out his yells. He is pulled down into the dark ocean and a pool of red blood starts to emerge atop the water as the man is dragged under and disappears.

Zander is by the side of the boat and sees a shark fin. He turns and quickly swims, his hands flailing as he tries to work to the front of the ship. A big wave strikes Zander and he goes under once again, struggling to swim. The torn off arm of the thug floats by him and bounces off the side of his face. He is panicked, and swims toward the anchor. Zander reaches the large rusted chain from the dropped anchor and climbs upon it. He clings to the chain just above the ocean's surface, holding on for dear life as the storm blows against him. He is shaking, both cold and scared, his eyes widened, out of breath, trying to ascertain his next move.

Pratt looks over the side of the ship and sees the crushed jon boat. "Dammit!" he yells. Pratt turns back to his badly wounded ship, multiple barrels of rum crushed, his deck filling with alcohol, the sea and rain water. With a huge mast hanging half off the ship, it is dead in the water. Barrels of rum sit helplessly on the damaged ship. Pratt's lone remaining helper is standing nearby with a dumbfounded look on his face. Pratt is enraged and doesn't know what to do. He looks up at the chaotic sky and shouts, his scream competing with the loud storm. He moves up to the man and grabs him by his shirt collar.

"Do something you fool! What am I paying you for?" Pratt shouts amidst the terrible weather.

"You can swim for it," the man hesitantly states, his neck slightly retracting, his head pulling back away from Pratt like a child expecting a slap from his father. "I prefer to ride out the storm here, sir."

"No. You will swim for it. You will go first." Pratt turns to the man and pulls out his gun. "I need to know if I can make it. I'll give you a barrel to hold onto!" Pratt shouts. "Get a barrel and toss it in!" The man rolls the barrel toward the ship's edge. He rolls it into the water and the rum barrel floats. The man looks back, his face sagging with fear, shivering from the cold. He doesn't want to jump in.

"It looks cold, sir," he states.

Pratt watches the barrel in the water and has an idea.

"Do we have rope?" Pratt asks.

"What's that?" the man, too cold and scared asks, not hearing the question the first time.

"Rope you fool!" Pratt repeats with an insult.

"Yes! Down in the galley!"

"Get it! You don't need to swim. We're going to build a raft!" Pratt excitedly states.

"Yes, sir!" The man rushes away, taking no chances with Pratt changing his mind. Pratt smiles, a devious grin, titling his head back, drinking in the bad storm as if he could weather anything God threw at him.

"What else you got?!" Pratt shouts at the sky, laughing, ice starting to form all around his face.

OUTSIDE on the watching gallery, THOMAS is slowly walking around the circle, the weather pounding him as he moves. Whitmore is laughing as he walks around, slowly following Thomas with his bullwhip hanging by his side.

"This is so poetic, Dent! It all has come down to you and me!" Whitmore shouts, throwing back his head, drinking in the terrible weather as if he forecasted it himself.

Thomas continues to move around the watch gallery, waiting for an opportunity to duck back inside through the open window. Once Whitmore clears a point, Thomas makes a run for it, quickly moving to the window. He reaches the open window and goes to hurl himself inside when the whip is snapped around his wrist.

"Still too slow, Dent!" Whitmore cackles, holding the whip.

Thomas, with the whip digging into his skin, grits his teeth and boils with inner rage. He shakes his head and yells out a mighty roar, stepping back outside. He uses the whip to his own advantage, yanking Whitmore forward, pulling the former jailhouse head guard right over the edge of the tower. Whitmore hangs over the metal railing, holding onto his bullwhip for dear life. The whip is still attached to Thomas's wrist. Thomas bends his head back in pain as the whip is firmly tightened around his flesh, digging in deeper and deeper with the increased pressure of Whitmore's dangling body weight.

"If I go, you go, Dent!" Whitmore shouts as he helplessly dangles off of the tall tower, the storm relentlessly battering the two men.

"I can live with that! Each of the last five seconds of my life…I can live with that!" Thomas shouts down, his head bending back, his eyes squinting shut. His entire shoulder is being strained; his arm in a tug of war between his own body weight and Whitmore's. Thomas growls, a furious inner growl of anger and disappointment in himself. He gives in and uses his other arm and slowly starts to pull Whitmore up. Each time he pulls Whitmore closer, an angry growl festers under his breath. With little choice and much reluctance, he pulls him closer and closer.

Whitmore, hanging on the other end, smiles, his eyes and stare narrowing into a sadistic grin, as he is slowly being pulled back up over the watch gallery's metal railing. The storm rages around them, pain and anguish raining down upon Thomas as he finishes pulling Whitmore up.

"Good choice, Dent," the evil man crows as he climbs over the railing.

Thomas reaches back and punches Whitmore across the jaw just as he clears the railing, knocking him to the ground. He then untangles the bullwhip off his wrist and tosses the whip out the window and it flies over the railing and down to the beach below.

Thomas turns back into Whitmore's punch which catches him across his jaw. He stumbles backward and quickly gathers himself.

"If you don't succeed," Whitmore begins, reaching inside his coat and pulling out another bullwhip which had been holstered inside his jacket. "…try, try again."

"You gotta be kidding me," Thomas remarks, shaking his head. He takes off and rushes down the tower stairs with Whitmore behind him.

The snap of the bullwhip unleashes the dangerous weapon, but it hits the cast iron railing, narrowly missing Thomas. It wraps up there as Whitmore makes his way down. Thomas runs, moving as quickly as he can down the stairs.

"Run you rat! Run-run away!" Whitmore shouts, his voice carrying through the inner walls of the tower. Whitmore's haunting voice is further enhanced by the wailing storm outside the tower.

Thomas doesn't look back. He races down to the bottom of the steps and runs to the door, pushing it open. He bursts out into the terrible weather, his face struck by the mighty wind and icy precipitation. Thomas's view is obscured, the harsh conditions making it difficult to see. A deepening fog is settling in on top of the nasty storm, making it nearly impossible to see anything more than a few feet in front of your face. Thomas blindly runs forward into the fog, charging ahead, away from Whitmore.

Twenty One

PRATT tosses another barrel of rum overboard. It slams into the water below, momentarily sinking before rising back up. He has his lone remaining crew member lying on a makeshift raft using 11 rum barrels tied together with rope. His thug grabs the last barrel in the water and begins to tie it off next to the others.

The thug looks up and sees the top of a shark fin circling around the makeshift raft. His eyes bulge open, frightened, watching the fin methodically disappear below the water's surface.

Pratt smiles and nods, the storm violently whipping against his face. "Is it sturdy?!" he shouts his question through the storm.

"Sturdy enough!" the nervous crewman shouts back, looking around with great concern.

A rope is hanging off the side of the boat. Pratt grabs it to head down to the makeshift raft. His thug is holding the rope, trying to keep it steady, but Pratt is struggling with the bad weather. With the rolling ocean getting rough, water is crashing up against the stalled ship and the makeshift raft. More snapping wood from the ship, sound additional alarm bells in the thug's head. He has had enough, his nerves getting the best of him. He uses a piece of wood and pushes off of the ship, the makeshift rum raft floating slowly toward shore, away from Pratt and the broken vessel.

"What are you doing?!" Pratt screams in anger, quickly pulling himself back up onto the boat.

"Every man for himself!" the thug shouts at Pratt. He uses the piece of wood to attempt to steer the raft.

Pratt yells in anger, jaw clinching, his hands straining into tight fists, as he attempts to come up with an idea—any idea that could help him. One strikes him and Pratt takes three steps back and charges forward, hurling himself off the side of the ship and jumping as far out into the water as he can. He lands just short of the barrels of floating rum.

The thug sees Pratt and his eyes widen, his mouth twists in disbelief over the insane act. He watches, wondering if Pratt will emerge out of the icy Atlantic or if he is dead. He is holding the piece of wood up into the chaotic air, readying it to strike Pratt if he emerges out of the water. A pistol shot. Then another. The shots are coming up from underneath the raft. The thug moves around but has nowhere to go and is now frantically looking down. He can't see Pratt anywhere and is staggering around on the makeshift barrel raft.

"Surprise," Pratt sadistically states, his arms up on the side of the raft, his pistol extending in his hand.

The thug slowly turns with his hands held up in the air. "Allow me the honor to swim away. I just wanted to get to shore. I meant you no harm!"

Pratt pulls himself up on the boat. "Go—jump in the water!" Pratt, dripping cold, his face bright red from the freezing water and brutal ice storm, dares his lone remaining crew member.

The man, with his hands up in the air, is looking the water over closely for a shark fin. He turns and takes the plunge, jumping into the water. Pratt steps to the edge of the boat as the storm rages all around him. He aims his pistol down at the water, aiming for the face of the traitor. The man emerges up out of the water, freezing cold, shivering immediately, his teeth chattering and his breaths shallow and rapid.

"Bu-but you said I could go," the man, his words shaky from his temperature drop, begs. His eyes are sagging—his cheeks raise slightly in anguish.

"No. I said you could jump in the water. Now you know how it feels." Pratt bares his clinched teeth and he fires multiple times, the gun shots striking the man repeatedly, killing his last remaining crew. The man slumps in the water, his lifeless body moving up and down in the rolling waves. Another shark whips up and drags the man's dead body down under the surface.

Pratt turns back and grabs the piece of wood his crewman was going to use. He starts to paddle the makeshift raft though the fog and the storm, his eyes desperately scanning around for what he believes to be the shore. The world has grown unrecognizable; the fog is so dense and the storm so strong.

"Where are you?!" Pratt shouts at the top of his lungs.

His anchored ship starts breaking apart behind him as the swell of the ocean is quickly gaining in force. Another giant mast bends and breaks, cracking at its core. Pratt paddles harder and faster. He nervously tries to get away as the mast falls. He ducks down, diving to the side of the barrels. The broken mast slams into the very edge of his makeshift raft, puncturing one of the rum barrels. The wind picks up and shards of Pratt's boat are flying by him in the air, the scene becoming worse and worse. The raft holds and Pratt slowly rises back up. He looks over and sees the light from Old Barney and manically smiles.

"There you are," he grins in anticipation of getting to the shoreline.

THE Oceanic Hotel creaks and moans as if it were aged to near death. Its entire foundation getting pushed and pulled over and over again. Sarah is sitting in the ballroom of the second story behind the piano, wet and cold, holding Jackson tightly against her.

"I'm scared," he mutters, his face curled up into her gut.

"It's all right, Jackson. It's all right. I'm here, Jack. I'm here," Sarah rubs her hands through his hair to calm the boy. "I'm not going anywhere. I promise." Sarah's eyes pan up toward the ceiling, staring out into space. "Please help us," she mutters under her breath. She begs for mercy from anyone willing to listen.

The wind continues to roar outside and then, like a stick getting bent to its breaking point, a giant crack in the foundation of The Oceanic causes the entire structure to shift and move.

"Ah!" Sarah yells as the piano runs along the floor from one end of the ballroom all the way to the other, the nose of the room dipping diagonally down. Sarah is holding the wall for support, Jackson gripping tightly to her.

"Hold on!" she yells to him in panic.

The far end of the floor on the other side of the ballroom caves. The piano, old chairs and tables fall. They don't strike the ground, but rather they land in water, the splashing of the cold liquid causing Sarah a new alarm.

"Oh, no," she says to herself, both her eyes flare open as wide as possible, her mouth half-cocked as she pans her head around, attempting to ascertain her next move.

The water crashes down below, ocean spray flying up into the hole created in the second story. The Oceanic is being pulled apart by the inside and is dragged slowly out to sea; the ocean swell eating away at the hotel with relentless force.

"I'm scared, Sarah!" Jackson shouts.

Sarah tries to use one arm to help her up to her feet while the other remains firmly grasped around Jackson. Her breaths have quickened as she tries to slowly shift her feet along the far wall. The ballroom is angling down like the bow of a quickly sinking ship, half of it pointed down in the ocean below. With every crashing wave, wood crackles and the ocean's teeth pulling the Oceanic apart.

Sarah is carefully navigating the tilted room, attempting to keep her balance and make sure Jackson is safe. They scale the wall slowly. "Be careful," she urges him. "Don't rush."

Sarah's right hand is extended back as a chest-high security measure in case Jackson loses his balance. She uses her left hand to press against the wall as they make their way toward the entrance to the ballroom.

The floor splits, wood violently pressing up in the middle of the room. The entire ballroom creaks and shifts, impending doom about to cave in on Sarah and Jackson.

"Quickly!" Sarah now urges, her plans changing. Her sense of urgency is followed by her and Jackson shuffling their feet the best they can across the moist slippery floor. Sarah's foot slips just a little, but she maintains her balance. Jackson's feet both slide out from under him and he loses his balance, falling down and starting to slide toward the water.

"Jackson!" Sarah screams. She dives down and grabs his hands, holding him tightly. Her body weight against the floor is all that is preventing them from sliding down into the open floor on the other side of the room and getting swallowed into the shards of wood and icy ocean waters.

"Don't let me go," Jackson begs. "Please don't let me go!"

Sarah is holding on for dear life but has no leverage to use to pull Jackson to her. If she moves, they both go. She is paralyzed, uncertain of what to do next. Jackson's hands start to slip, the moisture in the room causing their fingers to slowly pull apart.

"No!" Sarah cries, her voice begging for an answer.

"Sarah!" Jackson shouts.

Sarah gives up her position and reaches with her other hand, grabbing a clasping her fingers with Jackson's free hand.

The floor loudly creaks and breaks in half. It breaks right in between Jackson and Sarah. He flies down, their clasped hands remaining together as Jackson dangles down. Sarah bends over the break, staring down at sharp shards of wood and flooring floating in the water below them. Sarah is holding Jackson with all her might as he dangles above the water.

"Hold on!" she helplessly shouts. She can't do anything but hold on for a few more seconds.

"I'm falling!" Jackson screams. "Sarah, I'm falling!" His eyebrows bend down, his cheeks pull up. Jackson is petrified, knowing he is seconds from falling.

"You fall and I'm going with you, Jack! I'm gonna go with you!" she yells to him, trying to provide him some comfort.

His hands slip a little more, just a few finger tips left between him and the water below.

"I can't hold on!" Jackson screams.

"Lord, help me!" Sarah shouts, her head desperately bending back as she transfers all her strength to her straining fingertips.

"Ah!" Jackson's hands slide and Sarah loses her grip.

"No!" she shouts just as a dark arm comes diving down and grabs Jackson by a single hand. She turns and sees the frozen, shaking Zander holding onto Jackson's one hand.

Jackson is dangling down as Zander reaches with his other arm and grabs Jackson by his forearm for a better grip.

"Hold my legs!" Zander shouts to Sarah.

Sarah quickly moves and grabs Zander's feet, leaning back to counter Jackson's weight. Hanging over the edge of the creaking floor, Zander starts to pull Jackson up. Sarah hears more shredding of wood beneath the floorboards. She looks down and sees a running crack right below her. She looks up with great concern, the entire floor just moments from collapsing.

Zander screams in pain, transferring every ounce of strength he has left inside him into his arms and pulls Jackson up from the awkward slanting angle. He gets him back above the hole and Jackson crawls over Zander to get to Sarah. Zander, aided by Sarah holding his legs, slowly backs away from the hole. The three of them carefully rise up to their feet on the slippery floor. They run toward the ball room entrance as the entire floor rips and shreds apart behind them. The floor disappears just as they safely reach the entranceway. The ground stops crumbling behind them, a gaping hole left in the heart of the Oceanic. Zander looks back, sad, watching the remaining pieces of a grand history disappear.

The ceiling starts to crack, tearing apart. The entire hotel is being ripped to shreds, gutted by the storm and the ocean.

"We have to go!" Sarah shouts, the storm at a deafening tone.

"Let's go!" Zander agrees.

They rush away toward the other side of the hotel, running away from the ocean and heading back to the front entrance.

THOMAS is making his way through the dense fog and mighty storm when he stops, seeing a faint figure walking toward him. He can't quite make out who it is through swirling chaos. The ice and wind are making it near impossible to fully open his eyes and focus on much of anything. With his arm out in front of him, Thomas is battling the near-hurricane force wind along with nasty elements to see.

The man gets closer and Thomas is hoping to see Zander stepping into his view. But instead, he sees Pratt.

"Dent! I can't tell you how happy I am to see you!" Pratt pulls out his gun and points it at Thomas.

Pieces of debris fly by their faces. Wood shards from Pratt's now destroyed boat are hurling through the air. The men dodge the pieces of wood as they fly by in the storm like a whirling tornado destroying the entire world around them. The storm is deafening, and after the broken pieces of wreckage fly by, the men fix their eyes back upon each other.

They stand facing one another like foes in a showdown. They silently stare at one another, ignoring the chaos whipping all around them. That is when another figure approaches from the side. Whitmore, with his bullwhip hanging down, emerges through the wind, ice and fog.

"I'll be a monkey's uncle. A two-for-one! I'll get a big award for this! Accommodations! Apologies! It's all mine!" Whitmore shouts with glee.

"Whitmore?" Pratt yells in surprise. "Isn't this a funny pickle?!"

Thomas takes small steps backward. Pratt's gun is still pointed at Thomas but his focus has turned to Whitmore. The two men are dealing with the shock of unexpectedly seeing one another. Thomas continues to slowly back away without anyone the wiser.

"We can make a deal!" Pratt shouts to Whitmore.

"What sort of deal?" Whitmore asks.

"We can become partners," Pratt's slightly closed-lipped smile and single raised eyebrow gives away his lies.

"That sounds great," Whitmore's deep voice trails, he too giving away his dishonesty.

The men are two gun slingers in the old west readying to counter their opponents first move. Their eyes don't move off one another.

Pratt whips his gun around in Whitmore's direction just as the former officer snaps his bullwhip at the criminal. A gun shot and the cracking of Whitmore's whip are the last noises Thomas hears. He turns and runs with the two men's attention on each other. He runs through the terrible weather, looking back over his shoulder. The showdown is cloaked by the fog and weather. His breaths are quickened, the world around him filled with madness. He turns ahead and nearly runs into another shadowed object.

Thomas runs right into someone. His heart drops for a moment until he realizes it's Zander.

"Come on," Zander urges, wanting them to get away.

"I'm so happy to see you, friend!"

"Hurry," Zander intensely states, his face starting to ice from the cold weather. His teeth are chattering, his lips turning blue.

They race to the keeper's quarters together. They step inside, a few lit lanterns providing limited lighting. Sarah is holding Jackson, both of them still dripping wet from the storm.

"What do we do?" she asks with a ton of concern.

Zander is freezing and removes his hood and looks around, exhausted.

"There's two of them," Thomas states, also short on breath. Everyone is exhausted and before an idea can be floated through the dark cold air inside the home…

"No, Dent, just one," Pratt states, standing by the back door. His gun is drawn, fresh cuts to his face and arm showing the extent of the damage Whitmore inflicted upon him.

"What happened to your partner—the Jamaican fellow?" Thomas asks.

"I buried him too. No room for partners, Dent. You know that." Pratt is looking around, looking over all the faces over.

"Why are you here?" Thomas asks.

"My rum. The storm blew us north and I saw the lighthouse. But we ran aground. I need to save my rum," Pratt insists.

"It's gone, Pratt. It's all gone."

"Shut up!" he shouts. "You're going to save my rum, Dent. I'll kill every single person in here until you get me my rum!"

"Okay-okay. I'll help you. Just let them go. They have done nothing to you." Thomas attempts to deal with Pratt.

"How about I make you a counter offer? I shoot all of them and you help me because you have no choice. No witnesses. It's like I was never here."

Pratt smiles and raises his gun. He points it at Zander first. Zander closes his eyes.

"No!" Thomas screams and lunges at Zander, tackling him to the ground.

A single shot sounds. Thomas goes flying on top of Zander. Sarah shrieks in horror as she watches Thomas fall on top of Zander. She helplessly stares at the motionless Thomas lying on the ground.

"Son of a bitch," Pratt says with a silly grin. He looks down and blood starts to pour out of his chest. Another blast is fired from behind everyone and Pratt flies backwards, dead.

Standing with his smoking rifle, wheezing, is Henry. He is barely able to stand and breathe. Once satisfied he fulfilled his duty, he falls face first to the ground.

"Dad!" Sarah shouts and rushes to Henry's side.

Zander and Thomas look at one another, thankful to be free of bullet wounds. The two men stare over at Henry and Sarah, both speechless and breathless.

Twenty Two

WHEN Henry's eyes closed on that chaotic evening, they never opened again. He lasted until morning and two days later, a ceremony was held at dusk by the water. Henry's body was carefully placed in a small boat. Over a hundred and fifty residents of the island and of Barnegat attended the outdoor funeral service, filling the shoreline by the broken up Oceanic Hotel. They came to see off a man who they all deeply respected; a pillar of their community.

A Scottish band began playing their bagpipes. I asked Sarah afterwards about the musical choice and she told me that is what Henry always wanted. He wasn't Scottish nor did he own a pair of bagpipes. He just liked the sound of them and wanted to be sent off into the ocean for the last time as the music blasted.

The boat was doused in carnosine by Zander and I stepped forward with the match. I looked back up at the lighthouse, thinking of the first time I saw Henry strike the match and lit the Fresnel lens inside Old Barney. I struck the match and tossed it into the boat. A few other men, using long ores, helped send Henry out to sea. While the music was playing, the boat was engulfed in flames. The backdrop was a darkening sky with colorful streaks of purple and blue clouds. It is a magnificent send off for a magnificent man. I don't remember crying for my father when he died. I don't remember having shed a tear but I know I had when I was young. I shed many tears the day we sent Henry off to Heaven.

ON A perfect March afternoon, Thomas walked down the aisle and married the love of his life, Sarah. With Jackson and Zander looking on from Thomas's side, the quiet marriage turned out to be a bigger party than expected. Over two-hundred guests attended, bringing over cooked meals, baked goods and amazing spreads of food and fun. It was more of a town-wide celebration than a marriage joining two people together. It was beautiful, a party by the sea.

The Sunset Hotel kindly hosted the evening which spilled over onto the beach. It was a perfect sixty degree day, a preview of the wonderful spring to come. To make things even more perfect, Sarah would find out two months later that she was pregnant. Thomas and Sarah would raise their children on the island and remain there for the rest of their lives, officially adopting Jackson as their own and raising two of his brothers. The family of five lived a good life; a life Thomas had always dreamed of—one he never thought possible.

WINTER gave way to spring and the weather started to turn.

"217 steps. There are 217 steps to an isolated, miserable, existence braving weather, fixing everything imaginable, surrounding yourself in solitude, farming, cleaning and saving lives at sea. There is no second best in this job. You either are the best or you don't belong. Do you think you can handle that? Do you think you can take the first steps of the 217?" Zander is standing, awaiting the answer from his new trainee. The wide-eyed young man nods and salutes Zander, unsure of how to respond as the sun begins its descent in the sky.

"A simple yes, will do. This isn't the military, young man," Zander explains.

"Yes, sir," the young man replies.

"Excuse me," a stern voice calls to Zander.

"Yes?" Zander curiously moves past his trainee over to the man who is dressed in an inspector's outfit. However, it's not Gus, the kind man Henry dealt with for years.

"I'm looking for a Henry Jones."

"I'm sorry, sir, but Henry passed away."

The man's face squishes together with confusion as he looks around, wondering if a trick is being played on him. He regathers himself upon seeing Zander's sincerity and dives back in for answers.

"Well, who is running this lighthouse then?!" the man angrily asks, showing little patience.

"Thomas, sir."

The inspector flips through pages on his clipboard.

"Thomas Bullocks?" he asks.

"Yes, sir," Zander replies.

"He is the assistant on this list. I wasn't informed of anything," the man's eyes raise up as he searches frantically through his paperwork, an annoyed tone ringing through his words. He follows his expression with annoyed grunts and groans.

"I think you're looking for me," Thomas, dressed in his uniform, states.

"Who are you?" the inspector asks.

"I am Thomas, the man you're looking for. I'm the keeper of this here tower. Can I help you, sir?" Thomas comes strolling down looking all the part with his finely pressed uniform and confident glare.

"I'm Inspector Williams. I was neither informed nor am I aware that Mr. Jones was no longer in charge. This is unacceptable."

"Sir, where is, I believe his name is, Gus?"

"He passed away a little over two months ago. That is why we're having some trouble playing catch up. That is why I'm here, Mr. Bullocks. I'm here to make sure everything is done just right. I have no qualms about making changes." Mr. Williams continues to speak like a rude arrogant professor, his words filled with empty threats and harsh candor.

"Henry…Mr. Jones, passed away as well. We registered the paperwork with the Mayor. Our city got hit pretty hard. We lost some lives, some structures. We almost lost the tower. But we have persevered. *We* kept the tower going."

Mr. Williams pauses, staring at Thomas and looking the area over. The garden looks perfect, the tower well-kept and vibrantly painted; white at the bottom half, red to the top. He thinks things over and stares at Thomas and his professional stance.

"I plan to do a detailed inspection," Mr. Williams challenges.

"I welcome it, sir," Thomas returns.

"I am harsh, son. Just know that," Mr. Williams continues with his veil threats.

"I had the best teacher possible, sir. Be as harsh as you would like." Thomas is up for the challenge.

"The keeper's quarters looks damaged. You have family in the house?" Mr. Williams asks.

"The storm, sir. We are doing our best to salvage the home. My family, my new bride Sarah and her son Jackson, live there. And, of course, Zander and our new trainee, Oliver."

Mr. Williams flips through more paperwork and can't find what he is looking for.

"I don't see either of their names. You are listed as assistant. This isn't going to work. These kinds of paperwork errors can't happen."

Thomas steps forward, chest out, chin up high into the air and looks Mr. Williams right square in the eyes.

"Sir, I am the keeper of this tower. Zander is my assistant. Oliver is our trainee. We can correct this paperwork now, or we can all step aside and you can watch the tower in our absence while we wait for these issues to be worked out on your end? Another option is that you can continue with the inspection. If Old Barney looks good, if she is in the correct condition and we pass, then I kindly ask you to take a seat at my dining room table and my beautiful wife can fix us a meal. We can clear up any issues there. I also have the Mayor of Barnegat City who can attest to what me and Zander have done here. We have saved lives, sir. We have risked our own and saved lives. We also have worked hard to save the tower. We have proudly done our duty. We will live with whatever decision you make."

Mr. Williams may be a tough cookie, but he immediately senses Thomas's sincerity.

"Okay. I'll do the inspection and we'll go from there." Mr. Williams relents.

"Thank you, sir," Thomas remains calm but is excited inside.

Mr. Williams continues with his inspection. The Barnegat lighthouse passes inspection with Mr. Williams shaking Thomas's hand and complimenting the work he has done. Documents are fixed and Zander and Oliver are listed officially as keeper assistants. They worked the tower until the day it closed down.

Afterword

THE storm took its toll on everyone. The ice storm of 1920 ripped through the island and the Jersey Shore leaving a trail of devastation. The Oceanic was nearly swallowed whole into the ocean, torn to pieces by the pounding waves and rising waters from the storm surge. The keeper's house also sustained significant damage. United States engineers were sent to examine the lighthouse and they reported it wasn't safe. They recommended tearing it down. Despite their concerns, Old Barney stood tall in the midst of many storm surges. The lighthouse was never swallowed into the ocean.

The waters of the shoreline began to recede after 1920. It was too late for the Oceanic which got swallowed into the ocean. The keeper's quarters also suffered damage to the point where the government decided to sell the property dirt cheap. The Sunset Hotel got a good remodel after 1924, attempting to build on the fisheries which popped up all over the island. However, a flood in 1932 and a subsequent fire which burned the hotel down a month later left just brick and wire. Slowly over time, the remaining structure was swallowed into the ocean in succeeding storms. The once bustling resort-like haven, which had sprung up against Barnegat Bay's six hundred square miles of beautiful shallow water, contracted quickly. Even the Tuckerton Railroad gave up on Barnegat City as the once growing vacation destination for those of the Northeast corridor. It would be a temporary speedbump for the beautiful island. Better days would come once again. The city had one tremendous resident that would never leave; Old Barney.

The Barnegat Lighthouse is the second largest standing tower in the continental United States. The Fresnel lens inside the lighthouse remained a first-class navigational light until August 1927. A lightship was parked out at sea and the lighthouse was converted to automation to save money on oil. The light proved to be far dimmer and less powerful than before, seeing a reduction of a whopping 80% in strength. The automated transition proved to be fruitless and paled in comparison to the work of the keepers.

The light inside Old Barney was deactivated in January, 1944 and the tower was officially given to the State of New Jersey. The lighthouse is registered to the National Register of Historic Places as Barnegat Lighthouse. Visitors climb the 217 steps from the ground to the top and peer out over the ocean, just as the keepers once did. The lighthouse is featured on license plates in New Jersey and numerous promotional items.

The lighthouse rises into the sky as a beacon of hope. Still today, Old Barney stands proudly and can be seen from the Barnegat shore on a clear day. It stands as proud as the keepers who once took care of it. Nearly a million visitors a year pass inside Old Barney, with millions more gazing upon it and all its glory. Although decommissioned, this symbol of strength and light was the saving grace of many wayward fishermen who prayed for a miracle on many wayward nights. That miracle shined brightly in their darkest hours, showing them a way to safety, the beacon lit by the keeper and the light shown from the top of an extraordinary tower. That was the lighthouse. That's what it meant.

Brett Scott Ermilio

Award winning writer Brett Scott Ermilio currently resides on the Jersey Shore with his eight colorful roommates: his loving wife, four beautifully chaotic children, two small yapping dogs and one moody fish.

OTHER TITLES BY BRETT SCOTT ERMILIO INCLUDE:

GOING PLATINUM: KISS, DONNA SUMMER AND HOW NEIL BOGART BUILT CASABLANCA RECORDS (2014)

The riveting story of music producing legend Neil Bogart comes to life in this amazing rags to riches tale. With in-depth interviews from close family and friends, this is the only biography of the music producing legend.

JACOB (2015)

This award winning family fiction tale chronicles the life to two brothers, Ryan and Jacob. The two brothers are complete opposites with older brother, Ryan, playing the role of brother and parent to his younger, more creative, sibling. Jacob sees the best in the world while Ryan sees the harsh realities. The two brothers constantly battle in this inspiring and dramatic tale.

THE CONNOLLY AFFAIR (2015)

The Connolly Affair is a suspense-driven romantic thriller that will take your breath away. Nicki Connolly is a mother and wife, successfully holding her position as a partner at her law firm. But she feels threatened at work and her dedication to her job is causing a long-fought stalemate between her and her husband. On top of all that, she is leading an intense class action lawsuit that turns dangerous. All of the moments in her life come crashing together in this heart-stopping romantic thrill ride.

www.ingramcontent.com/pod-product-compliance
Lightning Source LLC
Chambersburg PA
CBHW070859250626
47159CB00003B/1120